W9-AQZ-304

MOTHERS
AND
LOVERS

MOTHERS AND LOVERS

Maria Flook

roundabout ●

Boca Raton Public Library

Copyright © 2014 by Maria Flook
All rights reserved. No part of this book may be reproduced in any form or by
any electronic or mechanical means, including information storage and retrieval
systems without permission in writing from the publisher, except by a reviewer
who may quote passages in a review.

Roundabout Press
P.O. Box 370310
West Hartford, CT 06137

ISBN: 978-0-9858812-5-2

Library of Congress Control Number: 2014942746

Printed in the United States of America
10 9 8 7 6 5 4 3 2 1

for
Randi Triant

MOTHERS
AND
LOVERS

Blaze stands beside the highway in a windy bib of waist-high daisies where a sign says: WILDFLOWERS. DO NOT MOW. Last-chance bumblebees skim the tossing mop-heads and he swats them one by one. A cruiser lounges past him. He dodges the trooper, sinking chin-deep in the weeds until his wig wag lights disappear in the distance. Then he's on his feet and pumps his thumb. Cars rip past. Drivers keep moving when they see "betwixt and between" written all over him. He has the penetrating look of a young man who unfairly suffers the aftermath of something.

Pounded by the right-lane air wake, he's thinking of *her*, the way she curled her pinky finger when she wanted him to climb into bed beside her.

Another driver peels by, checking his rear-view without pity. Blaze twirls around, and tilts his arms, playing airplane to mock him. In the growing dark they can hardly see him let alone stop in time. Dressed in black jeans and a dark hooded sweatshirt, he's almost invisible, his colorless silhouette absorbed by the macadam.

Truckers might pull over to save a baby stray, braking when they think it's a teen who took off in a huff. But when he climbs into the cab and extends his long legs, he's six feet plus. He wears a halo of blue meanies. So they start telling him their own stories to knock him off his high horse. He's heard it all a hundred times.

When his last ride dropped him, the driver punched his shoulder as he climbed down, saying, "Kid, go home. It's crazy to thumb in funeral clothes. That's just asking pancake!"

The rig had said, YORK, PENNSYLVANIA, THE BARBELL CAPITAL OF THE WORLD. The driver had explained that his trailer carried Lat Bars, Curl bars, Power Lifter Bars and crates of dumbbells.

Blaze said, "What's the difference between a dumbbell and a barbell?"

"I guess a *dumbbell* doesn't know the difference."

Blaze looked out the windshield to see a vanity plate preaching, THNKGOD.

"*Think* God," Blaze said, "Yeah, right."

"Son that tag says 'Thank God.' Where'd you come from?"

After the hearing that afternoon, he had left the courthouse in the county van. Heading back to the mini-max in Cranston, he saw his chance. Stopped at a no right on red, he crashed through the window of the bubbler GMC after peeling back the rubber gasket. He pried its lip, popped it loose, and swung his legs out first, like a monkey.

He was a tall drink of neon in his juvie hall jumpsuit, with two officers in pursuit. He lost them behind a strip mall when he climbed into a Salvation Army bin on chock blocks. He wormed under the heap of tangled clothes, waiting for them to crawl in after him. They didn't go in. He buried his hot pink pajamas in the give-away vault and walked away in his second hand jeans.

Standing on the rumble strip, he pictures her again. *Ruby bubbles of foam sputtered on her lips. Wet, red paisleys had bloomed on the top sheet, her body still warm when he left her.*

Just then, a big Kenworth car hauler downshifts and veers into the breakdown lane. The semi doesn't stop. It plows straight into the wildflower patch beheading a section of daisies, like a monster Weedwacker aiming for the tallest bloom. That would be him. The trucker blasts his direct-compressor air horn, two shorts and then the long, and blurs into the straight away, never slowing down. Blaze rolls clear just in time, pinging his collar bone.

Brushing thistles off his jeans, he sees more trouble coming. From out of the twilight, about fifty yards away on the apron of the highway, it's already gaining on him. A freak creature lopes in wild pounces, heading right for him—a big silver dragon. Half animal, half alloy, like an Xbox serpent or something from a Terminator movie.

He doesn't wait to see. He sprints down the breakdown lane, but the dragon gallops abreast of him, hissing and rattling its scales. It's just a loop of flameproof dryer hose—a squirming tube of shiny accordion foil—that tumbles with the wind. A cast-off, just like him, an escapee unattached to any legitimate dwelling or proper situation.

Chapter One

In the morning, the mountain was higher. New deliveries of sludge arrived after dark. She heard the diesel as it down-shifted and turned into her neighbor's lot. When she pulled her curtain to look outside, the driver cut his beams. He wasn't fooling anyone. The forty-ton articulated dump truck rumbled and vibrated her window panes as the driver maneuvered a gear-grinding, three-point turn before backing in. The hill was blacker than loam, almost like coal. Flurries dusted the peaks but snowflakes melted on touchdown. The mound was steaming.

April had already called town hall to complain. They told her to contact the board of selectmen, or maybe the zoning board who managed these unexpected contests between abutters. She was new in town and she was shuffled from one phone number to the next, never learning whose jurisdiction it would fall under. No one policed the black market bio sludge, a steamy pyramid of composted solids, almost roof-high. Every day the mound inched closer to her house. More of the teeming product was delivered next door before her neighbor could sell it, haul it, and spread it for his customers. Its odor wasn't overwhelming, but both bitter and sweet, like burned molasses. The hill was rising to the level of her dormer windows. She watched each illicit delivery and once she thought she saw a body tumble out of the truck bed, or perhaps it was a discarded dress dummy, a filthy life-size rag doll falling end over end. It was just her imagination.

Early spring had brought temperamental ice storms and nor'easter squalls, but the mini blizzard was half-hearted and dissolved at daybreak without enough snow to bury the eyesore. The toxic marl was a scourge on the New England countryside and an insult to her new house, a pristine antique Greek Revival. She had recently moved from Providence to East Westerly, a little backwoods hamlet once known for its productive granite quarries. A rural stretch of rocky field, forest and cranberry bog, it was still mostly undeveloped. Its comic oppositional name, East Westerly, was its most famous distinction, and a statewide joke. If someone "went off his rocker," or had "lost his marbles," Rhode Islanders would often say, "He's gone *East Westerly.*"

She wore a raincoat over her clingy nightgown and stepped into her furry boots. She walked outside into the cold pewter half-light near dawn, but the driver was gone. She heard the truck bed rattle and clank like an empty box car as it climbed the shoulder onto the highway and accelerated down deserted Route 91.

Watching where she placed each step, she circled the apron of the newly replenished heap. It was starting to drift and topple into her drive.

She was surprised to see she wasn't alone. A figure stood in the doorway of the place next door. Her neighbor's teenage son had been sent home from reform school and was living with his father under house arrest to await his next scheduled family court date, later that spring. The local school bus rolled past at six-thirty every day but didn't stop for him.

He was tall and slender, only a shadow in the poor light. She couldn't see his face behind a curtain of long, dark hair. Even in his hiding spot, the kid oozed a lot of attitude. He stamped his boot heel several times as if to kill a spider. He was merely snuffing a cigarette. He smoked menthols. She had noticed some of these white-white Kool butts sprinkled along the worn path that made a desire line between their properties. The kid prowled the path and flicked his burning stubs willy-nilly. Mentholated brands were popular in prison. The minty rush of flavoring adds an extra jolt. She imagined that in the monotony of the day-by-day lock-up, inmates seek every "extra jolt" they can get.

The boy turned to look in her direction. He was giving her the up and down. He didn't have a greeting. This was what she had to deal with. Father and son without so much as a "Hello, how are you?" She looked at the hill of bio-fertilizer. Tiny funnels of mist erupted over its bulk like wriggling ghost worms. The stuff was supposed to be rich fertilizer for weekend gardeners and gentleman farmers who puttered in their backyards on Sundays. Hazmat authorities monitored the transfer of cured waste coming from sewage treatment plants in Boston and Providence, but there was something sinister about the substance. It sifted, steamed and bubbled as if it were alive.

When she bought the farmhouse from Holt Townsend and his ex-wife, Janice Gallen, last September, she hadn't foreseen the trouble ahead. She hadn't known that Townsend planned to stay put next door. Townsend had refused to sell her the property with its adjoining barn and out buildings as one parcel. He had plans to renovate the weathered stables to make a rustic live-in bachelor castle. He wasn't going anywhere, he was digging in. But April loved the farmhouse. She had liked it the first time she saw it. A white clapboard nineteenth century Greek Revival, temple like; its solid, geometric form had the beauty, breadth, and simplicity that the classic design is praised for. The house was a simple rectangle really, with an el in back, and a screened-in porch. The short end of the rectangle faced the road, creating a two-story temple front with its distinctive pedimented gable and flat entablature. Its eaves were finished with a cornice and its gable side was embellished with a cornice return. These details made the temple-inspired house at once elegant and familiar, very American, reflecting the Jeffersonian ideal of the individual within the larger whole— the independent citizen, singular but not alone. A woman on her own would be happy, prosperous, and safe in such a house.

She had been very grateful to find her new farmhouse in move-in condition. The walls were freshly papered and the woodwork was painted. At the walk-through she was surprised to see some of Townsend's furnishings left behind. She found a cast-iron black cat doorstop, probably not a real antique, but charming; a Franklin stove in one corner; and a Shaker table with matching side chairs. She discovered a folding highchair in the kitchen closet and a tiny toy car on the top shelf of the hall closet. The little car was a familiar VW with flower stencils on its hood and front doors, like a hippie Bug of the sixties. She imagined the wayward son as a baby. She wondered what had turned a little boy into a juvie offender. Finding the high chair in her new kitchen was strangely unnerving; she felt it at a personal level, like discovering another woman's earring in your lover's bed.

Neither Townsend nor his ex-wife seemed to want these abandoned items. A shrink might say that leaving an item behind signifies "a resistance to let go" and "a dream of return."

And she was surprised to discover several black lines on the kitchen wall. The parents had documented a child's gradual growth spurts and ascensions of height using a ruler and a Magic Marker. The sentimental pentimento of a growth chart and the couple's cast-off furniture made April nervous. She didn't want to think of their sullied marriage or sit at *their* table. After she had moved in, she called a local antique dealer and asked him to take the dining set. She couldn't disconnect the wood stove without disturbing its stove pipe, which might release a cloud of black grit and dust. The stove would remain with its belly full of ashes, like an urn for the Townsends' burned-out matrimony. She decided to keep the heavy cast-iron door stop. April had a slight fear of real cats and had never owned a kitty ever since a teacher had once told her the legend of what happened to the British novelist Thomas Hardy. Upon the writer's death, his heart was removed and buried separately from his corpse in Stinsford, England. The story says Thomas Hardy's house cat dug up the heart from its isolated crypt and scampered off with it.

The iron cat had come to seem like steady company whenever April found it at her feet, and it wasn't going to scratch her furniture, or bolt out the screen door, as a real cat might.

Of course, the farmhouse needed April's touch. She unrolled her kilims and arranged her authentic, if a little beat-up, van der Rohe Barcelona chair of hand-welted leather with its matching ottoman, placing them to the left of her most prized antique, an overstuffed French settee. She was pleased to showcase her idiosyncratic collection of furniture in the Greek Revival, when it had seemed cramped and over cooked at her condo in College Hill.

When April moved into the house in September, Townsend had not yet launched his landscape and driveway business. By March, it was in full swing but his renovation project was stalled. His "post-and-beam château" was still more barn than bungalow, and worse, the string of mismatched sheds and storage bins next door reminded her of the mysterious Waco compound where David Koresh had run his spooky commune.

April knew that many reasonable people were restoring abandoned barns. She had seen several of these vaulted milk sheds and chicken coop cathedrals springing up everywhere in South County. Farmers were not only putting their gingerbread Victorians on the market, but also selling their dilapidated out buildings and pig sheds to dot-com wonders and bankers sick of their cramped condominiums. All of rural Rhode Island was becoming a bedroom community for Boston, and even for New York City. These new countrified homeowners still had to have their Sub-Zeros and central air but they were unwilling to give up a smidgeon of the status that came from owning a renovated barn. April had met a couple at the post office who bragged to April that they had found a property with "its own covered bridge." Townsend assured April that his barn, too, would maintain its ramshackle facade with furious attention to its weathered details. Her realtor said that having a luxury remodeled barn as her closest neighbor would only be good for real estate values, even if it caused an eventual hike in her property taxes.

That was before the mountain of sludge.

In the kitchen, April started her coffee machine and washed last night's dinner plate at her double sink. She dried her silverware and put it away. She was finicky and kept her teaspoons and tablespoons separated in parallel bins, with the teaspoons facing the opposite way of the tablespoons, bowl to stem. When she opened the silverware drawer she'd never reach for the wrong one.

If only she could use the same precaution as she sorted her personal affairs, and her contracts with people could be managed and monitored, held at bay, "bowl to stem."

Outside, her neighbor's fenced pasture opened wide into the distance. She was always surprised to see Townsend's two quarter horses streaking past her window. She liked to hear the muted thundering of their hoof beats, audible through her single-paned antique leaded-glass windows that offered no sound-proofing. The horses were quite a different sight from what she would have seen from her apartment in Providence. She had moved to the country trying to extract herself from an affair with a married man. He was the provost at Sinclair College, where she was a faculty member.

It had started at an informal Oktoberfest party on campus when the provost had tried to spark a conversation about a recent biography of Mark Twain. He said he wanted to "pick her brain," but she told him she had not yet read the new book, nor did she plan to order it from Amazon. He cornered her to introduce himself, saying "Miss O'Rourke? Fielding Mirhege. Not a giant elm, but a *mere* hedge." As he described the correct pronunciation of his name, he swept his arms wide open to suggest a big tree with its spreading canopy, and then cupped his hands as if to hold a more diminutive specimen. "See? 'Mere' hedge." He offered the impromptu lesson as if he had no clue how to convince a girl to pay attention to him.

She believed that he often performed the pantomime without success.

"Oh, I get it," she said, "not a giant sequoia?" She let him know she was taking the bait. She was already in awe of him. She had devoured his book of essays on the Romantic poets while in graduate school. His groundbreaking chapter on Coleridge was the first to compare the poet's "conversation poems" to the work of the poet Frank O'Hara, bringing Romanticism from the eighteenth century to the twentieth. His prose was supple and had an un-academic lilt that excited April. Mirhege said that O'Hara was the Coleridge of his day, having achieved a "rhetoric of camaraderie" with fellow poets, just as Coleridge had done with Wordsworth. Mirhege linked O'Hara's essay "Personism: A Manifesto" to Coleridge's conversational language and his premise of "One Life," a belief that all humankind is intertwined. If Mirhege had unearthed these connections, April thought he must be really something! O'Hara believed that in poetry the poem is between two persons instead of two pages. He said that instead of calling someone on the telephone, you write a poem to him. He said you should write a poem the way you buy a pair of pants. The pants should be tight enough so that "everyone will want to go to bed with you."

She stared at the provost in that way now. His slacks were snug and he looked pretty good. She allowed herself to imagine that he might one day, like O'Hara, write a poem to her. He wore a wincing half-smile, as if embarrassed by the same agenda. She was charmed by his bashfulness and thought he was handsome. His face was youthful, yet he wasn't too young. He looked well-rested and well-fed, a married man with all his creature comforts secured, except one. He seemed to know she was between men. The previous year, her boyfriend had been killed in a freak accident. Faculty had sent a wreath.

When Mirhege asked for a date, he joked, "It's *academic* that we hook up." She couldn't keep from thinking of Coleridge's lines "A delight / Comes sudden on my heart" and "Like some coy maid half yielding to her lover" in her excitement about accepting an invitation from the renowned critic. Their affair had been sparked by a very natural, almost organic attraction that began in that fall semester, and in an awkward progression of mild nuance and flirtation it carried over into the spring term. By then they were lovers. They continued to see one another for the next two semesters, including summer break, except during August when the provost went abroad with his wife and children, leaving April behind. When she said that she wished she could see Paris beside him, he confessed to her the same burning wish. He asked her to feel sorry for *him*.

And last semester, when the current chair of her English Department announced that he wanted to step aside, the provost asked April if she was interested. She was a tenured associate professor and was admired in her department. Her colleagues would support her, but she felt a little awkward when she was asked to consider the appointment by the provost himself. He was dangling a carrot. The job came with a substantial stipend, and if she nibbled it, he might think she'd be indebted to him.

In Providence, April had lived on the second floor of an old Victorian triple-decker, right off Hope Street, only a few blocks from her lover. His house was in a better neighborhood and it reminded April of a famous local verse that jabbed at Providence society by deconstructing its street names: "In Providence, Friendship is a one-way street. The rich folks live on Power Street, but most of us live 'off Hope.'"

She didn't like running into his wife at the corner bakery, or seeing the provost as he walked his Irish setter, "Peck," named after a has-been Hollywood legend once beloved by April's aunties. Gregory Peck was the actor who had played the sanctimonious lawyer in *To Kill a Mockingbird* and the provost had told her that he had admired the Oscar winner's portrayal of the Harper Lee character.

If she saw the provost walking his setter, "Peck," she would say to herself, "There's the pecker, *and* his dog."

She tried to be dismissive of him.

April told her friends, "If you date married men, you can't have expectations." They knew she was still in mourning after the recent death of her boyfriend, Riley. They said April felt no one could replace Riley and that's why she avoided a real relationship.

She didn't wish to re-enter the bothersome routine of hunting and gathering at the university night spots, at downtown bars, at faculty soirees, or at those maddening student parties in tight studio apartments. She tried to spend more time alone. She signed up for a gardening class to learn how to nurture exotic orchids which are very fussy. When she mentioned this to her lover, he teased her, saying that the fussiest jungle exotics couldn't compete with *her*.

She began to see how he, too, had contrived his own fantasies and belief systems about her—she was his cartoon concubine who he hoped would pry him out of his dismal rut at home. They both understood that she couldn't remedy his situation. He had signed the dotted line long before April entered the picture. Once, sitting face-to-face in the hotel room after having sex, they had smiled at one another in bittersweet compliance. In silence, each shrugged, as if in agreement, as if saying, *It is what it is.*

But she decided to leave town in order to distance herself from him. She couldn't stay in the city and be single again. She told her friends, "I refuse to become a crone in a condo."

Old maids in garden apartments were an ever-increasing population. She wasn't yet forty, but felt she was being funneled closer, soon to join their ranks. Some of these types became animal hoarders, like a woman on her block whom her neighbors called "the ferret lady." A spinster or a hag, April was a long way off from that. But she was alarmed to come across the *C* word in the dictionary, and to find out that the derivation for the word "crone" was "carrion."

Space Junk Hits Car
A local woman was found crushed in her Toyota after it was struck by flaming debris from soviet Skylab–type satellite. . . .

April often invented little escape-hatch scenarios to battle her self-critical observations. Instant death seemed the only way she might be rescued from her shameful entanglements. At moments of obsessive anxiety and hysterical self-loathing she liked to invent newspaper headlines.

College Prof Disappears
A Sinclair College faculty member has not been seen in two weeks. "It's as if an occult hand reached down and grabbed her," a colleague at the college told Providence police sergeant Constantine Tedesco. A Missing Persons report has not yet been filed by friends or family members. . . .

As she watched her kitchen window, one horse came galloping back in the opposite direction, chased by Townsend's dogs, a Border collie mix and a brindled mongrel. A quarter horse is part Arabian, part Thoroughbred. She saw its elegant Arabian traits in the horse's large cupped nostrils and dished face, beautiful in profile, as it turned to confront the bothersome dogs. The scruffy mutts lined up for the stare-down.

Townsend's other horse was a golden sorrel with a big white splash on its face as if it had just been struck by a snowball, right between the eyes. Its white face was pretty but this horse had a deformed leg. It might have suffered a broken bone that had never been set, and its shortened hind leg gave it a stuttered gait, its hindquarters sinking lower, like a hyena.

The crippled horse stirred up uncomfortable memories. When she was a little girl, April had suffered from a slight limp due to a mild case of scoliosis. She had been forced to wear the dreaded Milwaukee brace, with its embarrassing neck ring. She had hated the contraption, but had hated more that her father liked to supervise the daily routine when she had to put it on. Her mother tried to help April, but her father shooed her away, saying that only he knew how to adjust it correctly. April shivered, standing in her training bra and panties, as her father adjusted the device. He spent a good deal of time fussing, before he allowed her to finish dressing for school.

Even with the brace, she had spent hours in the backyard "playing horse." She broke off branches for riding crops and galloped around the house. April snapped the willow whip against her leg. Its sting helped to remove the gnawing tingle of her father's touch. Her mother warned April, "You'll be wearing that neck ring forever if you don't stop galloping like a pony." As an adult April had no telltale limp and had developed perfect posture. She walked with her back straight and her shoulders squared. Having once had a twisted spine she had worried it somehow correlated to a "twisted mind" or other perversity. As a child she had blamed herself for whatever she had done to spark her father's secretive routines with her. A doctor, when looking at an MRI, might be able to notice the little crink in her vertebrae, but she was relieved to know that any residue of her father's touch couldn't be documented on X-ray film or magnetic images.

April realized that the small, golden quarter horse outside her window was almost a three-legged freak. Horses were usually destroyed after injuries as bad as this. She tried to give Townsend the benefit of the doubt. Perhaps he had not been cruel to keep the animal alive but surprisingly sentimental. When she was a horse-crazy girl, her father had called all horses "Indian ponies." He had called any pinto or piebald horse "a paint." His poeticized colloquialisms had taught her to romanticize everything about horses, and later, everything about men.

Chapter Two

April opened her freezer door and took out two previously steeped tea bags from the ice cube bin, little pillows of green slush. She walked into the parlor and collapsed on her sofa. She was hatching a headache. She wanted to go back to bed. But she closed her eyes and placed the frozen teabags on her eyelids. She was certain that the increase in her morning headaches was being caused by the toxic sludge pile. She hadn't been sleeping well. Even now, with her eyes closed, she was vulnerable to vivid, high-contrast reruns of her difficult sessions with her lover at the Westminster Hotel.

She had to teach a one o'clock class and after that she had an appointment for yet another sex quarrel with the provost. At that appointment she hoped to have a meeting of the minds and together call an end to it, without hard feelings.

Her start-of-the-day headache wasn't like a crunching hangover, nor like the heavy, throbbing helmet from a long day at work. Instead, it felt like a narrow band of hot steel that wormed behind her eyes, from temple to temple. The tea bag trick sometimes worked wonders. She would rest on her sofa with the economical remedy for only a few minutes, for just a little nap, she thought, before she gathered herself to start her real day.

The black hill shivered outside her window. *My God*, she was thinking, unsure of what she had just seen. Again the huge pile quivered and throbbed, like a mammoth beast twitching its hide. A flock of sparrows exploded from the bare branches, startled. She heard a low internal rumble, like the deep reverberations of a crumbling fault line, as the mountain of sludge shifted closer. It was moving! Her windows grew dark as the pile swallowed one side of the house, moist clumps of it tipping against the eaves and thudding onto her roof.

She woke up from her insty-nightmare.

Someone was tapping the brass door knocker in flurries of clinks and clanks. She was on her sofa, still unable to surface from her dream. When the knocking became more furious, she put the soggy tea bags in a saucer and went to see who it was.

She stopped to look in a small mirror she had hung in the kitchen hallway. April fought against a pernicious vanity. She blamed it on forty-itis. At the mirror she could apply her lipstick or quickly smooth her hair whenever someone arrived unannounced. April looked at her face, wiping a little dab of nap-drool from her chin. It always surprised her to see herself when she was at home, alone and solitary, after shedding all affect, and without the happy mask that she wore in public. Her job at a small college sometimes felt stifling, it sapped her, and she felt her energy dwindling. Women's magazines said to expect it, the first droop that a woman feels as she climbs onto the plinth of middle age. There she was. Toneless as putty.

And next to the mirror was the growth chart bleeding through, as if to remind her that she was childless.

The unexpected visitor kept banging on the door.

She had thought it might be the provost, arriving for one of his rare small-and-early surprise visits, but it was a newcomer. He had one foot already wedged on the threshold as she pulled the front door open. Half way inside already, he stood there uninvited. Shoulder-length hair framed a very pretty, yet solidly square-jawed face, his skin so white he looked pale as a geisha.

It was the boy from next door.

"Oh, it's you?" she said in her neutral and tolerant schoolteacher's voice. She didn't invite him to come in.

"I'm testing my cuff," he said as he brushed past her and walked into the foyer.

"You're doing what?"

"Testing the hardware."

"Your cuff?"

"My 'Virtual Arrest Solution.' You know, it's got its stamp of approval from the American Civil Liberties Union."

"You have to wear that electronic device?"

He showed her a rubberized cinch snapped onto his ankle. "It's a wireless 'tamperproof transmitter' synchronized to a box at the house and to my Track Mate right here, see?" He lifted his thermal sweatshirt to show her a small device he wore on his belt.

"Looks like a cell phone."

"My dad has one, but I'm not allowed to have my own cell phone. I get to wear this this thing called a 'global communicator.'"

"It's a what?" she said, completely at a loss. "Global communicator" sounded oddly too rhetorical for the law enforcement hardware, and it reminded her of a literary inside joke about an absurd reference to the female genitalia, a famous line that said: "I've heard it called a lot of things, but never a waffle iron."

He told her, "GPS receiver. It shoots to the outer-space satellite, back to the cell tower, and then to the monitoring center."

"Shoots what?"

"Every move you make."

He said, "I can't leave the property without sending an alarm to Big Brother. I'm surrounded by an invisible fence just like a dog pen."

She wondered what drug he was taking—maybe Ritalin—that made him such a motor mouth. She had learned that students who spent a lot of energy explaining themselves were not to be trusted. If he was looking for sympathy, he wasn't breaking her heart. As he continued to explain his ankle device, she sensed that he hadn't yet learned how to tally its insult. He said, "I move one inch. Left or right. It's mapped on the terminal at the monitoring center. If I'm not where I'm supposed to be, it pops onto a screen and those Betsys alert my

PO. Then he calls my dad, or he calls the state police barracks. Those fucks."

"How long do you have to wear it?"

"Ninety days in all, but I'm short time now. My review date is next week. If I get any add-on time at the training school, these dog-pen months count against my sentence."

"Well, you're not very locked up now," she said.

"That's the beauty part. It's usually a hundred and fifty foot radius. They gave me more room since they put me on the rock pile to work with the old man. But you're inside the radius. It's good here," he said, "and here—" He inched into her parlor. He walked in tiny bride's steps, until he was all the way into the room.

April followed on his heels. Then he turned around.

He grinned. "Oh," he said, "I should introduce myself. I'm Blaze." He extended his hand.

When she reached out to shake hands with him, he licked his palm, grabbed her hand, and pumped it up and down.

She was surprised by the flash of his pink tongue, followed by his cool, wet tug. He had tricked her. Her wave of repulsion felt more like a thrill.

He was making a crude joke, at her expense, but it was more than a joke. It was not just a teenager's harassment of her refinement and decorum. It was deeper. She felt its adult threat.

He plopped down on her sofa, brushing her saucer of wet tea bags onto the floor. "What's with the tea bags? I thought I smelled coffee."

She didn't offer him a cup of coffee. He must be imagining some kind of dream breakfast and she wondered if he was getting fed at his dad's. The boy's offbeat invasion was making her head swim, triggering her innate maternal reactions, or *something*.

She didn't sit down but stood beside him.

He put his arms behind his head. "We're golden," he said.

"Golden? You mean that the sofa is within the confinement map? It's safe?"

"You tell me. Is it *safe*?"

She looked at him in awe. He was acting like a precocious Casanova, and he seemed as confident as his elder, the sludge tycoon next door. She wondered if the kid had learned it from his father. Other men might talk to her like this, but they were usually hat acts, all talk and no real threat.

He leaned back on the sofa, resting his long arms across its sloping back. "Is this a fainting couch?" he said. "It's so *Antiques Roadshow*."

"Not a fainting couch, no. It's French Empire," she said. She understood his confusion because the antique French settee had a sculpted back that was higher on one side before it dipped gracefully to the lower end, like the matronly curve of a hip. The settee was very feminine. Teen boys and grown men looked almost silly sinking into the cushions. She could have told him that real fainting couches were popular when ladies wore tight corsets and they often collapsed from poor circulation. She said, "*Antiques Roadshow*, you say? Did you really watch PBS in jail?"

"No, we liked the MAP Channel."

"You mean National Geographic? I like that too."

"M-A-P. Mature Amateur Porn. My favorite. I guess that's why you look so familiar," he said.

She felt a queasy pleasure-tug in her stomach. It was a silly insult, or perhaps it was a back-handed compliment. She tried to ignore it.

"This is nice. I like it," he said, patting the sofa cushions. "It's comfy. So, in the old-en days, why did women faint so much?"

"Like I said it's not a fainting couch. But go ahead, be my guest. Feel free to faint if you want to."

He reached out and grabbed her wrist. "No, *you* will. You're going to faint all you want." He smiled, staring into her face.

She tugged her hand away, watching him more closely. His eyes were colder when his mouth was shut. She sensed a raw fear under his silence. His chiseled expression looked older than fifteen or sixteen; he was a hardened animal right out of a jungle of small cons and headaches that she didn't want to imagine. But he jabbered like a sugar-jazzed kindergartner. And there was something childlike about the way he had plopped down on her couch. Like a kid ready to watch Saturday cartoons.

Men are happy to kick off their shoes, wing tips or Nikes. Once shoeless, when they are in their rumpled socks, they are like innocents. She sometimes liked to imagine the boy's handsome father, Townsend—*Coming here to sit down, camp out, nudge me into the bedroom or fall on me right here.* Men often sleep where they finish, in bed, on the settee. Unwilling to acknowledge his claim or his commitment to her, she would be expected to sort it out on her own. She smiled. Her fantasies were fiction but felt good swarming through her mind. She'd savor them later when writing in her bedside journal with its velvet board covers. She had learned that velvet covers kept her journal from sliding off her bed. These were unwholesome thoughts to have at this hour in the a.m., she scolded herself. She knew that these surges were in direct response to her current dead-end affair with the provost.

She didn't know what to do with the teenager. If he was really under house arrest, she wasn't supposed to babysit him. She said, "So what do you do all day? If you aren't going to school, shouldn't you have a job?"

He told her that he was helping his father remodel the barn. Between lock-ups he'd had a real job at Dunkin' Donuts. He said, "The manager was a Nazi. He put up signs everywhere that said, 'If you can *lean*, you can *clean*.' Even when the place was perfect you had to act busy and wipe everything with a rag. That rag has to keep moving."

She recognized the familiar story. Work is a grind, especially when you are low on the totem pole. "That rag has to keep moving" was how she had often felt at her academic job.

She was impressed by his ability to put his finger on it.

She wanted to ask him directly why he was under house arrest. She said, "So what's the story with the bracelet?"

He locked eyes with her. His unnerving peepers wouldn't let go. "You really want to know? Okay, I'll tell you," he said. But first he held up one hand before her face. With his other hand he plucked each individual fingertip as if he were removing a tight glove. His slow and deliberate pantomime suggested that if he were to tell her about his arrest record he would be forced to bare himself to her. She found his performance almost charming until he said, "It's called aggravated assault."

She didn't exactly know what categorized an "aggravated" attack. She thought it meant that a weapon was involved, even a bare fist. Boys always fought about girls. She didn't want to imagine drugs, armed robbery, or something worse. So she said to him, "She must have been really something. Was she pretty?"

His eyes narrowed. "Not talking about *her*."

She had opened a can of worms.

"What's her name?" she said.

"Hey, do I need a pop-up blocker, if you keep asking questions?"

"What girl wants an offender like you?"

"Lucinda's my true love. She's future-proof."

April was surprised to hear him using computer slang like "future-proof" and "pop-up blocker," phrases she had learned from her boyfriend who had been a techie.

She asked him, "Lucinda? Where is she?"

"Was in college. Got confuckulated when she dropped out her first semester."

"She dropped out? Why?"

"Flunked out, I guess. Now she's living with her gran in Hartford. That gray box keeps a moat around her."

His crude slang stung her with its sexism, or its *ageism*, but April knew that students didn't flunk out after just one bad semester. She said, "So, your girlfriend's in Connecticut?"

He said, "I see that Camry has a moon roof? That's a nice feature."

She realized that his unauthorized plop-down might be because he wanted her wheels. She warned him, "That car is a lemon. Every time I park the thing, its taillights won't turn off. So I have to remove a fuse from underneath the dash with needle-nose pliers to shut the lights off." The mechanic had told her it would be fifteen hundred to replace a circuit panel, so for the time being she would have to drive the beater.

He said, "Maybe it's red squirrels. They like to build nests in the engine block where it's warm. They chew through the ignition wires. Here's what you do. First you catch them in a Havahart trap, and then you drown them in a rain barrel."

She winced in appreciation of his brutal little story. She said, "Sometimes I drop the fuse behind the dash and I can't find it. They're tiny."

"I could find *your* fuse," he said.

She recognized his sexual antagonism. It was a turn-off or a turn-on. She didn't want to decide.

She hoped that Townsend would come over to round up his son. "Is your dad working on the barn?"

"It's a teardown. He's got big ideas. They backfire. Like he finished the pantry shelves with this fancy nosing—but I can't pull a cereal box off the shelf, it gets caught on the quarter-inch overhang. And last week he installed a wall safe but he lost the paperwork with the combination. He had to rip it out again to find its serial number."

"He installed a wall safe?"

"He's loaded."

She hadn't seen proof of this; there was nothing ostentatious about Townsend's lifestyle, as far as she knew, except that he had purchased several sparkling new tractors for his landscaping business. She was annoyed when he lined up the cumbersome machines too close to her property line.

Blaze said, "He likes to count his cash and put it through the burster."

"The burster? What's that?"

"It's a little tabletop machine that sorts money and tips the corners of the bills so they don't stick together. The cash makes that nice purring sound like when you shuffle cards."

She said, "Well, you know what they say, you can either make money or you can make history."

He grimaced at her as if she were his preachy grammar-school teacher.

Just then, a bird hit the window, a loud plunk. They went to look and saw an indiscriminate ball of brown feathers lying in the garden bed, with its glossy bead eyes and its beak opened slightly, panting. "That's a grackle. It's conked out. You should have a ribbon hanging, one of those bird-safe ornaments. Or it's going to happen again. That's murder," he said.

"You from PETA, I guess?"

Blaze said, "You kidding? We used to butcher lambs every spring."

"You raised lambs?"

"This was a sheep farm in the way back. Sheeps make lambs. Next, we kept laying hens in the yard to sell cage-free eggs."

April smiled. She thought he was something like a "cage-free egg" himself.

He said, "My dad thought he was Farmer Mackenzie"

"You mean Mr. McGregor."

"That geezer in *Peter Rabbit*. Whatever."

"Do you know when your dad is planning to move that sludge pile? It's like that movie *The Blob*."

He told her, "You're right. That mound is like an X-file. It's like Stephen King compost."

He was mocking her.

"Sweird," he said, smearing the words. "Yeah, I'd keep an eye out. Things can happen. Like 'House Drops on Witch.'"

He liked watching her process his snippy chides. The boy had stretched out on her sofa. He was reclaiming his space. He might have reclined like this before the warmth of the parlor stove in better days. He got up and walked over to the stove. He opened its door, getting powdery stove black on his hands. He looked inside the cold box as if to stir the ashes of his once-happy family, but he latched the door again. "You're not using wood?"

"I have to clean it first, don't I? I've put it off all winter. I think wood stoves are messy."

"We always knew when to add more wood just by watching the cat. He'd curl up closer and closer to the stove door when the fire was going out. My dad has two new stoves over there but that barn never heats up. It won't ever be a real house."

She didn't argue about that.

"My mom ditched me to run off with a contractor who builds strip malls. Hoo-er," he said, imitating the cold jargon he must have heard on TV shows or maybe at the kiddie prison. "The new one is worse—"

"She has a new boyfriend?"

"John Two. He builds submarines at Electric Boat. Acts hot shit, but he's just a welder."

"He's a pipe fitter?"

Blaze said, "The first John was a fuckwit but this one's pure evil." The kid's sentimental jag about cats in front of stoves had turned into brimstone. April ignored that he had called his mother a whore, but she thought it was interesting that he had said, "My mom ditched *me*," instead of saying she had spurned his father.

"You don't get along with your mom?"

"Bitch doesn't pass the food-bowl test."

April had met his mother a few times but she didn't recognize the reference he was making.

He said, "You know how the ASPCA evaluates shelter dogs? The trainer reaches for the food bowl with a plastic arm. If the dog bites the arm? End of story."

His icy summary of his mother's vicious streak was disturbing, but his absurd invention of the food-bowl metaphor seemed shockingly authentic.

"Then what happens?" she said.

"Lassie gets 'humanely euthanized,'" he said.

She asked him about the crippled horse.

"My mom calls him a freeloader."

"She says that about your dad?"

"No. The horse. Since nobody can ride him."

April imagined Townsend caring for the maimed horse. It was heroic or heartless. "It's amazing that horse survived."

"When a horse is kevorked, they shoot a pellet into its eye. Not exactly humane. He's had that broken leg for years. He's older than me." He shifted on the sofa, stretching his legs out. She rescued a hand-embroidered pillow from under his dirty shoes.

April sensed that the horse was kept alive just because Townsend was stubborn. She had a growing affection for the crippled animal. It often hobbled up to the fence, throwing its head over the top rail to greet her, when she left for work in the morning. "Despite his lame leg, he's real sociable," she said.

"How about you?" he said. "Are *you* going to be sociable?" He patted the velvet seat cushion.

"Okay, look. I'm getting a pretty good instinct about you—"

"Oh, yeah? It's everything you imagine *plus* a couple inches."

Perhaps he had talked like this to high school girls who knew nothing about men, and their ignorance had only worked to empower him. It wouldn't succeed with her. His coarse, almost scatological remarks about his size-chart prowess hinted at classic coprolalia, an uncontrollable condition she had read about in a psychology text back when she was in college. She felt a sympathetic stitch unravel.

She refused to feel sorry for him.

So she glided across the room to a sideboard to get a little distance. As she backed up against the antique breakfront, she felt one of its brass drawer pulls dig into her buttocks. She recognized that her escape to the sideboard was a mannerism common to Turner Classic Movies with Joan Crawford. That melodramatic actress always twirled around her parlor furniture showing her angst or ire by leaning against massive mahogany credenzas or swooning across velvet divans.

She faced him. *She* was supposed to be the experienced one. She should have authority over this full-of-himself teenager who was under house arrest. As a college professor, she often took the upper hand in tense situations with young men, even if her tactics sometimes had Gothic, Jane Eyre mannerisms. Her male students sometimes tried to find a chink in her armor. They watched her closely as she walked between the tight tables in the classroom, trying not to bump her hips against the crowded chairs. But when she talked about the knot-tying chapter in *Moby-Dick* or when she read a passage out loud from Emerson's essay "Self-Reliance," she just looked too curvy.

On the website RateMyProfessors.com, where students critiqued teachers, she'd often been awarded a little red icon beside her name, a "hot pepper." If she noticed her male students' stolen glances, their ogling, she didn't actually flaunt her beauty, nor did she flinch from it.

Blaze was way ahead of her. His silly insults had confused her, first with his wet handshake, and next with comments she might have heard before, but always from a seasoned player, not from a kid.

It was as if he expected to see her melt, ignite, and sputter like a saucer of cheap suet. *This will be simple*, she could see him thinking.

Blaze didn't have much faith that his father's remodeling job would heal the rift between them. His visible distress about April living in his childhood home (the kid felt it still belonged to him) made her recognize that she had moved not only into a family crypt, but into a living organism.

He didn't seem to want to leave. He complained some more, mocking Townsend's plans for a three-car garage without any promise of the three cars. No, Blaze would never have his own car because his folks had withheld *everything* from him. And he looked at her as if he was trying to decide where she belonged. If she wasn't on his side, he might add her to his guano-encrusted list of enemies.

Chapter Three

747 Wheel Carriage Plummets 3,000 Feet,
Crashes through Farmhouse Roof
A woman was found dead in her home after a tragic aviation
accident. Boeing grounds seven hundred jets. . . .

April finally told her brazen young neighbor, "You have to leave. I've got to meet my class."

"You work at Sin?" he asked. "Yeah, I heard."

She hated it when people lopped off the second syllable of Sinclair College. The slang nickname had special meaning to her because of her connection to a married man at the college. Even their love notes were exchanged to and from "sin.edu," an e-mail address they shared because of work. It was a long-running joke at the college. The story went that the webmaster at Sinclair's IT center had wagered he could get the shortened e-mail address past the administration, and he'd been successful. Some parents complained. She wished she taught at a college with a benign, respectable tag like Caltech, UMass, MIT, or NYU. There was a famous joke that students liked to recite to her in singsong, and with fresh jeers each term: "We just go to Sin, but you have to *work* at it."

Blaze didn't move. She said, "Look, I have a class at one o'clock. I have appointments." She was meeting the provost that afternoon. In her jousting match with the kid, she hadn't even thought of it.

"Okay, I'm going," Blaze said. He rolled slowly off the sofa in one languorous collapse to her carpet. Then, in a cat-like motion, with the spry hydraulics and silken movements of the beastly, beautiful young, he was on his feet. Seduced by his dreaminess, artificial or not, she walked him to the kitchen door with added formality. She felt off-center and tried to regain control by relying on her ladylike decorum. "It was very nice to meet you, Blaze," she said. "Thanks for stopping by."

She watched him walk down the path to the driveway where her car was parked. He stopped to peer into its driver's side window, steepling his hands as he pressed his nose to the glass. Her Camry looked a little shabby. It was a '99, with doilies of rust on its front fender. And of course she had to remove a fuse each time she parked it. But its interior was neat as a pin. Whatever his appraisal, she had nothing to be embarrassed about. Then she remembered her pump bottle of hand sanitizer that she kept on the console. She always cleaned her hands when she got into the car after student conferences. He'd think she was a fussy hypochondriac. She didn't have any stuffed animals on the dashboard, no silly air freshener baubles hanging from the rearview, no religious trinket or laminated holy cards that some people displayed on their dashboards. Even with its moon roof feature, her vehicle was nondescript.

Blaze turned and smiled at her. He was twirling something on his pointer finger. She recognized the little flat plastic cube of her lock beeper.

He had pocketed her car keys.

She always left her keys on the kitchen counter, beside the door. He couldn't resist the temptation. Despite her description of its electrical problems, she'd left her "Oh, What a Feeling" Toyota right there on a silver platter! She was outside, running to catch him. Blaze had already climbed into the Camry. He had found the needle-nose pliers in the cup holder and replaced the fuse. Sinking into the driver's seat, with a comfortable grin, he cranked the ignition. It purred. He toed the gas and rolled the car in a half circle around her, careful to keep her in his vision, in case she tried to grab the door handle. He avoided the empty flower beds, steering clear of their borders, as if in mock respect for their naked canes and dormant bulbs. The Camry peeled down the country lane, its gears shifting smoothly, responding to its young driver like an all-too-willing cohort. It was easier for April to blame the car than to accept the stinging recognition that she'd been duped by the kid.

Townsend wasn't home. He was probably at the Hilltop for an eye-opener. She had often seen his truck at the tavern at the crack of dawn, and later at midday it was parked there once again. She imagined that the kid's GPS ankle gizmo would alert the police. She didn't have to do anything. Yet Blaze seemed to want to prove to her that *she* had to deal with him now.

She went into the house to call 9-1-1 to report her car was stolen. If the girlfriend he had mentioned lived in Hartford, like Blaze had said, the state police could pick him up anywhere on route. She lifted the handset and stared at the keypad, trying to calm down. She couldn't remember the exact six digits of her plate number and wouldn't know what to tell the 9-1-1 operator. And she worried that the police would ask her why she had tried to have a civil conversation with the young criminal instead of booting him out of her house and bolting her door. Her loneliness was always getting her into trouble. The police might assume she had encouraged the boy to take advantage of her and they'd think that, like all women, her naïveté was feigned just to mask her secret agenda. Her good friend Milt would have said to her, "Dial the number! Don't psychoanalyze everything when forming a plan of action!" By second-guessing, April could never enact the first step.

She punched 9-1-1. She didn't press "talk" to connect the call.

She stared at the emergency number on the phone's LED screen. The number gained a sudden absurdity in its terse and glimmering read-out. She walked back into the parlor and arranged the scattered sofa cushions. She fluffed a pillow and crushed it to her face to breathe it in. He had deposited his boy chemicals on the velveteen, but she wasn't going to let it drug her. She recognized the early signs of trouble just as easily as she knew how to grill a fritter. *Yes, it's time to flip it over when bubbles start rising to the surface.*

She retrieved the wet tea bags which had left damp smears on the carpet. She tried to get Townsend on his cell phone. They needed to have an emergency powwow. She would tell him that (1) he would have to control any further deliveries to his sludge pile and (2) he would have to rein-in his brooding son who had wasted her time that morning. The delinquent! The resident car thief!

As she searched her Rolodex for Townsend's phone number she heard her e-mail chime. She had a message. It might be a love note from the provost and she had to steel herself to look at her in-box. She never got used to seeing his biting e-mail address, "f.mirhege@sin.edu." Yet lately she'd been receiving a lot of spam. Endless Pools kept sending her sales promotions. Her name was on their mailing list because of a confusing mistake. Their harassment was driving her crazy. Each time she clicked on the rogue e-mails, pictures of the sparkling death trap contraption materialized on her screen. The subject line might say "Jump right in!" or "Order before such-and-such date and receive a motorized pool cover!"

When she opened the new e-mail, again it showed a bright picture of the glittering pool, but the subject line said, "April, I want to meet you!"

The personal note alarmed her. She looked for more text to explain the remark or some kind of disclaimer, but there was nothing. She'd been receiving these sales pitches for months. It was the first time she'd recognized that the promotional e-mails weren't just sent automatically from the company's data-base. She couldn't think about it now. She hit the delete button.

Her Camry had a full tank. *He'll just love that*, she was thinking. And on her key ring she had a Mobil Speedpass, so he'd never have to worry about getting gas. She envisioned Blaze in her car, in her seat. His narrow hips would hardly make a well in the cushioned upholstery. He was so lanky he had had to move the bucket as far back as he could. When he'd circled her, he had released the backrest to drive in that slouched low rider posture.

It was one thing that the boy had invaded her home—a plop-down was an annoyance—but the crowning moment when he swiped her car had veered into an unknown arena that she didn't know how to absorb. She was alarmed, but it was somehow tantalizing. By taking her car, Blaze reminded her of the romantic pranks of high school boys who burned rubber, leaving a patch on the street outside her house.

April had a colleague at Sinclair, Claudia Perez, who worked on campus as an adjunct teacher. Claudia had urged April to break off her relationship with the provost. Claudia was also a case load administrator at the DSS offices in Providence and April believed she might know something about her neighbor.

She found the number for the Department of Social Services in the white pages, under the Rhode Island government listings. Claudia picked up her extension. "So are you making any progress, I hope?" Claudia said, curious about April's plans to extract herself from her affair with the provost.

April said, "Today, I do it. He gets the heave-ho."

"Good for you," Claudia said, "but you've said it before."

April knew she had a love-hate relationship with the provost. A love-hate relationship is the most passionate kind of union, and the hardest to disentangle from. She loved the provost's mind and admired his important work. Each time she tried to disengage, it was as if the poets he had written about in his well-received books jumped out of the pages to convince her not to leave him. She thought that a man who expertly parsed both Romantic and modern poetry, and who offered the most informed readings of diverse poems by both Thomas Hardy and Frank O'Hara could not be so easily dismissed. "I know I'm hemming and hawing about Mirhege," she told Claudia. But she asked her colleague to see what she could find out about Blaze.

Claudia told her, "That would be confidential, you know? I can't just pull his file. Even for you. Why do you want this?"

She didn't tell Claudia about her stolen car. DSS would get on the horn. The police shouldn't learn about the Camry. From her. She was startled by her reflex to hush up, but she didn't fight it. Already, she was covering for the boy.

"Like I told you, he walks right into the house. He's got these crazy ideas. He's wearing one of those ankle bracelets. I just want to know—is this kid dangerous or what?"

"You say he's wearing a cuff?"

"He's not very locked up."

"You should go to the local sheriff, ask him what he knows. Kids like this have a file that's a square foot thick. Let's see what comes up on screen."

April heard her friend typing on her keyboard. "You say it's Blaze Townsend, right?"

"That's correct. Blaze Townsend," April said, surprised to hear herself speaking with an odd, proprietary tone of voice. She cleared her throat. She had started to think it was a beautiful-sounding name.

Claudia said, "Here he is."

"What do you have?"

"Pretty typical stuff. In and out of juvie lock ups." Claudia told her that at the age of fourteen, Blaze had entered a revolving door of training schools, teen tanks, and last-chance sleep-away camps, both private and state operated. "Recidivism is common with these kids. Says here Blaze grew up in a 'verbally abusive household, in a charged environment . . . with running water . . .'"

"With running water?"

"The court takes into consideration the depressed economics or the austerity of certain family settings as possible catalysts to a client's violent flare-ups. Police have been out to the house a lot. Usual divorce inferno." Claudia explained that the reports said there was often something broken when the cops arrived. Chairs overturned; a lampshade ripped; a TV screen kicked in; a full dinner plate of food inverted on the kitchen table; a plate of spaghetti crashed against the door lintel. Strands of pasta dangled like a curtain, left to dry into yellow spokes.

Claudia said, "Jesus, he's been in and out of boot camps. He's one of our environmental refugees, you know?"

"He's a what?"

"It's when people are forced to leave their homes because of an earthquake or rising water, Katrina situations, Hurricane Sandy. In his case, it was a mom and pop volcano. He's been moved around a lot."

Claudia gave April a generic gloss of Blaze's JD resume— truancy, drug possession, trespassing, and petty theft. She said he had "prior bad acts" but that they appeared to have been pretty harmless, like one time noted when Blaze had borrowed a neighbor's Arctic Cat snowmobile. Blaze took it for an exhilarating, wintry tour. At dawn, he purred through the woods and pastures, across the white fields until the sun lifted higher. He was heading back to his neighbor's house to leave the beautiful machine right where he'd found it. Taking a short cut, he drove into a frozen pond obscured by a lid of snow. The ice was thinning in a February thaw.

Cats don't like water.

April was thinking that if Blaze drove her Camry into a lake that might be one way to stop him. She thought if he was capsized, it would be better than if he kept running.

She listened to Claudia's list. She herself had "prior bad acts," in a manner of speaking. The provost wasn't the first married man she had seen, and he probably wouldn't be the last.

"Blaze is text book O-D-D," Claudia said. "Oppositional defiant disorder. That's pretty common for kids in and out of the training school. It's more like a fever than a disease, and it's usually symptomatic of something else, or *several* something elses. Note here says that the mom said she's not responsible for all these something elses. And she has her own story. She was raised by her four brothers after her mom died. She found her mother dead in the backyard."

"Dead from what?"

"Alcohol problem. It says she was too drunk to hang her wash outside in the dead of winter when she collapsed. No coat on. Froze to death or something. "

"Finding her mom like that? That's pretty tough."

"Getting raised by four older brothers—that's worse!" Claudia laughed. "Give me an hour or two and I'll dig up the actual paper file. But it goes nowhere, right?"

"It stays with me. On my word," April said.

"I'll see what else I can find out."

Chapter Four

April's day had not even started but she'd had a plate full already. Her friend Milt Phelps, a colleague in her department, had said that April's most unsettling character flaw was her organic to-a-fault predisposition to be consumed. By men!

She had told Milt, "Oh please. You're just projecting."

Milt had been her first acquaintance when she was a new arrival at Sinclair. Milt pulled her into his office to share some important campus phone numbers—the extension for the secretary who didn't monitor how much copy paper faculty swiped, and his speed dial numbers for the best Thai take out, and for the Indian sandwich shop called the Deli Lama.

At the start, Milt had surprised her by saying "Greetings, sinner!" as he rolled right into a cheerful stanza from W. H. Auden:

> *"Welcome to our well-run desert*
> *Where anguish arrives by cable*
> *And the deadly sins*
> *May be bought in tins*
> *With instructions on the label."*

She often sat in Milt's office as they graded papers or filled out book orders, and they shared the department's one copy of the local paper, the *Providence Journal*, or the *Pro Jo*. His office was decorated with souvenir broadsides and familiar lit posters, like the annoying one that commanded, POETRY MATTERS!

"Real poets don't have to preach," she told him.

And Milt came into *her* office, bringing half a sandwich or a whole pot of green tea.

April endured her friend's needling jabs and his all-too-well-meaning criticism about her dating her boss. Milt knew that Provost Mirhege was a family man who would never budge. He believed that after the death of her boyfriend, April should try to meet an eligible bachelor. April knew her lover had a wife and two sprouts. He was framed and hung up on the wall already, and she didn't have to finish the masterpiece on her own. The canvas was stretched, the paint was dry. No muss. She told her friends, "I know he won't leave his wife. I'm not asking him to." But she sometimes allowed herself to imagine being the significant other of the revered literary theorist.

The indistinct boundaries of their love affair were in fact quite rigid. The provost never telephoned her from his home, and she in turn didn't bring him to her apartment. At first, these rules fostered not a disillusionment about love but its opposite. Within their predictable regimen, in its repetitive setting, April was assured of a kind of constancy, or what TV shrinks might call "a habit of captivity." Her sessions with Mirhege at the Westminster Hotel presented no sudden turns of mind and no heightened transitions. It was a steady, unalterable habit, a stasis of predictable pleasures without expectations for attaining raised consciousness or gainful insight. Infidelity requires no such growth.

And April had learned to tolerate the provost's annoying mannerisms. He did not name his penis as some men like to do, but when he called her to make an appointment, he'd say, "*We* are dying to see you," as if he and his cock were partners, a super hero duo, or a team effort. Once he even said, "Meet *us* at two o'clock?" She believed he was too conflicted to assume responsibility. He needed to blame the other one! The provost requested the same room at the Westminster each time. He liked a particular suite on the fourteenth floor at the far end of the hallway, where it came to a dead stop. The corner room at the end of the hall had an added aura of secrecy. His nervousness elicited her empathy and made her feel sorry for him. Until it became transparent.

When she lived in Providence the provost had never made love to her at her place, because her condo was just a few streets over from his own house. He said that if he met April in close vicinity to his address, his wife would send him "tuning-fork vibrations."

"You can't expect us to perform when I'm right down the block from Sarah. No, we can't meet in the neighborhood."

Even after she had moved into her farmhouse, he had come out to East Westerly only a few times.

He said, "If you have to be on campus anyway, why should I drive out there?"

The provost's cousin was the hotel manager at the West-minster. A recent transplant from Germany, he spoke impeccable English, but his accent was alarmingly familiar. His voice sounded like snippets from documentary footage of Third Reich principals or perhaps it recalled villains in James Bond movies. Whenever she entered the hotel lobby she saw his cousin behind the high mahogany front desk where guests lined up at reception. On her way to the elevators, he acknowledged her without making conversation. His indifference always made her feel both anointed and snubbed, the way a spy must feel when accepting an assignment that requires pristine anonymity but that, in fact, carries with it worldwide consequences.

Afterwards, when she and the provost departed, they rode two different elevators. If they were forced to descend to street level together, they exited without chitchat, and walked to opposite ends of the lobby. April knew it was even more conspicuous this way, but she indulged him.

The provost met her only at the hotel. April had often bumped into his wife at the Stop & Shop, or they faced one another across a busy East Side intersection, sitting in their cars, waiting for the light to change.

Unlike the poor wife, April could pack up and live wherever she chose to reside. With her move to the country, April liked to think she had achieved her "foretaste of freedom." Then again, her rival didn't wake up every morning to find a sludge pile outside her bedroom window.

The Westminster Hotel had an idiosyncratic bistro on its

lobby floor. The restaurant was a sunken den that had once been the actual granite vault of the now-defunct Old Stone Bank. The bistro was called The Vault. The space was a half story deeper than the first floor, and it had an aura of submerged liaisons and illicit partnerships of both today and yesteryear. It was decorated with antique lanterns, adding machines, and other nineteenth-century money-lending paraphernalia. The safe's large brass door, with its tumblers and gears exposed, was left ajar so that diners could admire the complicated locking mechanism. She had dined there with the provost only once, but he occasionally allowed her to order room service from their menu when she complained she was missing her lunch to meet him.

Yet after each tryst, before leaving the hotel room, the provost performed a little pantomime. He pinched his fingertips against his lapel and twisted his fist a half turn. "This stays in the vault," he'd say, warning her not to speak to anyone of their liaison. She should lock it up in her heart.

She was his mistress, plain and simple.

Milt told her, "No, honey. You're not his mistress, you're his *dis*mistress."

"Oh, that's pretty good," she said. "Go find someone to play Scattergories."

"You just don't like to hear it," Milt said.

"Fuck you. Try some Boggle."

If Milt called her "*dis*mistress," it was because she had told him stories about her lover's behavior. Mirhege had tried to prove she mattered to him. He bought her occasional gifts. He rewarded her with a few impromptu trips. On an overnight to a seminar at Gettysburg College, Mirhege sat across from her at a local dining room in the small Pennsylvania town. The menu had said, "Turkey with filling." Mirhege asked the waitress, "What's in the filling?"

"Filling," the girl said.

"Yes, I see that, but what kind of filling?"

"Just filling."

April recognized that in her relationship with the provost, she was exactly like that. She was the indefinable filler on the menu.

Last semester, he had surprised her with an illicit "honeymoon" weekend in New York. He wanted to take her to Fire Island, where the poet Frank O'Hara had died, hit by a dune buggy on the beach. He planned to read a poem out loud, standing on the exact spot where the accident had happened. The memorial trip to New York to visit the site at the beach seemed very important to him, and again she admired his deep immersion in the art spirit. He told her that he had other business ahead of time, so she traveled alone by train to meet him. The hotel was modest, if not seedy, but within walking distance from Penn Station. As Mirhege quickly dressed after making love to her, he told her, "God, that was so nice. We love New York!" using the familiar plural pronoun. He was saying "he and his cock," or maybe he meant his "cock and balls."

"Now for the bad news, sweetheart," he said. "I still have meetings this afternoon."

"You have to leave? What about reading the poem on the beach? I thought that was the whole reason we took this trip."

He peeled fresh cash from his wallet and left the bills on the bedside table as if he were settling the tab with an industrial debutante working a midtown convention. He named a few restaurants where she could have dinner. "Try that Greek place up the street. Great octopus salad."

"Octopus salad?" She saw the creatures squirming on a bed of lettuce, and again on a salad plate of undulating fifty-dollar bills.

That afternoon she didn't visit a museum, her lover's recommendation, but decided to window-shop. She walked east and turned onto Madison. She crossed the street and went on towards Fifth. She bought a soft pretzel and was chewing its hot doughy ribbon, when she saw Mirhege at the curb, hailing a taxi. His wife stood beside him trying to rank several unmanageable shopping bags. The woman decided which bags could go into the trunk of the cab and which she should keep in her lap. She had big carry-alls from Barneys and Bloomingdale's, and a few tiny, high-gloss totes from Madison Avenue boutiques. April watched the couple on the sidewalk cause a minor disequilibrium in the flow of pedestrians. Even at a distance, she recognized his sport jacket, a windowpane plaid she had never admired. She recognized the slant of his sideburns, the symmetry of his features, his fine-tuned gentlemanly tics as he instructed the cab driver.

He looked miserable.

After their side trips to Gettysburg and New York, April had rolled with the punches. And Mirhege had sometimes showed her genuine warmth and intimate courtesies that suggested what he might be like as a family man. He had come over to her condo to fix her garbage disposal when her sink was stopped up. He was lying on his back, on her kitchen floor, with his head under the sink. He had rolled up his sleeves, and he was getting his oxford dirty. He had some trouble reconnecting a PVC elbow, but he got the job done. He had brought a mini acetylene torch to heat up the pipe collar.

There was something different about him when he was acting like the man of the house, fixing her plumbing. She started to believe he might one day really leave his wife for her.

Only recently had she discovered that Mirhege might be putting the kibosh on her appointment to be chair of her department. The entire departmental committee had endorsed her candidacy. Mirhege was holding it up. April soon learned that he had swiped her heavy box of documentation from the chair of the committee. The box had her updated resume, her journal publications, her class syllabi, her letters of reference, and everything proving her record of pristine and orthodox industriousness. But since her boyfriend Riley's death, she had not attended conferences and had not been writing much criticism. She had not yet published her paper on Emerson and mysticism. She wasn't a star in her field, but her student evaluations were always good, both in the personal comments and in the numerical Scantrons. Her only blotch was a ceaseless rumor that her boyfriend had not died in an accident but had committed suicide.

The chair position included a $20,000 stipend. She needed the extra money to buy a new car. Without it, she'd be driving her old Toyota a-while longer, with its electrical problems and a dysfunctional defroster that never cleared her foggy window. In bitter winter she drove to work, straining to see through a windscreen of spun sugar. Even the provost had once commiserated and said, "With all their genius, you know, from the get-go with computer chips and transistors, the Japanese just can't make defrosters."

In the months since he'd first asked her if she was interested in the position, Mirhege had stalled the process of appointing her to be chair with extra red tape. He had re-examined his initial recommendation about what role April should have at the college, and he decided that he didn't want her to enter his arena as an administrator.

He wanted her for his secret life.

She planned to confront him later that day and get him to explain what was holding up the decision. The $20,000 pay hike wasn't small potatoes to her. She had been grateful to join the English Department at Sinclair College. Nestled between, or some might say overshadowed by, Brown University and Rhode Island School of Design, Sinclair was a fifth-rate factory, not much better than a community college. Yet, like its glamorous neighbors, some of its walls were ivied. April was a worker bee and taught a grinding "three and three" course load, three different classes each semester, mostly survey courses in American literature, with occasional higher-level classes she designed on her own. She was meeting her self-designed seminar that morning, Introduction to American Transcendentalism. And at three o'clock that afternoon she was scheduled for one final tutorial with the provost at the Westminster.

Chapter Five

The car smelled of honey or vanilla. April must have dropped her grocery bag and her herbal shampoo had spilled on the car floor, soaking the rug. The sugary pastille primed Blaze for his destination. Its girly smell evoked Lucinda.

He'd get to Hartford in less than two hours doing the five-five, but if everyone else was speeding he'd attract attention going too slow. This was how he rationalized driving twenty miles per hour over the limit. Cops call it "high-speed fleeing and eluding." He didn't see a trap, but he eyed every ghost car and plain wrapper. It would help if he could pair up with a hitcher to perch on the passenger side. No one was thumbing.

When he saw the I-95 on-ramp just ahead, he was wavering. He was wobbling.

If he fled in the cuff he was pulling open another trap door. The chute sluiced directly to a cot at the ACI. It was grand theft auto even without the ankle bracelet infraction. But he wanted his girl. Lucinda. He saw her body. She's wearing nothing but a crimson thong. He saw her face. He followed it onto the highway.

His cuff was the problem.

Yes, he was nabbed. He was under some invisible thumb. He had tried to think of his house arrest in a lucid conceptual frame.

But *thinking* made him fume.

Theorizing turned him into a time bomb.

His father had encouraged him to accept the cuff as a small nuisance, an irritant, "the grain of sand that creates the pearl." And it was nothing compared with the in-your-face chain-link fences and concertina wire at the high-security training schools and mini jails he'd been shuffled through. After two years of detention centers, gladiator boot camps, and Christian and wilderness reform schools—with their military, religious, service-based, or adventure-camp settings— one after another, he couldn't really complain about the cuff.

Blaze had been enrolled at three different outsider operations. The church camps were the worst. He had never had religious training. When he was a little kid, he saw rough-hewn crosses erected alongside the highway, often in clusters of three. He asked his dad, "What are all these 't's' doing out here?"

Townsend laughed and said, "Those aren't *t*s.' That's Calvary, where Jesus was nailed up with his two sidekicks, the good thief and the bad thief." Townsend gave him Bible facts in little snippets like this, but when Blaze had pin-balled between different schools he had often been forced to participate in prayer activities. He was herded into Outward Bound treks, blind-folded relay races, fire walking, creative writing workshops, state park sleepovers, dog grooming for no pay, soybean shucking, and haiku contests. At one school they had kids building Native American sweat lodges.

At Twin Rivers, in Meadville, Pennsylvania, kids were dragged out of bed every morning at daybreak, before breakfast, to perform elaborate drill practice. The drill instructor counted cadence, "Cheaters, liars, dopers, cons, *left.*" "Nancies, pussies, queerbait, fems, *right.*" Or Blaze inserted his own twangy marching command: "*Die*, two, three, four. *Die*, two, three, four. *Die! Die! Die!*"

Every day, different kids tried to do something worthy of an expulsion at a public school. But sending these kids back to Mom and Dad meant the checks stopped coming. To be expelled Blaze had to torch something. Firebugs had to be deported out of state, back to where they came from.

Blaze swiped a secretary's Cutex polish remover and dribbled it in a thin line down the carpet in the busy administration office. He lit the carpet with contraband matches and watched the flames feather. The polish remover made a flouncy, ankle-high rope of fire the length of the room. The women assistants screamed, and then giggled as the headmaster himself stamped out the long, hot stripe.

So the boys were lined up before the fire chief, and he went from one to another with his sniffer device. When he stopped at Blaze the sniffer identified hydrocarbon vapors on the cuffs of his jersey. Blaze was nabbed.

Blaze grinned at the headmaster. He'd won. He was expelled.

He was getting out of Meadville.

After he was sent back home to live with Janice Gallen at her new A-frame, she agreed that perhaps the military atmosphere might have been cross-purposes. She didn't try to get him re-enrolled in the public high school. She was tight-lipped as she examined her options. Janice told Blaze he would have to accept her routines and follow her house rules. He would be respectful to her friends, including her new boyfriend John Two whom she called her fiancé although no wedding date had been set.

John Two was his mom's second consecutive boyfriend named John since she'd separated from his dad. Blaze had named the first parasite Jaundice, or he called him John *Boss* because the intruder kept ordering him around, his warnings and caveats usually handed down through his mom. She'd say, "John *wants* that music turned off." "John *wants* his carton of Marlboros put back where you found it." "John *wants* this messy backseat cleaned up."

Janice said that her boyfriend couldn't be expected to put up with "baggage he didn't pack himself." She seemed to know that Blaze kept up his sullen attacks against John Two because he didn't like the man sharing his mom's bed, despite the fact that her boyfriend contributed to the household cash pot. She didn't have an answer when Blaze asked her, "And how'd you get that bruise? Is that something we should talk about?"

So Blaze critiqued John Two nonstop, pointing out to Janice the man's all-too-familiar faults. But she closed up if he asked her about her puffy lip, so Blaze asked her about John Two's habit of wearing his wristwatch buckled on the *outside* of his sweater cuff.

She had no built-in answer for that.

John Two was smacking Janice around and he tried to intimidate Blaze. If John Two wasn't trying to pop him, he was bragging about his lame-ass job outfitting nuclear submarines, trying to teach Blaze the specs: his sub was 377 feet long; it displaced 7,800 tons of water; its maximum diving depth was more than 800 feet; its periscope had been replaced with a new photonics mast.

He boasted about the stunning costs of building just one sub; each had a price tag of $2.3 billion.

Blaze said, "Oh, right. I'm saving up for mine. Or maybe I'll just lease one."

Janice gave Blaze a worried look, warning him not to push his luck.

The climate at the claustrophobic A-frame got worse. John Two asked Blaze to help him repair a kitchen door. The door wasn't hanging right and it was rubbing. John Two told him, "Well, kid. We'll just leave you here to solve the problem."

The man was giving him some sort of ultimatum.

John Two said, "That should be fixed when I get back if *you* don't want to be fixed. Know what I mean?"

The man drove Janice to work, leaving Blaze with the job. Blaze saw that the door needed planing where it was rubbing against the threshold. He had to get it down first and he tapped the pins loose from the hinge leaves with a ball-peen hammer. He lifted the door and waltzed it off its frame, careful not to bang into anything. He smoothed its edge with a hand plane, curls of fresh fir collecting at his feet. He checked it with a spirit level, and then planed its edge a second and a third time until there was a nest of sweet-smelling ribbons across the kitchen floor. Finished, he lifted the door onto its frame, dropping the hinge pins back into the brass knuckles.

He saw John Two standing on the opposite side, coming out of nowhere. "Good job, shitbrain," John Two said.

"I fixed it."

"You think so?"

"I planed the door. Like you said, it was swelled up."

"Okay. Let's try it."

Blaze pushed the door shut surprised to see it still rubbed the threshold; the knob shivered in his hand with the same friction.

Blaze looked at the door. A blinding stripe of white light slashed across the top. There was a half inch of daylight where he'd planed the wrong end.

The door was ruined, unless they replaced the hinges.

A pipe-fitter's upper body has a certain bulk. John Two's arms were so muscled that they never fell straight to his sides, but hung ape-like on either side of his trunk, with his palms facing backwards. Thin as a rail, Blaze wasn't a threat. John Two pinned Blaze against the refrigerator and crammed the hard tip of his elbow between the knobs of his spine. Blaze yelped. John Two kneed him in the buttocks. Blaze sprung free and the man chased him around the cook top. Blaze grabbed the spirit level. He lifted it high and could have crowned John Two, but he brought it down on a bowl of grapefruit, splitting open the pulpy white rind on a yellow globe.

From then on, Janice tried to keep them apart. But the next time she'd hung the wash, she looked out the kitchen window to see her clothesline on fire. Blaze had walked down the line squirting lighter fluid on John Two's Carhartt work shirts, his trousers, thermal socks, and boxers. The separate clothes were distinct at first; then the whole row erupted in a bright, golden wave.

One day, Janice came home from work early. She found Blaze stretched out on the sofa, his pj bottoms sliding down his hips because the waistband was shot. He tugged his pants higher. He was watching an info-mercial where girls were on their backs, bicycling their legs, to show the results of a tummy cruncher DVD. Janice punched the mute button on the clicker. She sat down beside him. "You should get dressed," she said.

"Okay."

"Hugs first," she said. She tried to squeeze him, but he squirmed away.

Next she'd want a back rub or she'd ask him to wash her hair. She could never get her boyfriends to do her any favors. Blaze didn't budge. He thought, *Let John Two be the workhorse.* When he looked at Janice, her face softened in a familiar way.

She smiled at him with a guilty hunger, a mom job, and he didn't want it.

When she divorced Townsend she had told Blaze, "It's you and me. We've got each other." Then the Johns had started to stack up.

He looked at her sitting beside him and said, "Now what?"

"Nothing," she said. Her face had that trembling, elastic look.

He went to get his jeans, and when he came back, she told him, "Honey, you're on your own tonight. John wants me to go look at kitchen tile."

Later the couple went shopping, and Blaze was glad to be solo for the night. He was alone for only five minutes when he heard someone on the front steps. He thought Janice had come back to get her Best Buy credit card that he saw she had left on the sideboard. He went to the door. A pretty, blond-haired girl, like a hot coed from a Pantene commercial, was standing on the porch. She said, "I'm Lindsay," and then she introduced someone she called her "driver," a beefy man dressed in gangsta sweats. Together they told him that his mom had said he might be interested in going to a "rock concert."

"Rock concert" was a lame expression Blaze never used.

"It's your favorite group," Lindsay said.

"No kidding," Blaze said. "Who would that be?"

"Sunny Day Real Estate?" the girl said, as if she was still uncertain she had been told the right name. Blaze wasn't surprised that Janice knew the name of his number one band, because she used to go to shows with him. She'd often come to watch him when he had his own band. They played at the Sons of Italy lodge or at the VFW. She stood in the back of the room watching him play his guitar, avoiding the mosh pit in front of the stage. She looked like a golden era groupie, from a different world, older than the teenybopper goths and skinheads who crowded the floor. At a Battle of the Bands at the Elks, a drummer from another band asked Blaze, "Who's that cougar who keeps waving at us?"

Janice might know his favorite band, but he told the blond girl, "Sunny Day Real Estate? They broke up."

Blaze followed individual band members on the web, and he would have read about it if the group had resolved their feud. And it was unlikely they'd do a commercial gig. The event would have been hate-blogged up and down his hardcore-punk sites. The girl explained that she represented Sound City, a national chain of sound equipment super-stores, and she was recruiting a live audience for a TV promo. The girl wore a tight-fitting yellow top with the Sound City logo. Her T-shirt was a size too small for her substantial gifts. She was like a Howard Stern rubber-stamped porn star. He was thinking, *I can tap that*, if she gave him the slightest opportunity at the big corporate rave she described. He hadn't yet found his pussy legs after coming back from the all-male world of Twin Rivers. And he had just learned that his girlfriend Lucinda had enrolled as a freshman at Macalester College in Minnesota and he wasn't sure where the campus was, or how he could find her. Wherever it was, Lucinda might as well be in a girls' dorm on the moon. Maybe this PR princess, in the throbbing yellow T-shirt was an opportunity not to be ignored. He imagined a work-out with her would leave him uncuntious.

He got into the minivan with the weird couple. It was a ho-hum Plymouth Voyager, but when he sat down in the bench seat and the driver yanked the panel door closed, Blaze saw that the passenger cab was secured, front and back, like some kind of super-sized Havahart trap. He tried to force the slider open, but it had a safety-lock and couldn't be budged. A Plexiglas screen separated the front buckets from where he was sitting in back, just like the cage in a cruiser.

He'd been kidnapped by the mod-squad hottie and he was in transport.

His chaperones knew that few teens went willingly to Elm Park Baptist School unless they were tricked or taken by force. He watched the traffic smear past. He saw they were snaking down I-95 South. After a few hours they hit northern New Jersey and peeled onto I-78, heading west. They stopped in Allentown, Pennsylvania to grab another kid. They snagged a third boy in Akron, Ohio, and kept driving west. Blaze tried to fight his way free at a rest stop but the beefy jock driver fought dirty, twisting his arm and grabbing his sack.

The boys compared notes, and each kid described how he had been smooth-talked, yanked from bed, or brainwashed by his own kin. Blaze remembered what Janice had told him: "Hugs first" and "You're on your own tonight." He swore to his new cellmates that he would hate Janice Gallen for the rest of his life on Earth and hate her "full-time from hell."

They were delivered to the infamous Elm Park Baptist School in Kirksville, Missouri. Less than ten hours ago he'd been in East Westerly, minding his own business, thinking of Lucinda. The next morning, his eyes red, his clothes rumpled, his hair sharked in awkward clumps, he jumped down from the van in the Show Me State!

Missouri was unregulated. It was magnet for cash-cow reform schools that were not permitted to operate anywhere else. Schools with unacceptable practices had set up shop in Missouri after being exiled from their own home states. The Elm Park Baptist School had a mission statement that promised to "separate teens from the ungodly" and vowed to enforce "the radical separation of teens from their lifestyles." The school followed a program called Bible Discipline which included forced memorization of texts from the Bible and paddling if these chapters weren't accurately "assimilated to memory." Even if students memorized texts, did their chores, and sang hymns with perfect pitch, they could be punished for their "sullenness."

When Blaze once tried to call his father to explain the conditions, the telephone was ripped from his hand. It wasn't the staffers; the brainwashed youngsters swarmed around him like angry bees protecting their hive.

After hopping from school to school, his last lock up was Greylock Integrity House, a wilderness-adventure treatment center for "teens at risk." Brochures claimed that a "forested mountain setting removes urban distractions and simplifies options." And, in a "rustic classroom, logical consequences of daily living are clearly understood."

The school was named after the highest peak in Massachusetts. At 3,491 feet Mount Greylock spiked up between Pittsfield and North Adams, farther north on Route 7. An instructor told Blaze that both Melville and Thoreau had camped on Mount Greylock. Melville had "partied" at its summit when he finally completed *Moby-Dick*. Area motels and ski lodges, community centers, nursing homes, strip malls and taverns were named after the tourist attraction. There was Greylock Comb and Curl, competing with a beauty salon called BerkShears. A sign on panel trucks said MT. GREYLOCK STRIPPERS. Blaze was disappointed to learn it was a company that refinished furniture and stripped antique wood doors, sinking them in vats of solvent to remove layers of lead paint.

The campus was claustrophobic, bordered on all sides by the foothills of the Berkshire plateau. One boring, empty vista without a city skyline.

Everywhere he looked, the horizon was like a big green waffle.

To escape, Blaze had had one problem to conquer. A significant hill, almost a mountain, lifted up behind the dormitory, an impenetrable pine forest, a bramble wall without a clear cliff, or promontory. It was a green blob of pine bough and bristle called Little Hen. If he could get over Little Hen, he'd be free. The perfect fade wouldn't be easy.

After the "incident" at Greylock and his half-baked escape, he was sent home with the ankle cuff, still in the system, but he was relieved to be out of boot camp. The barn was his native ground. Before his parents' divorce, he had sometimes skipped school to work with the two horses and other livestock, when Townsend still had sheep and a couple head of cattle. Blaze admired the muscled sires, and he liked the nomenclature—bronc, ram, bull. These terms were very male and were used as superlatives.

He did his daily chores mucking stalls, filling feed bins twice a day, and scrubbing the water troughs in the sheep pen, two antique claw-foot tubs that his dad later sold for two grand a-piece when Restoration Hardware started a trend for Victorian plumbing. Blaze had liked working the farm.

He took pleasure in solitary work. He liked to snip the wire string from a bale of straw just to watch its compressed leaves fall apart like a golden accordion.

If he weren't wearing the cuff he could have saddled the bay horse to ride until dusk when Townsend came back. Before he was nicked, he did a lot of thinking on horseback. Riding fences, pasture to pasture, into neighboring fields that didn't belong to them. He was learning a kind of interior life that might help him later on, or it might cause worse problems. An examined life without any mentor is a kettle of slithering worms, but he liked thinking about serious things. Of course, he also thought about sex. And guns.

Under house arrest, he was permitted outdoors only to slave with his father within the confines of the barnyard.

His life was yard work, restocking the woodpile, and looking after the two horses Townsend kept stabled for sentimental reasons. Townsend wanted him to operate the lawn tractors and learn to use power drills, chain saws, and lawn-edgers, saying to his son that all Blaze needed to advance in Townsend's new business was a little hand-and-eye coordination. He said it wouldn't hurt for Blaze to acquire some common sense to match his brawn, and with a little more tinkering on his attitude problem, he should think of himself as an actual partner in the operation.

Early that morning, before Blaze barged in on April, Townsend came back from a driveway job and parked the truck. The dogs jumped to the ground. He told Blaze, "They've got chickens over there so they don't want me bringing my entourage." He walked to the wood pile. He asked Blaze, "So are you getting somewhere with this disaster?"

The splits surrounded them in loose piles and tumbled ziggurats. Townsend said, "When you're done with the wood pile, you have to finish moving the sludge. Our lassie next door is getting pissed. We don't want her freckles to fall off."

Blaze had not yet met April, but when his dad talked about her freckles he was sure it was one of Townsend's metaphoric wraparounds.

The sludge pile was intimidating. Blaze had already had a little problem driving the Bobcat, trying to make a dent in it. He rode the mini loader like a go-kart, making wild turns, dropping the bucket too abruptly. Grinding gears and tearing in reverse, he had backed into Townsend's newly stacked cords of wood, toppling them. Townsend had kept his cool. But he seemed to think that Blaze had done it on purpose. He asked Blaze to sort the splits and rebuild the stack—but this time, the cords should go on the *other* side of the drive, opposite the original pile.

"You say I should move it from *here* to over *there*?"

"That's right."

"The fuck I will."

"You knocked 'em down, you build it again. Where *I* want," Townsend said.

Blaze started to select pieces of wood, lobbing them across the driveway to the other side like his father wanted. "You want the locust mixed with the oak? How about this hickory?" Blaze said.

"No need to sort. It's good to have them mixed in. You want to use the best with the worst."

Blaze nodded.

Townsend said, "Try to make an even cord about four feet deep, and same in height. About eight feet long. Leave enough room between rows for the wind and sun to penetrate."

When his father preached about "enough room for the wind and sun," and to be careful to use the "best with the worst," his lessons seemed to have double meanings. They were moral instructions directed at Blaze.

Townsend and Blaze worked together on the first row, constructing a neat, sweet-smelling monolith a little less than shoulder height. Stacked any taller the splits would topple.

"Now that's a pretty sight," Townsend said, stepping back to look at their work.

Blaze was usually embarrassed by his dad's displays of optimism.

Townsend said, "That's BTU-ti-ful. A row of firewood curing in the sunshine earns interest all summer. That's money in the bank."

"I guess that means we've got money to burn."

Townsend said, "That's a good one."

Blaze knew that his father didn't like irony, but he liked word-play. He had told Blaze that in the day-to-day grind wordplay was a succor and it was good for his son to learn how it's done.

Townsend went back to his job, and Blaze was left alone. He looked up from the woodpile to see the crippled quarter horse standing outside the barn. The horse nosed the heavy slider, where it had once had free access before Townsend started his project. Just like the dogs wanting table scraps from Blaze, the horse always seemed to show up if Blaze was nearby. Blaze didn't have time. The dogs, too, got under his feet as he tried to stack the wood. Blaze knew that animals can sense a change brewing even before you've made your first move. Ever since he was a child, that horse had always seemed one day ahead of him. The dogs, weaving in and out of his legs, were pests. Their unbridled joys reminded Blaze of his own furies, and he didn't like the gang-up. He kicked the brindle in its rib cage. It yelped and shrank away, then turned around. It crawled back on its belly, its tail brushing back and forth in the dirt as it inched forward, wanting love any which way.

With only one row stacked, the split wood sat in a heap like a collapsed log cabin. It added to the generally gloomy effect of their barnyard kingdom, like a Hollywood set of a deconstructed ghost town, a low-budget film that's been shelved long before it has finished production.

He began another row and felt a little confidence when he had successfully arranged splits for the bottom plinth, making a saw-tooth cradle for the next layer he stacked. He inhaled the astringent scent of raw wood. It cleared his sinuses, or maybe, for once, it was a job well done that made him feel like he could breathe.

Blaze merged onto the expressway. He'd go through New London and then drive north on Route 9. April's Camry had the go juice, but he didn't drive with his toenails in the radiator and he avoided the show-off lane. He would go real easy. Lucinda might hide him, but she didn't expect he was coming. She didn't have his time table or know what she was in for.

Blaze knew he was just buying time. GPS would ID him on a bank of screens at Short Message Service. They'd call his PO, Dick Yarborough, to inform him that Blaze was running, and Yarborough would decide if and *when* to get the cops after him. That's the relay team.

Blaze would have to remove the cuff. It wasn't hard to cut the plastic strap. "Removal of the unit" was a major infraction and could put him right back into RITS, the Rhode Island Training School, or into the ACI. Whenever it came off, he had to be able to disappear into thin air.

Suddenly his leg felt weak and paralyzed cramming the gas pedal, as if he couldn't mash a button mushroom. He felt funny all over, like a sock monkey filled with rag stuffing.

Dick Yarborough had called it "somatic symptoms" when Blaze described his dizzy spells and feeling light-headed. "These happen when you aren't facing the problem. These symptoms try to get you to pay attention." He told Blaze that instead of his bracelet they might insert a chip instead. Offenders were getting GPS chips implanted under the skin, to be worn for the rest of their lives. "Do you want something like that?"

Yarborough always asked Blaze to talk about Janice and Lucinda. He said that Blaze had to address his troubles with females that had triggered the incident at Greylock that Blaze refused to acknowledge. Yarborough said, "Sex anxiety is at the core of all teen violence." It was hard for Blaze to look at his PO without laughing because Yarborough had showed up at his office with one of his eyebrows shaved. He told Blaze that he was having cosmetic surgery that afternoon to remove a patch of basal cell skin cancer. "From all those years without sunscreen," he said. It was an out patient procedure, but the pre-surgery checklist had asked him to clean off his brow with his own razor. It was difficult for Blaze to take his probation officer seriously when he looked like Mr. Potato Head.

Trying to ignore him, Blaze looked out the second-story window and counted the power lines.

Yarborough said, "So let's go back to Greylock right before the shit got shredded. Where were you exactly? In your head, I mean."

Blaze lit up a Kool. Against court house rules.

Yarborough said, "Look. Work with me. Girls don't exactly think that thing's a friendship bracelet."

"I can get more pussy in a strait-jacket than you'd ever get in those Calvin Kleins."

"You're not getting any now, are you?"

Blaze decided the meeting was over. He often got up to leave after just a few minutes, ending the session. He'd say, "I'm fleeing the interview," borrowing a famous line from a madcap police movie.

A cruiser drifted abreast of the Camry. The trooper was shouting on his cell phone. That's a cop book violation. The trooper was having a raging fight with his girlfriend or some kind of family drama of his own. He wasn't interested in April's stolen car. The black pearl peeled off.

Blaze felt a sudden warmth filtering through the chaos. A recognition. A change of heart.

It was the sun overhead coming through the *moon* roof.

So he pulled off the highway at a scenic lookout to find a payphone. He dialed Dick Yarborough collect, just like any fuckhead standing in line at RITS or the ACI.

When he was put through, the PO told him, "I just got the alert two minutes ago. Your father will be pissed. Idiot, you've only got a few days left! SMS has got you on Ninety-Five South, near Groton. Driving to Hartford, are we? That girl rolled up her carpet, didn't she? So what are you going to prove?"

"I made a mistake. I'm coming back. You call the cops yet?

"I drop the dime, it's in motion."

"I'm turning around."

"*I'm* punching speed dial."

"Liar," Blaze said.

"I'm typing up the noncompliance report."

"You are not." Blaze hoped that April hadn't called the cops on her own to make it go hinky.

Dick Yarborough said, "If you come right back, there's some breakthrough value in that. So watch your speed. Don't be half-assed and get picked up. We don't need to broadcast this to everyone down here. Shit, you're an embarrassment, you know that?"

"Boo fucking hoo," Blaze said.

He drove the Camry back to East Westerly, watching the speed limit. He approached the barn, but he drove right past.

He kept going.

At his mom's A-frame there was a vinyl he wanted, left in a

box in the bedroom. It was an indie-label Operation Ivy classic, a rare record that he could sell on eBay. He'd seen other ones going for a hundred fifty. Janice had her own PayPal account and might believe his story.

The A-frame was in a land-compact community, a tightly knit organization of freeze-dried hippies and green grandpas, and Blaze knew he wasn't always welcomed inside its rough-hewn gate. Janice didn't really fit in either, despite her newly acquired bumper stickers she'd slathered on her van preaching EAT LOCAL FOODS, KNOW YOUR CARBON FOOTPRINT, and VOTE WIND FARM. Janice had bought these stickers all at once at a health food store.

Her adoption of these slogans seemed to be a pose she was trying on, in order to clean up her act after her Chernobyl with Blaze and Townsend. She was settled in the A-frame, but according to Janice, her neighbors didn't want a trouble-maker shacking up with her. She could have been talking about Blaze or John Two. Blaze was banned from the compound, she had told him.

When he turned in the drive, he saw her van. She was late for work, or sometimes she stayed home from Electric Boat because of one of her headaches or maybe it was girl troubles.

He got out of the Camry, leaving the fuse in and the taillights burning. The A-frame unnerved him because of its bizarre conical architecture—a claustrophobic pyramid, half silo, half party hat. It had an open area on the first floor, but he hated its cramped upstairs rooms, the walls lopped off on both sides as the steep roof pitched tighter. He tried the kitchen door but it was locked. He looked into the first-floor bedroom window. He saw that Janice had left her flimsy nightgown in a ring on the floor as if she'd just stepped out of it. She always hurried to get dressed for work each day, and every night she stripped, leaving her dirty clothes in little piles. He followed a trail of her panties, like silky water lilies and pink dahlia blossoms dribbled out the bedroom door and down the hall.

The familiar vision was hot and sour.

He stared at her panties. Then she was at the bedroom slider. She tugged open the door on its gritty track, getting it tangled up in her bathrobe hem.

"You didn't go in today?" he said. He saw why she didn't show up at the office. Her black eye was still fresh and hadn't faded to butterscotch yet.

"Is that satellite following you?" she said.

"It's chill."

"I don't want them showing up here."

"Relax."

"Well, just for a while," she said. She pulled him inside the room. He closed the slider and leaned against the cold glass, deciding what to do now.

Driving back to the barn, he stopped at the Mobil Mart to use April's Speedpass and top off her tank. The cashier was a girl he once knew. She squealed with nervous delight at the sight of him standing in line. He shushed her, inching his chin slowly left and right, until she knew to close her mouth. He came up to the counter and asked for a carton of Kools. She started to ring it up, but he placed the flat of his hand on the vinyl mat beside her register. He said nothing. Hypnotized, she punched open the drawer to cancel the sale. She slid the carton over to him, for free, her face as white as a china plate.

As he was leaving the store, he saw a big galvanized tub of fresh tulips beside the door. He sorted through the wet clumps, each bouquet wrapped in a cellophane bonnet. He helped himself to a double bunch of fat ones, a dozen waxy pink knobs that had not yet opened.

Chapter Six

April had dialed a student who lived in Watch Hill to ask her for a lift to campus when Blaze turned into the drive. She clicked off. Blaze parked her Camry and removed the fuse before he climbed out. He was leaning against its hood. He had a new carton of cigarettes tucked under his arm. Without fanfare, he ripped it open and peeled the seal from a single pack. He lit up. She stood on her kitchen stoop. They looked back and forth. He was pale, almost starved looking, as if his little escapade had taken a lot out of him. Again, she saw the raw fear under his quiet.

"Aren't you asking for trouble?" she said.

"I'm okay. I'm not DWLS, if that's what you mean."

"You're not what?"

"Driving with license suspended."

"Your license is revoked?"

"It's not suspended. I never took the test."

That he had taken her car without a legal ID wasn't the point. By confessing his Division of Motor Vehicles status, he was just trying to distract her. "Can I have my keys back?" she said.

"Left them on the dash," he said. He walked over to the barn, slapping the carton of cigarettes against his leg. He had borrowed the car to go to the Mobil Mart for smokes. "No big deal," he seemed to be implying.

She walked over to get the keys and was surprised to find a wet clump of tulips crammed behind the steering wheel. She tried to remember the last time a man had brought her flowers. The provost was more inclined to surprise her with nonfiction titles or periodicals.

Pale pink tulips were unusual. Supermarket bouquets were most often a sickening mauve or gaudy yellow. She wondered how much they had cost. And a carton of cigarettes wasn't cheap, so Blaze must have had some spending money. Maybe he got into Townsend's secret stash or pilfered some bills from the burster. April remembered that she had left her handbag in the living room, right beside the sofa. Just the day before, she had gone to the bank. She should have two fifties, and another hundred in smaller bills tucked into her wallet, but she didn't want to dig it out to count her cash.

She found a large vase for the tulips, a nice cranberry glass flute, its wide mouth roomy enough to allow the bloom-stalks to fall open in a full circle, uncrowded. That's the only way tulips should be displayed, she thought. Because tulips are short-lived and pouty.

In the meantime, she understood she would have to ask Townsend to control his son. She didn't have much hope that Townsend would cooperate since he had yet to respond to her complaints about the sludge pile.

When April had first griped about it, Townsend had said, "Well, what do you expect to see when you're way out here in the sticks? You're going to have mud. You're going to have manure."

East Westerly had very few regulations. Townsend said, out there, if she felt inclined, she could do just about anything. She could fly a "rainbow flag" (he was prying); she could hang her wash in the *front* yard, if she wanted; she could raise chickens, hobble sheep; she could set up a farm stand and sell strawberries without getting a vendor's license; or, if she was industrious, she could refurbish one of several abandoned cranberry bogs up for grabs.

The closing on the house had been held at a strip mall law office right off I-95, where Townsend was a client. The meeting included Townsend and his ex-child bride, Janice Gallen, the usual suspects from the realty offices, and a financial planner from Townsend's bank who was there to collect some of the profits owed to him. April sat down at the table and Townsend asked her, "So, where's Mr. O'Rourke? Don't we need his John Hancock?"

April's broker said, "Come on, Holt, it's *Miss* O'Rourke. You sound so old fashioned."

"That's me," Townsend said. "Old timey."

His ex-wife, Janice, made a face for everyone. The brittle couple could not mask their impatience with one another.

Townsend told April, "So, you're saying there's no mister? Well, okay." He smiled.

"A third of my clients are women," her agent said.

"That's *me*," April said, echoing Townsend's wry vernacular to try to ease out of the fray.

"That's you?" Townsend said. "*One-third* woman? Sorry to hear that. That's too bad. I like women to be a hundred percent."

April was usually careful not to divulge information about her personal life to strangers, especially the fact that she was a virtual widow. More than two years before, her live-in boyfriend, Riley, had died in an unusual accident when he was swimming in an Endless Pool. The circumstances of his death seemed bizarre to most people and whenever she tried to explain the details, it brought a pall of absurdity to her tragedy. If she talked about it, she'd be forced to describe the mechanism, a high-tech, crypt-size exercise tank with a fast-moving current. When the pool company had learned of the accident they had sent her a sympathy letter. Her friend Milt told her, "That's a hush Hallmark card. They want you to keep your mouth shut."

She had continued to get company e-mails, insensitive feelers for swim tank sales, because her name was never wiped off their system. It started to appear to April as if someone was trying to harass her, on purpose. She had e-mailed Endless Pools to have her e-mail address unsubscribed, but within a week, she was getting more messages. There was something creepy about it. She Googled information about the Rhode Island cyberstalking law. The law described cyberstalking as a "willful course of conduct directed at a specific person which seriously alarms, annoys, or bothers the person, and which serves no legitimate purpose, but would cause a reasonable person to suffer substantial emotional distress." That described it, all right. The e-mail reminders had prevented April from adjusting to her tragic loss. April couldn't move on as other bereaved women might.

Some people felt her widow status wasn't legitimate because she and her boyfriend had never been legally married. If she didn't have the marriage license that might have authenticated her widow status, she did have in her possession Riley's certificate of death.

April looked out her window to see that Townsend had returned from the tavern and was loading his truck for his workday. She had been interested to see a faded bumper sticker on Townsend's truck that had probably been placed there by his son in his high school days. Instead of WESTERLY SPIRIT Blaze had altered the tape so it said WESTERLY *SPIT* .

And she was amused to see that his trailer hitch had a rope tail, a colorful nylon braid that brushed the pavement until its tip end had become a ball of fluff. The scruffy tail was some sort of redneck flag or man-power emblem with absolutely no practical use. She was relieved to see that Townsend didn't have a much more coarse display of manhood prowess that she had recently seen on one or two vehicles around town. Other men had the poor taste to display on their bumpers "tailgate testicles" or "truck nuts," realistic plastic gonads you could purchase on-line and attach to your car.

Townsend looked ready to get to work. When his gear was stowed, Townsend walked in a circle around the truck, staring at his feet as if searching for something in the gravel. Then she understood he was lost in thought. He latched the tailgate with the same distracted look.

Like his son, he was tall and attractive, neither too slight nor too beefy. Townsend was at least sixty years old if he was a day. He still had a good head of hair, streaked dove-white across the temples. April believed that men looked good when they went salt and pepper, then into brush-strokes of chromium, then into a blast of white. She knew that women fight each silver strand like it's a fuse to a time bomb that explodes into cronedom. On occasion, she had found a couple silver threads in her dirty-blond locks, but she could never find exactly the same hairs. They might be new ones! These secret strands drove her crazy if she stopped to search for them.

Townsend was at least twenty-five years older than his ex-wife, Janice Gallen, who was even younger than April. He had married a baby bride. Janice was probably already knocked up and it might have been a shot gun kind of thing. When April first met his ex-wife at the closing for the house, something much deeper than an age difference seemed to evoke their quite visible disequilibrium. Only blood or money could create such ire.

April got to know Janice better at a surprise visit in February when Janice showed up at the kitchen door. April pushed open the storm and leaned out, fighting the pneumatic closer mechanism that was adjusted too tight. April said, "Can I help you?"

"Oh, I wasn't sure if you were at home," Janice said. "Remember me?"

Janice was a pretty girl, with contradictory aspects. She wore her hair in a high, flouncy pony tail, like women in the grandstands of a Winston Cup challenge. Her jeans were pencil tight and looked veneered to her body, like a more urban slice of trash. April saw her car slathered with bumper stickers and peacenik decals like a hippie taxi from a different era. The preachy emblems on her vehicle and the woman's attire didn't seem to jibe. April said, "Of course I remember you, we met at the closing, right?"

"Sure did. I'm here to get the cat."

April had once or twice seen an orange tom stalking through the back garden. She had thought it was an outdoor cat that belonged to an elderly couple down the road. She told Janice, "You mean that big orange tabby with the tattered ears? Is he yours?"

"Oh, Jesus, not that alley cat. I'm talking about the doorstop." She pointed to the cast-iron kitty propped against one of the French doors in the archway to the living room.

"Oh, right, that's yours. I didn't think you missed it."

"Blaze wants it. We found it at the flea market in the way-back-when. It means something to him."

April thought that the hokey cast-iron tchotski wasn't something that would be typically prized by a juvenile delinquent. The cat was a piece of Americana that had been manufactured to keep *doors open* and seemed like an ironic token for a kid under house arrest. And when Janice said "way-back-when," April was certain that Janice had meant before the kid turned bad, *before* everything fell apart in their happy family.

Janice came into the house, her eyes darting back and forth as if in an instant critique of a spinster's fussy nest with its high-end antiques. She said, "You getting settled?"

"It's slowly coming together."

Then Janice said, "Got any kids?"

April was startled by Janice's bold question. April had not had a baby with Riley. She had once become pregnant with her first husband, Thurlow Johnston, years ago, but it was an ectopic pregnancy that had had to be terminated with minor surgery. The doctor assured her that ectopic pregnancies were not that uncommon. Yet he alarmed her when he explained that in rare instances these abnormal gestations could result in a "stone baby." He said the disorder was called lithopedia, after the Greek word for "stone," and it happens when the fetus, growing outside the womb, is rejected by the body and becomes encapsulated by calcium deposits.

A fossilized fetus was hard to forget, but with Riley she had always been careful not to get pregnant again. She never missed a period.

"No, I don't have children," April told Janice, taken off guard, although she often stopped to look at infants cinched into supermarket baskets, even when they fussed. "Not yet, but someday, who knows? I mean, I love kids."

"You love 'em? Well, if you're in this house, living next door to my son, you'll learn."

"Excuse me?"

"If you're looking to borrow trouble."

Janice lifted the heavy doorstop and cradled it in the crook of her arm.

"Be careful, you'll get stove black on your blouse," April said.

Janice wasn't in any hurry to leave.

April said, "I hope you don't want that table and chairs. I got rid of them. They're at Crosby's Antiques. Of course you should take the consignment, not me. I'll tell him."

"What can it be worth?"

"Mr. Crosby said a couple hundred at least."

"Those old chairs were booby traps."

The women laughed as if they were both in on a little joke, as if they had together hatched a conspiracy against the stuffy antique dealer. Or it might have been laughter about Janice's forsaken marriage, symbolized in the abandoned dining set.

"It's a big house for just one," Janice said, prying. "But congratulations. What's a dinosaur to me might just be paradise for you."

Janice walked over to the barn lugging the heavy doorstop. She was going to see Blaze. She ducked inside the rustic house and April saw a shade tugged down. April didn't see any reason to pull a shade when the day was so overcast.

Thinking of Janice now, she remembered the boy's harsh appraisal of his mother. He had also described the housecat inching closer to the stove when the flames were dying out, as if he was nostalgic for its dying embers. *Well, the fire is out now,* April thought.

The boy was an SOS in the flesh. If she tried to rescue him, she knew that sometimes it's the lifeguard who gets drowned.

She had to be at Sinclair in two hours, but she couldn't move. She stood in her living room. The hundred-year-old plank floor sagged slightly, pitched higher on one side than the other. When the house was inspected before the closing, the contractor had told her that the floor joists should probably be shimmed.

She tried to ignore the slight grade in the floor, but finally she went to look for a marble she had seen in her sewing box. It was a cat's-eye keepsake from childhood that she'd saved in a little jar of buttons. She found the marble and placed it on the bare boards in one corner of the living room. The marble started to roll towards the center, slowly at first, then accelerating, until it hit the fringe of an area rug.

The tilted planking was dizzying, and April couldn't help thinking that the slanting floor was a metaphor for her life tipping in a mysterious direction. It would have to be looked at by a professional.

She pivoted in a circle to study the room. Her furniture didn't seem to fit. She moved an end table. She ceremoniously repositioned a standing lamp that was lost behind a chair, pulling it forward where it could be admired. Next, she shoved her sofa across the floor so it rested at the diagonal. That, too, wasn't the answer. She tried to re-create the balanced and cozy arrangement she had achieved before the kid had arrived and slouched on her settee. Something had changed. The homey feeling she had worked hard to create had somehow evaporated, but she didn't know why. When she looked outside, she saw the sulky teenage boy standing in an opposite window in Townsend's unfinished barnyard condo. The kid was in some kind of gloomy huff with his forehead pressed against the cloudy pane of glass. His face had that familiar *Go ahead. Just try to save me* expression she recognized from her years as a teacher. He watched her for an instant in frozen time. Before she could react to his glower-some Edgar Allan, he dipped his shoulders and turned away. The window was empty.

Chapter Seven

Blaze stood before the antique pedestal mirror that his mother had left behind. He pushed his jeans down and was almost naked, except for his Virtual Arrest ankle cuff. With his pants unbuttoned, he browsed, unrushed, through a stack of his dad's retro *Hustler* magazines. He'd found them in a sliding tower on the new pantry shelves Townsend had just finished sanding. After Janice left him, Townsend didn't bother to hide his magazines. The ancient fold-outs were tame compared with current Internet porn. The carefully air-brushed photos seemed almost prudish, but the novelty of these leftover pussy shots had a pervy attraction.

Blaze tried to imagine these girls *today*. They'd be hot-hot forty-somethings, about the same age as his new neighbor next door. After meeting April that morning, he found the magazines seemed stale. So he stood at the window to spy on the old farmhouse. The newcomer hadn't put up all her curtains. He wanted to think that maybe she liked him watching her.

When a cruiser didn't show up, he was certain she hadn't made noise. The tulips were a success, when he had expected she'd throw them in the dirt. And when he had returned the car, he saw it in her eyes—that look that says, *What are you doing to me? Keep doing it.* She was hypnotized. That's what he wanted to see.

He watched her push her girly sofa across the room. With its one side higher than the other end, it wasn't a practical item like the geometric sectional his mom had bought at Crate and Barrel. But his mom took the couch with her when she moved out, leaving them with nothing to sit on in front of their new flat-panel TV. So Townsend picked up a huge, scuffed leather couch from Jordan's Furniture Warehouse. It was brand new, but looked beat up. Townsend told Blaze it was called "distressed leather" and it was supposed to look "lived in."

Blaze didn't think April would like it.

April shoved her French sofa in the other direction, back to where it had been. She couldn't make up her mind.

And just the other day, Blaze had found Townsend's good binocs in an old box of hand-carved bird-calls, field guides, and shot gun shells. On a clear night he knew how to find Aldebaran, the brightest star, despite all that navstar hardware all over the sky. He went outside and climbed onto the barn roof. He wasn't looking for constellations. Tucked behind its north-side ridge he had a good view into April's second floor bedroom. Her café curtains came up only half way. He watched her sitting on her bed in just her bra and panties as she pulled on her knee-socks. He adjusted the Bausch and Lomb trademark Twist-up eye cups, thumbing the center focus knob until she was sharp, sharper, sharpest.

He pulled her in.

Her tight bikini underpants were printed with tiny flower buds. He focused the binocs until he saw her gorgeous little camel toe, perfectly defined. But he was fighting the roof's steep twelve foot pitch and he almost slipped down the asphalt sheeting.

Now, he steadied the glasses to watch April re-arrange her living room. Her jersey was riding up higher as she bear-hugged the antique sofa. The little knob of her tail bone was visible above the waistband of her low-riding hip-huggers.

Her lonely tussle with her furniture bothered him. Women's secret domestic chores were mysterious, and worse, he didn't like it when, out of the blue, people started plucking his heartstrings.

Townsend called it "girl trouble" when men let feelings about women intrude on their common sense. He told his son, "Prioritize like this: paycheck, vehicle, season tickets, whiskey, prime beef, then, okay, maybe some distraction like that." Townsend avoided crude idioms and never said "pussy" or "tits and ass," but used words like "distraction" and "extra curricular" when he instructed Blaze about women. Townsend never acknowledged that Blaze had already had his fiery baptism. He refused to listen to the stories Blaze told him, exhibiting his disbelief and disinterest with mock repulsion and a bit of genuine rivalry. Regardless of his father, Blaze had navigated the rough waters and fjords of sex. Then he hooked up with his first real girlfriend, Lucinda.

Blaze thought of her now as he sampled the cornucopia of fresh pink from yesteryear, following his progress in the tilted reflection of the pedestal mirror. It was almost a done deal before he'd even gotten started. The ankle cuff didn't distract him as it had in the very first days he was rigged when he had felt like a rooster with its leg caught in a chicken-wire fence.

That's how he often felt during each ordeal with women. He'd start out with his presumptions—he liked to believe it was catch and release. He was the trapper, but then it got turned around, and it was he who was trapped. Lucinda was sometimes the trigger, the gun powder, and the target of his fantasies. Now he had to deal with the hottie next door prancing around her living room. She was aloof and too cerebral, but even so, he saw her as a fascinating bull's-eye, reminding Blaze of an incident at the Westerly Rod and Gun Club when someone had tacked *Penthouse* centerfolds on the target boards until feminist Nazis wrote to the newspaper about it.

The telephone intruded. It was Townsend's new Droid with a bitchy jangle. Like oldsters all over, Townsend still hadn't got the hang of taking his phone with him, and he sometimes left it behind. Blaze looked at the caller ID. J. GALLEN. Maybe Janice's neighbors had seen him nosing around her A-frame. He didn't pick up. He was in the middle of his rewind of Lucinda. And then he had the pussy prof, his new taboo entrancement. He didn't need his mom to distract him.

He remembered when April had said, "I'm getting a pretty good instinct about you." He had thought he heard her say she had a "pink-stink." He loved that warm sweetness girls have between the legs, a familiar yeasty scent, like when Janice lifted a dish towel off a bowl of rising bread dough.

He tried to maintain a mind and body disconnection as he spied on his neighbor next door. Women of interest evoked the same kind of dead-or-alive, bait-or-repellant reaction in him. You *want*. You *want to avoid*. Townsend had said it's never good to show you're aroused if it's mutual on her part, or too lovey-dovey.

Sex was a hate thing.

He tried not to think. It was better just to close his eyes.

With his eyes shut, he saw familiar sparks and patterns, the busy print of Janice's Wamsutta bed sheets, swirling like vitreous floaters.

Just thinking of the quirky word "Wamsutta" triggered wood.

Watching April, he remembered a time before his folks divorced when he'd intruded on his mom in the bathroom. Blaze had just started shaving and wanted to use Townsend's old shaving mug to soap up. Janice said, "You can't use this sink right now. I'm washing my hair brushes." He saw her hair brushes lined up on the shelf above her head.

She was washing her *panties* in the suds.

When he was a little kid Janice would take off her blouse so he could drive his Matchbox cars through the Johnson's baby powder she sprinkled on her back. She'd lie on the couch in the heat of the day and unclip her bra so that Blaze could roll his cars up and down her spine. He liked to push the cars, making looping tracks in the talc. The air would fill with a cloud of it and would sometimes make him cough. "Don't use too much," she said. "It isn't good to breathe baby powder. Don't inhale it." That's how it started, as an innocent partnership that began on a humid summer day.

Listening to April's fears about the sludge pile he understood her anxiety. He had his own nightmares about being buried in a mountain of white dust, or he dreamed he fell into a mine shaft of snowy silt. He'd wake from these dreams smothered in his pillow. He still thought of Janice as a mystery attraction, harsh and beautiful, fully dangerous and not just "high maintenance." Now it was this stranger in the window where his mom used to be.

He pulled up his jeans and cinched his accessorized belt. He tried to accept the annoying Virtual Arrest contraptions as mere hardware.

As soon as the cuff came off, he was going to find Lucinda.

He had met the girl in high school, when he was sent to live with Janice's sister, Cheryl, in Providence. His aunt had had her own problems. When he moved into her house Blaze entered a dime novel already in progress.

His Aunt Cheryl's place was a busy den of out-of-work friends and free-range roosters who came and went. It was under her roof that Blaze took his first drink, J&B in a colorful Homer Simpson's tumbler, the same glass from which he drank milk at breakfast. At his aunt's house Blaze picked up his hard-core cigarette habit, keeping his carton stashed in a tube sock, so no one would steal his smokes. His aunt never cleaned the cluttered rooms. The long, rectangular sock didn't seem to intrigue her.

Nights, he fought for the best chair in front of the TV to watch Howard Stern but he had to endure *Sports Huddle* chats with the older men. Blaze ran off more than one time. Each time he tried to hitch home to East Westerly, staties always picked him up and brought him back to his aunt's. Kids stick out loitering on exit ramps. Blaze was tall but skinny as a turkey baster. He didn't beef up, but seemed to grow an inch taller between breakfast and dinner.

While living with his aunt, he attended Classical High School in down-town Providence. At Classical, he developed an obsessive attraction to a senior, Lucinda Mackey. Lucinda was two grades ahead of him. She fell under his spell despite their different social spheres and academic levels.

He showed up at her modern, architectural mansion and jimmied a window to get inside. Her father was a physician at Mercy Hospital, and Blaze knew she was a rich girl. Yet he was surprised to see that the foyer was like a hotel lobby with a vaulted ceiling and the floors had overly padded, plush carpeting that he had trouble walking on to get to Lucinda's bedroom. Once there, she plucked off her baby-doll pajamas in teasing slow motion. But her father crashed into the room and chased Blaze out. Blaze wasn't wearing any trousers as the man trailed him two blocks and across a busy intersection.

He ducked inside someone's breezeway to hide from Dr. Mackey. He was surprised to find that a pet collie was curled on a pillowy dog bed in one corner of the porch. She was whelping a litter, right there and then. With four pups already, the bitch was mouthing a new one, cleaning off its glistening cellophane birth sac.

The house was dark and the dog's owners were missing the red-letter moment.

Blaze knelt beside the collie, awed by the miracle, and he tried not to interrupt its natural cycle. He didn't notice Lucinda's father until he was standing right behind him.

"Jesus, what do we have here?" Dr. Mackey said when he saw the collie tribe.

"You think she needs a vet?" Blaze said.

"I don't know about her, but you're going to need a hospital—"

Blaze scrabbled onto his feet and shot out the porch door, dislodging the screen panel which flip-flopped after him as he stumbled off the stoop.

The man chased him down an alley before giving up. Freezing to death, wearing only his boxers, Blaze searched for a pay phone in several empty Verizon shrines. Each time he found the familiar Plexiglas shack or a wall-mounted shell, the telephones had been removed. When he finally got lucky, he made a collect call to Townsend.

"Okay. I'll get there," Townsend said.

"Bring me some pants."

Both Townsend and Janice drove into town to get him. Janice said, "I told you that girl was trouble."

"Maybe she's a little too fast," Townsend said.

"She's an upper crustacean. A Miss Deb slut." Janice sounded brittle.

"She's teaching me how to French-kiss without slobbering."

Janice said, "Well, I guess it's good for you to practice now. Not like your father who never learned how."

Blaze saw she was jealous that Lucinda had kissed him. Janice's envy was annoying, but it also reassured him to hear her prickly two cents. Her disembodied scolds and caveats always had that familiar squeeze to them.

In the spring, Blaze and Lucinda disappeared together. They decided to hitch to the West Coast, but had made no preparations. They got as far as New Mexico and camped in a desert meadow near an old folks' trailer park. Blaze made a teepee tent from sheets of Tyvek weather wrap he had found at a construction site. He called it Rancho Lucinda so the girl wouldn't complain. He promised to get her into a condo when they hit Los Angeles. But she was thinking of her parents' palace and all its amenities. She talked about her folks like they were all members of a private club. She'd had a tiff with the organization, but she'd be going back if he didn't get the garden apartment with the swimming pool, like he promised her he would.

Instead, Blaze convinced a retired senior to let them into her double-wide trailer when Lucinda complained about seeing a scorpion in their tent. The old woman fed them supper every night in exchange for chores. Lucinda did laundry, baked meringues and lemon squares. Blaze repaired furniture and covered a rusty refrigerator with contact paper. They greeted spring in the desert, watching cactus flowers erupt in drifts. Monks' hood and prickly pear, and one called dwarf's chin, which grew alongside the trailer. The crone who befriended them taught them the flowers' memorable names and told them wives' tales about their medicinal uses.

Lucinda missed her period. She was nervous and told Blaze that she wanted to go back to Rhode Island. Lucinda had had a science teacher who had explained that human gestation mimics the process of evolution—from worm, to fish, to a lizard with scales—and this progression was repugnant to her.

Blaze tried to calm her down. He knew her pregnancy was his scratch-ticket jackpot. If a baby was really coming, Lucinda wasn't going to throw him over. She'd *have* to belong to him.

She told him she needed to see her mom.

When they hitched back to Rhode Island, she was too scared to face her parents, and Blaze took her to East Westerly. They found Janice in the garden shack. She was using the Shop-Vac to collect a furious constellation of spiderlings that had hatched, like thousands of hairy peppercorns spinning in all directions. Janice almost didn't recognize her son with his deep bronzed skin and his long hair bleached from the desert sun. If she was pleased to see him alive, she didn't show it, and kept jabbing the vacuum nozzle across the plank floor, sipping up spiders.

She looked at Lucinda and said, "Returning the merchandise?"

"I'm pregnant," the girl said with dizzy confidence. Then she burst into tears.

Janice sat back on her heels, the Shop-Vac still roaring. "Poor babies," she told them, lumping the two of them in with the unsuspecting unborn, and perhaps with all the teensy spiders expanding in wider circles.

"We're keeping it," Blaze said.

"Men aren't the ones who decide about babies. You did your part, now it's her choice. Right, Lucinda?"

"My choice? I don't know—" The girl seemed frightened of her advantage when Janice spelled it out. Feminist ideology was a luxury she couldn't adapt to if it actually required her to have an active role.

Blaze looked back and forth, from his *un*bride to his *un*mom, searching each face to see where he stood. Just like he feared, the females seemed united. Their shattered intimacies with him had formed a bond between them.

Janice told the girl, "We'll go to Planned Parenthood. It's easy. It's almost like a drive-through. But honey, your mom has to sign something."

"Can't you sign it?"

"This state is top-heavy Catholic. They need parental consent."

The clinic said that the procedure would take place over a period of two to three days. It required that Lucinda have a sponge inserted to dilate her cervix before she could have the vacuum extraction. Janice was concerned that if the girl waited for the sponge to expand, she'd have time to change her mind. Janice brought her home with them to make sure the girl kept the little thimble of sponge tucked in. Blaze told Lucinda, "Look, you don't have to go through with it."

Janice said, "That sponge isn't listening to *you*."

Blaze didn't understand the procedure. He thought Janice was calling Lucinda a stupid girl.

His hayride with Lucinda was over, he knew.

At first he had thought that the unexpected baby was like hitting a speed bump too fast; the bump might take it out of alignment, but it was fixable. But with Janice in the driver's seat, the whole chassis comes off the axel. The wheels toe in; the engine block breaks loose and collapses onto the concrete. Everything comes to a screeching halt.

After the abortion, Lucinda's parents shipped her off to a famous upscale psychiatric compound just outside Boston, not much different from a finishing school or spa for wealthy problem kids. Because of her unauthorized months with Blaze her parents wanted her emotions sanitized, massaged, and toned. Every trace of Blaze, his wicked soulfulness and poisonous pheromones should be erased from her consciousness, which wasn't of great magnitude, and therefore was wholly tabula rasa within a few days.

During her confinement she wrote Blaze a platonic note. She didn't even say she missed him.

Blaze hitched to Belmont and walked into MacLean Hospital after hours. He never got close to Lucinda's wing. In a confrontation with two uncompromising uniforms he overturned a potted palm and threatened a busy-body therapist who tried to defuse the eruption. The mini palm had a price tag of $1,100. He was taken off and grilled in district court then handed over to Rhode Island staties. He was dumped on the doormat at Rhode Island Training School.

Blaze hated cops. His dad had once been stopped by a trooper who lost a contact lens when he was writing a ticket. Townsend helped the trooper search for it on the shoulder of the road; they spent a good while combing the blades of grass and sorting the gravel, but Townsend still got the ticket. And Blaze remembered watching a segment of the syndicated TV show *COPS*. Police tried to sweet-talk a jumper off a bridge, saying, "Come on, get down off that ledge, we'll talk about it. You're not under arrest. We won't cuff you." Liars! As soon as the jumper climbed down, the cops kneed him in the back, wrestled him to the ground, and slapped the cuffs on him. Endangering himself was a crime, they told the despondent soul. Every scratched suicide, no matter how amateur, goes on the books.

At his intake interview at RITS, while absorbing the austere monochrome of his new surroundings—the tile grout was prehistoric, like a cave mosaic of yellowed cigarette breath, slime mold, urine mist and, yes, airborne fecal dust—Blaze asked for a piece of blank paper. He wrote the first of many terse missives to Lucinda, short and sweet. "If you're hoping that I'll forget about you, I hate to burst your bubble."

Janice and her sister, Cheryl, said it was because of Lucinda that Blaze had been nicked. When Townsend visited RITS, he told his son that Lucinda wasn't the first female to cause Blaze injury. Janice had had him rubberstamped as trouble before he was ever born.

Blaze had always known he was an accident. He had also learned that his name had come from an argument. When Janice was expecting, Townsend told his wife that he wanted the privilege of naming his firstborn Jack, in honor of his father. He told Janice she could choose the name if the baby turned out to be a girl. The doctor had already read the ultrasound picture and told them it was a boy. Janice had never liked her father-in-law, Jack Townsend, the reigning patriarch at the farmhouse where she lived with her new husband. Day to day, she was wedged between Townsend and his father and was under their dual scrutiny and constant criticism. She never had any say in household decisions, and her father-in-law restricted her use of the car. She took the car out anyway, and the man wasn't happy when she had a wreck. It wasn't her fault, she told him. "I was driving and a huge wolf spider jumped in my lap. It crawled into my shirt cuff!" She ended up in a ditch. The old man didn't believe her story. He told her that woman drivers lived up to their name. Townsend's father abruptly passed away from pancreatic cancer—the span of his illness was fast as lightning. During the mourning period, Janice didn't buy extra Kleenex.

The winter before their baby was born Townsend took delivery of a quarter horse colt, a gift for his wife. The two-year-old was a gorgeous sorrel with one white sock and a big white face. Townsend started working with the colt, breaking it slow and easy. It would be a fine pleasure horse for Janice when she was ready to ride again and the colt would be civilized by the time his son was old enough to have his first saddle lesson.

Janice was pleased with the colt. "God, he's handsome," she said. She had a funny smile on her face, like the cat that ate the canary, when she told Townsend, "Just so you know, I'm calling my horse Jack."

When Janice squared off with Townsend, she was seven months along, her belly between them. Townsend was forced to relinquish the name.

Six weeks later, Townsend sat next to Janice's hospital bed holding his little son in his arms. He looked into the infant's fresh face, cooing baby talk. At almost fifty years old, he was surprised to hear himself shift to soft murmurs and sugary back-of-the-throat growls as he purred to the cunning newcomer. He nuzzled his prize and told Janice he had decided on a name for their son.

She sat up in bed. "You have a name?"

"I'm calling him Blaze."

Janice recognized the switcheroo. Her ruse had backfired. She told Townsend that she wished she'd never laid eyes on that quarter horse colt with its white splash from its forelock to its muzzle. She said, "Okay, very funny. So tell me the real name?"

He didn't blink.

"Hey, you're going too far with this—"

He was serious. The horse was Jack, and the baby was Blaze.

"You can name the next one," he told her.

"Don't dream of it," she said. "He's the first and last."

For years, just to needle Townsend and to make sure to remind him, she called their son First and Last. Janice insisted the horse be sold but Jack remained in the family, even after the accident and its leg was maimed. It was a survivor, despite a bitter joke. It became their disabled mascot, a harbinger of their crippled marriage. They didn't yet know that the horse meant to hold on longer than they would.

Chapter Eight

April saw Townsend loading his truck. She found her boots and pulled them on. She'd try to catch him before he left, but she had no intention of telling him about his son's joy ride. That was a little pouch of powder that she wanted to keep in reserve. She wanted to talk about the sludge pile.

Blaze appeared beside his father's truck. She watched the two of them square off in some sort of argument. As they stood nose to nose, April recognized how much the father and son looked alike, long-legged, lanky, their features chiseled with an identical cleft of the chin. They both had the same nice cheekbones.

Blaze was pretty deadpan. But as the duo tore into it, his father maintained a natural grin. His demeanor was neither as tarnished nor as wounded as his son's. Townsend oozed organic charm. He proved to have a comfortable seniority and the upper hand.

Blaze stomped away from the truck. Whatever the snit was, Townsend had won the contest.

Townsend sensed he was being watched by his neighbor. At the closing for the house Townsend had tried to learn April's statistics, asking her if there was a "mister." She, too, seemed to want to know about him. For instance, he had recently been forced to retire from his corporate job as account executive and administrative manager at Diggs & Snyder Industries in Providence.

D & S, a local toy manufacturer famous for its board games, had refused to become the newest acquisition of Hasbro, which had already absorbed Parker Brothers and Milton Bradley. Milton Bradley had in fact once stolen an idea from Diggs & Snyder in '42. Milton Bradley's famous game Chutes and Ladders was modeled after an original Diggs & Snyder game called Dumbwaiter. Staying independent had caused hardships at the company, but Townsend had been linked to an office scandal. He was miffed to learn that the realtor had told April everything.

He had his own ammunition about his neighbor. At the closing he had learned that April had a birthday coming up. She had said "I'll celebrate a milestone next summer in my new house. The big Four Oh."

"No kidding? You know, *'Forty is the youth of old age, fifty is the old age of youth.'* I guess you wonder where that puts me?" he had asked April.

"Over the hill," Janice said, "and through the valley of the shadow of . . ."

That morning, Townsend had been instructing Blaze,

"Look, before I get home tonight I want all that wood stacked. Just work on that pile without wrecking anything. Maybe when I come home we'll go to Warwick Bowl with your Brunswick apple. We'll call Dick Yarborough and get him to adjust the GPS on your bracelet."

Blaze said, "You think I want to go to the lanes with you like a nine-year-old?"

"So don't act like one."

"I'm not bowling."

"How about candle pins?"

Blaze left him jabbering to the empty ground. Every time Townsend tried to tickle the on-and-off switch with his son, he hit the wrong button. Townsend was still finding his legs after losing his corporate job, trying to adapt to his life, not just as a novice entrepreneur starting his own business, but as a single parent.

He had resigned from Diggs & Snyder after he had helped a junior colleague launch a six-month spree of illegal transactions. He paired up with the black-sheep son of the company's CFO. The thirty-something junior executive–slash–Enron wannabe had been in charge of contracting factory help for outsourced work orders in India. Townsend set up a graft operation with a point person overseas, and when the kid went abroad for a meeting he came back saying that the "towel head" was tickled pink with Townsend's mock-up of a secret spread sheet. Together they invented schemes involving ghost employees, inflated payroll directories, and fabricated invoices. Expenses were attributed to phantom pallets of Diggs & Snyder mini bowling sets, Velcro dart boards, travel-size magnetic chess sets, and other small ticket items, by a half million gross. Good sums were skimmed with every wire transfer of money, and they raked in a lot more because Townsend had "check-signing authority." The youngster was feeding his gambling addiction at Mohegan Sun and Pocono Downs, but Townsend was cautious and filtered his take into invisible piggy-bank accounts. Most of the work was electronic, and Townsend had helped the baby VIP go in and get out, creating fake codes and passwords that evaporated in timed segments to cover their trail. Townsend was the graybeard brains of it. For a substantial gratuity.

An internal audit eventually proved that Townsend himself had entered figures; not every entry had been washed clean. When the theft was discovered, the younger executive's amateur heist was swept under the rug because of his family ties. He was the offspring of both a Snyder niece and a second-generation Diggs, who was in fact a prominent shareholder and who literally ruled the company, on paper. The kid had his blood umbrella and his father bailed him out. Townsend didn't have any safety net when a PI forensic accountant proved that Townsend must have received a percentage of the stolen receipts in the amount of $500,000. It was even more than that. Federal and IRS investigators, if alerted, would have fried him. Diggs & Snyder couldn't pursue Townsend without exposing the chief financial officer's scoundrel son. The CFO had come forward to fork over the amount his son owed the company, keeping it under a cloak of executive privilege. The board was never informed of the disembodied cash flow. The CFO soaped windows, but his son would be expected to meet a rigid payment schedule thereafter. Townsend resigned from Diggs & Snyder without any gold-watch emendations to his retirement benefits but with his fraudulent bonus intact. "That's a gag pension," his boss, an old friend, teased him. The worst of his problems was Janice. She'd try to get her share if she could.

He planned to let her in, as soon as she decided to come back to him. A nest egg needs a hen. He was giving her a little more time to wake up from her nightmare with John Two and to decide she couldn't live without Townsend. If not right now, for his later years, for what Townsend's ailing father had called "the long walk home," he wanted Janice beside him.

His barfly kin at the Hilltop Tavern said it must be taxing for a man his age to manage a teenager single-handedly, especially a troubled kid. He corrected them, saying that Blaze was "sensitive," not troubled. "It's a delicate balance—trying to juggle the *good*, the *bad*, and the *ugly*. A blood horse isn't a donkey."

He was behind the wheel when April trotted over to the Tundra. The dogs jumped down from the truck bed to circle her legs, happy to see her. She shoved them away repeatedly as they nuzzled her pockets looking for treats.

Townsend thumbed his window button and nestled into his captain's chair, grinning, and waited for her to mouth off. He could see she was revved up.

"Do you have a minute?" she said.

"For you? I've got minutes or hours, you tell me," he teased her.

He climbed out of the truck, careful not to stand too close to her so she wouldn't be hit with the give-away scent of gin. It was only the mid-morning. Her coffee pot probably hadn't even clicked to its automatic shut-off and she didn't need to know he'd already been to the tavern. He often went to the Hilltop to join the retired stone cutters who liked to greet the sunrise with their elbows up.

She said, "Do you have the paperwork on that manure?" She gently kneed the jittery brindle who circled her legs, but the dog kept worming back to her.

"The paperwork?"

He'd had his fill of zoning board Nazis; he didn't think she'd be the type.

"Aren't there restrictions about hazardous waste?" she said. "In California these sales are banned."

"Are we in California?" he said. "Besides, Surfer Girl, this is green product. It's not yellowcake uranium, you know."

"It's too close to the house. It's shifting."

Townsend studied the hill of sludge. He unclipped his measuring tape from his belt and together he and April walked over to her place. He hooked the tab on a window well and walked back to the hill, unrolling the spool. The tape said that it was only twenty feet from the foundation to the sludge heap.

He said, "Jesus, what's happening here?"

"I told you there's something wrong. That pile is toppling. What are you going to do about it?"

"Question is—what is *it* doing?"

He watched her face freeze.

He said, "Look, out here it's live and let live. That's sort of our Appalachian oath. Our boonies code. Want to come aboard?" He was warning her: *You can't beat us, so join us.*

Recently, there had been newcomers, the occasional gentrified exec or college prof, like April, who had found a little country retreat. Getting gas at the Mobil in town, Townsend had met a new resident, a stuffy academic who commuted to work three times a week from East Westerly all the way to Sarah Lawrence in Bronxville, New York. The fellow had bragged that he crossed three states in under two hours. Townsend noticed books tossed on his dashboard, *The Essential Kierkegaard* and *The Origins of Totalitarianism*. These titles were lined up where everyone could see them. He was just another snobby four-eyed neighbor, but East Westerly was still the sticks.

Townsend told April, "We've got silos, we've got livestock. It's the country out here." April told him that she liked the "rural setting." Two squat silos nearby looked like a salt and pepper set. Big rolls of baled hay resembled popovers or brioches. And she wanted to start a garden. She noticed the common names of flowers mirrored simple human joys and fits of pique, moral quandaries, icy judgments, and deceptions. There was one called mock orange and another called false indigo. There were old-world favorites that suggested daily plights, like one called obedience plant and another called loosestrife. She was amused by two flowers with opposing names: bee balm and bugbane.

A half mile down the road, a neighbor raised llamas and miniature horses. April told Townsend that when she first drove by the place, she had thought the tiny horses were salvaged carousel ponies that people often bought at antique barns. In Watch Hill they claimed to have the oldest operating merry-go-round in the country—maybe these were originals, salvaged from that tourist trap. The diminutive herd was arranged at random, just as some homeowners displayed fake deer or mirrored balls on their front lawns. As she rolled past the merry-go-round cast-offs, the little horses lifted their heads and pricked their ears. They swished their silky tails and shook their heavy manes.

She said, "That mini zoo is almost a mile down the highway. It isn't in my lap like your septic heap."

"I've got a business here," he told her.

April asked him about a hand made billboard at the entrance. "Can you translate? Sounds like a Chinese riddle."

He told her, "Sleep. Creep. Leap. That describes a garden's stages of growth. First year, your saplings take hold but don't gain in size or height. The next year, new shoots erupt and there are signs of progress. Then pow! The third season, there's a blooming blitz. Shrubs get fat, they leaf out, and everything flowers."

She seemed unnerved by his fanaticism.

He said, "How about you? What stage are you at?"

"Excuse me?"

"Sleep? Creep? Leap? Where are you?"

"Me? I'm trying to dump my boyfriend. I guess that's the leap phase."

"You want to leave your boyfriend?"

"I'm in the leap stage, because *he's* in the creep stage."

"Then cut him loose," he said. "'Growth follows the knife.'"

She stared at him as if she mistook his charming maxims and sage advice for a menacing condescension. He was always revising his approach with women, trying to find the exact combination of fruitful flirtation and necessary caution. He often used his iron-fist-in-a-velvet-glove technique when he negotiated, and he had always found it helpful to add a pro-phylaxis of needling criticism. He tried to ignore how pretty she looked when she was trying to perfect her scowl. He could see she wasn't a scowler by nature, and was just a dabbler. In her battle mode, she became very attractive. Her heart-shaped face was pronounced, with her pointy little chin thrust out, and she wore a very erotic lip-nibbling pout.

She gestured to a patch of weeds that traveled along the post and rail fence between their properties. "Is that poison ivy?"

He said, "That's not ivy, that's wild grape, or what they call fox grape."

"But it's creeping across. I thought grape likes to climb. Doesn't grape want an arbor?"

"It's *wild* grape. It doesn't come with its own arbor. This grape travels laterally until it finds something to grab on to.

It has to do some sideways searching. Now you look like someone—"

"I look like what?"

"Like someone who might have done a little sideways searching."

He used his corny garden talk to pry into her. In fact he liked to read nature poetry. He could easily quote from Wendell Berry or recite Robert Frost.

> *Nature's first green is gold,*
> *Her hardest hue to hold.*
> *Her early leaf's a flower;*
> *But only so an hour.*

"Maybe you can get some Weed-B-Gone?" she said.

He looked at her. He was thinking that, in his experience, women this bitchy wanted an *itch* scratched.

"That pile of mud has to be moved," she finally said, "and calling it mud is generous. Can't you use one of these tractors? It's like a John Deere showroom out here."

"Well, I do tree surgery, stump grinding, brush removal, stone walls, driveways, koi ponds. I need the equipment." He looked at each machine with satisfaction. The Bobcat mini backhoe. The Gravely brush scourer. The Ditch Witch trencher. He wanted to order a tree spade. With that one, he could clear-cut the Amazon rain forest. He didn't tell her that he had already sunk a couple hundred thousand in the business. He didn't think it would impress her.

April told him, "That waste is laden with chemicals, cadmium and cyanide, heavy metals and, of course, it's got the unmentionable. I get these headaches."

"You have headaches? I can beat that. I've got acid reflux. I have to sleep sitting up. You don't want to know my list of complaints, do you?"

He patted his breast pocket hoping April didn't notice he had a little pill organizer hidden in his jacket.

Okay. She wanted sympathy for her headaches. A woman with borderline hysteria was often attractive to him; it sometimes meant a little extra voltage in the bedroom, although he knew from his sex squalls with Janice that high-strung women were a handful. He believed Janice would eventually come crawling back, but in the meantime—

April turned on her heel and started to walk away.

"Wait," he called after her, "if this pile is really eating you up, I think you need an outlet. Maybe you need to get out more. Maybe tonight, you'll come over for a drink?"

She turned around. "You're inviting me for drinks? Will your son be home? Because we have to talk about him."

"You want to help him with his GED?"

"He's not my problem."

"Okay. Maybe *I'm* your problem."

"Did you know he was over at my house this morning?"

"He told me."

"What did he say?"

He thought she seemed a little breathless, whether from an irritable consternation or some sort of bubbly anticipation, he couldn't gauge.

She said, "That electronic cuff isn't working."

"He's trying. Give him some time."

"He's supposed to be *doing* time. Not wasting mine."

She had touched a nerve. His kid's ordeal was the one little chip on his shoulder that he couldn't brush off. He was supposed to be on a job in Coventry, but if she wanted to know the story, he'd unroll the papyrus until she was sorry to have stuck her nose in. He told her, "Family court is a racket. It's a salaried cottage industry. They make a paper trail of fantasy stories they cook up just so they can punch a clock." He explained to April that Blaze was teetering before a possible stretch at the ACI, the adult corrections facility in Cranston.

The antiquated maximum-security crime bin was a long-standing Rhode Island landmark visible from I-95. It housed the typical hard-core specialists and wasn't a safe setting for MINS or CHINS.

"MINS or CHINS? What's that?" she asked.

"Minors or children. *In Need of Supervision.*" The ACI's gloomy brick towers, its chain-link fences and coils of razory concertina wire that stretched across the perimeter like a nightmare slinky, were always in his mind.

His son might end up like some of these young men who kept doing bit after bit, doing life on the installment plan. "He doesn't belong in that rat hole," Townsend said.

"So who decides where he goes? Family court or DSS?"

"They're in cahoots. They're a beast with two backs."

Townsend described his son's last session before the Family court judge. "He stands there like a man. He doesn't put on a courtroom smile like those other kids when they stand up, as if butter won't melt in their mouths.

"Of course, we've had our own combat history," Townsend told her, "but DSS says, 'The child is non-amenable to further services.' *Non-amenable*. Jesus. So they give him to me. That's good. I'll take him."

"So his mom didn't want him?" She asked the burning question.

Townsend explained that Janice said her peace-loving neighbors at the land compact didn't want her combustive JD son to ruin their settlement's hard-earned sanctuary. "Janice's new boyfriend doesn't like Blaze in the house. He'd just as well have him locked up at RITS."

April knew that RITS was the unfortunate acronym that rhymed with zits, for the Rhode Island Training School in Cranston.

One of her students was working on his MSW and had asked her to advise him with a thesis project. He had created a sort of Scared Straight website to be used as a new deterrent to gang involvement. The student had installed the Internet site complete with digital photographs and video links to the training school. He called it "Virtual Tour of RITS." The photos showed the institution's worst aspects: razor-wire basketball courts; close-up shots of cafeteria goo and slop; thin mattresses on concrete racks; stainless steel toilets without toilet seats or paper holders. The web site was a room-by-room, face-to-face pictorial visit to juvie jail.

The horses had come to the gate. The white-faced freak pricked its ears and nickered in tender clucking notes that were almost like a bedroom sound. "He likes you," Townsend said.

"He says he likes me?"

"I'm talking about the horse," Townsend said.

He watched her face flush pink.

She quickly changed the subject. "So you left Diggs & Snyder to start up this business with your son?"

He told her, "I came to realize I was a mere speck within a wide slice of the pie chart, in white-collar paralysis. It was a simple decision to turn my attention to my son. And the judge liked the idea. He told me about Robert Reich—"

"President Clinton's secretary of labor? That one?"

"Reich quit his post in D.C. to return home to Massachusetts just to raise his two boys. He chose his sons' well-being over his own career."

April said, "Reich's kids must be white-bread Ivy League eggheads."

"Oh, you think it's a pipe dream for us?" He heard himself sounding defensive, and that's a bad perch when you're wrangling a girl.

She said, "Those Beltway patriarchs are notorious failures. I'm sure you'll do fine."

She was just dishing applesauce, but he liked her already. April had a little word fire that he enjoyed. He imagined their conversations if he could get her up on a bar stool or nestled in the bucket seat beside him. He'd take her to the Sand Bar, a romantic cocktail lounge on the water, rather than bringing her into the Hilltop, where she'd be surrounded by bar-flies. She wouldn't appreciate that. And Janice often came into the Sand Bar. His stock would go up if Janice saw him sitting with April. He'd show Janice he could spread his wings—he could flap them! And he was thinking that if the court sent that guardian ad litem busybody to sniff out details about his parenting skills, dating a college prof would be a strategic move.

"You know the label those DSS pencil pushers give to kids like Blaze? They say he's 'unredeemable.'"

Non-amenable. Unredeemable. It was like having your child called terminal by an oncologist at the cancer center at Children's Hospital. Townsend refused to accept the prognosis. Townsend said, "I know Blaze can jerk a chain, rubbing people the wrong way. He plays tough. You have to laugh. But these agencies have never seen his better side."

Sensing her disbelief, he said, "Like when Blaze started a punk band, you know what he called it?"

"I imagine it's pretty shocking."

"He called his band All Smiles."

"That's sort of temperate for a punk band," she said. "Are you sure it's not just ironic and the joke's on us?"

Townsend told April that All Smiles was the same name

that Blaze had christened the beloved family dinghy that they had kept moored nearby. He didn't say that the skiff was currently at the bottom of Chapman Pond or explain to her how it had got there.

April said she sometimes saw record reviews in the student paper about punk bands with those in-your-face names like Asshole Parade, Rancid, or Me First and the Gimme Gimmes.

"I know. There's skinhead punk, thrash, power violence, and even vegan punk. Blaze once did a cover of 'Mack the Knife.' It was blistering. It was genius."

He told her that the court didn't know Blaze in his tender moments, like when he had volunteered to work with disabled kids at a horse camp called Mon Ami le Cheval. And in summer, he sometimes wore the hummingbird-feeder hat. He would put on the floppy fedora with a beaker of sugar water attached to its brim and sit stone still in the garden, waiting for the hummers to come to him.

"He has the patience to do that?" she said.

"You see? He's not trying out for the Crips or the Bloods."

She said, "I guess you're happy to be out of the office and to have your boy at home?"

"I don't miss the eye strain from those buzzing strip-light panels, or those three martini headaches after business lunches."

"I bet you don't need a business lunch to enjoy a drink. You smell like you mop up gin with your shirt-sleeves."

She must have seen his truck parked at the Hilltop. "I guess you're my mother?" he said.

"Maybe you need one." She stared at him.

His jeans were filthy. That morning he had looked for his cleanest dirty shirt. His lumpy winter jacket wasn't top-of-the-line Gore-Tex but was made of matted boiled wool. He brushed his sleeves. "Yeah, my coat is kind of shedding."

She told him, "It's like Thoreau's description in *Walden* of a coat called a 'fear-naught.'"

"You teach Thoreau?"

"Thoreau. Emerson. Sophia Peabody. You know, the wacky Transcendentalists. I have to do some general survey courses, too."

He wanted to tell her that his work clothes were not an affect, not like the contrived get-up worn by so many weekenders he saw at the pricey country market. Those poseurs liked to wear rag-tag L.L. Bean chamois shirts and cable-knit sweaters with unraveled cuffs, *on purpose*. Instead, he told her he was glad to put on his tool belt. He said, "It's funny. You pick up a hammer, and you see nails sticking up everywhere."

She didn't understand the metaphor, so he explained that he was also on call for plowing driveways or cutting tree limbs 24-7.

He unlatched the tailgate and whistled for the dogs. "They can jump *out* of the truck, but they need the tailgate to get back in." The dogs scrambled aboard and he latched the gate again. He climbed into his cab, ready-Freddy. He had a promising contract in Coventry with a big deposit in hand. He told her, "The dogs like to come to the job. They're company. Maybe some time you'll come along?"

He watched for her reaction. He had revealed he wanted her to be one of his "pets," but she wouldn't acknowledge that she understood.

It was early and the ground was still frozen. He should be careful with her. If he used one of his new spades in the hard till, he might break its shiny tip.

She said, "God, it's getting late. I have to get to work too."

Townsend said, "Remember, we'll do drinks tonight. You'll need to unwind from your Ivy League grind."

"Maybe. I will if I can," April said.

"Oh, I'm sure you *can*," he said. He employed every opportunity to use the double entendre, and he liked to watch her squirm.

She, too, grabbed the chance to put him in his place, saying, "Why do you need that gaudy rope on your truck? It's like a peacock tail without the cock."

"Well, you noticed it. So it works, I guess."

April didn't let him tease out any more thread. She pivoted and breezed away, almost stepping out of her boots.

Chapter Nine

April worried she might be late for her class when she finally sat down in her Camry. She noticed that something was written across the dusty windshield. With his fingertip Blaze had scrawled "MAP" in block letters, backward, so she could read it sitting behind the wheel. She used her wipers to clear the message with washer fluid. She found her pliers to insert the fuse for her lights, but the fuse wasn't in the cup holder. She brushed her hand under her hips, hoping to find it on the seat. She flipped open the console, then she leaned across the passenger side to rip into the glove box.

So, this is how he wants to play it, she thought.

Townsend had not yet left for his work site, and the dogs jumped out of the truck again, leaping waist-high on either side of her as she approached the barn. The rustic halfway house seemed stalled at its conceptual stage of renovation, perhaps delayed for its umpteenth revision of drawings, with little actual construction completed.

New rolls of fiberglass, the bright-yellow color of marsh-mallow Peeps, were parked on either side of the doorway in two long, upright stacks, making a tight grotto.

At the end of the itchy fiberglass aisle she saw Townsend's new front door, a big double-size job made of knotty alder, its swirling whorls the golden hue of sourwood honey. April was surprised by its idiosyncratic beauty. It was a legitimate trophy house door and promised a lot for the project, if Townsend were to try to match a standard like that. Well, at least he had his door hung, she was thinking.

She knocked. Her knuckles hardly made any sound against the thick plank. Townsend was pleased to find her. "I guess you want that drink ahead of the yardarm?"

"Of course not. I just need a minute."

"Oh, you just dropped in to see what condition your condition is in?"

"Very funny," she said. "Look, I'm late for work."

"Come in. Don't jump to any final opinions. It's a work in progress."

She stood at the threshold and surveyed the vast, wide open room. It was gutted. There were no interior walls, no sheetrock had been hung, just some roughed-out rooms framed with two-by-sixes, and of course there were the im-pressive, original weight-bearing posts and beams that kept the roof from caving in. Townsend told her that he hadn't completed installation of his new solid-state radiant heating system, but she could warm up in front of two wood stoves that were hissing and popping at either end of the big, empty barn.

The smell of wood smoke had an instant effect on her. Wood fires in her childhood had always accompanied winter holidays. Holidays triggered acceptable drinking binges that eventually led to screaming matches between her father and mother. Townsend saw her hesitate on the threshold and mis-interpreted her wariness. He said, "Don't worry, the barn is braced. It won't collapse." He pointed to the metal jack posts he had installed to shim the crisscrossing beams and ceiling joists at two troublesome spots.

She didn't see a suggestion of a working kitchen. A big double-door refrigerator was the lone appliance. It wasn't in-stalled but rested in the middle of nowhere, plugged into a bright yellow extension cord that spiraled away into an empty corridor.

Townsend saw her looking at all the extension cords snaking through the place and said, "Yeah, we're on a generator. For now. It's a thirteen-horsepower Honda DeWalt. I got a guy coming next week to put in our new circuit box. We need a new box for the radiant heat. I could do it myself, but we can't get the C.O. without a licensed electrician."

"You're here now without a certificate of occupancy?" she asked.

At the far end of the wide open, prairie-sized room, slouched on a scuffed leather sofa, Blaze pretended to ignore her. The sofa was shoved right beside a big spool of liquid-tight flexible conduit cable. Apparently, Townsend was doing the wiring himself even if he had to get a pro to do the circuit box for him. The cable spool was a makeshift computer table for the Dell that Blaze was using.

She saw a stack of pirated *Girls Gone Wild* DVDs or something similar, and she wondered if Townsend had sent away for them. Blaze wasn't watching *Girls Gone Wild* but was on the Dell instant messaging Lucinda.

Townsend called over to him, "Don't put all your eggs in one basket."

Blaze didn't listen to his father. When he saw April, he clicked his mouse on the bottom tool-bar and the screen flashed to a video game. She was surprised to see the graphics were similar to those of *Sniper's Diary!*, a first-person shooter game that Riley had worked on with his Ion Storm flunkies to compete with a rival game called *Postal*. Of course, any kid his age would like Riley's masterpiece alongside best sellers like *Counter-Strike*, *Doom*, or *Mortal Kombat*.

"What game are you playing?" she asked him.

"*Painkiller*," he said. "I'm not allowed to play gun games. How are they going to know?"

When April saw that Blaze was hooked up with a modem and was online, she realized that the boy could fish anything he wanted from the wide blue ether. He might challenge his rivals in a *Painkiller* marathon. Or he could harass her with pasted-in Endless Pools e-mails.

"So who were you talking to on line?" she asked him.

"Nobody you know. But this is from her." He pulled a note from his pocket. It wasn't a print-out of an e-mail but a yellow sheet from a legal pad twice-folded so many times it looked like a mini pleated shade. He offered it to April.

She carefully stretched open the fragile accordion. The handwriting was familiar schoolgirl penmanship. It said, *Come get me! Don't wait! Love, Lucinda. P.S. I like your poem.* The letter had a little drawing—a smiley face. *On stilt legs.*

"Do you write poems?" she asked him.

"Maybe I do."

"Will you show me one? I teach literature, you know."

He wasn't impressed. He pushed away his keyboard and he put on some headphones. He shut her out and started leafing through an Acorn brochure about how to build a prefab Deck House. Several oversized books about architecture were strewn across the sofa and dominoed onto the floor. Townsend said, "We're looking for ideas." The boy had one book open to a big monochrome photo of Wright's famous Usonian masterpiece, the one called Taliesin. The boy had put his Coke down dead center on the gorgeous picture, making a wavy ring of condensation on the crisp print.

She needed to get the fuse for her Camry.

But in one corner of the giant room, by the window, she was distracted by a gorgeous pedestal mirror. It was not what you'd normally see in bachelors' quarters, let alone in a stable. "Where did you find this?" she asked Townsend.

He told her that the mirror had once belonged to his

mother. He said Janice had asserted that the mirror was more of a woman's collectible and had wanted to keep it, but he refused to let it go.

April recognized it as a nineteenth-century mahogany cheval oval, with beveled glass and scrolled feet. She was impressed, not only by the mirror's beauty but by the fact that Townsend had retained some sentiment for his matriarch. He had not let his ex run off with the heirloom. Then she wondered if his unusual devotion to his mother might have been one reason his wife had left him. She imagined the two women's faces warring in the cheval mirror. Then she saw her own face, her own wide eyes, in its reflection.

Hooked on one side of the mirror was a comical headdress. It was a common straw fedora fitted with a sugar-water bottle and a red plastic floret nozzle. The hummingbird hat. It was the ridiculous contraption Townsend had told her about. Her assessment of Townsend's boy was constantly shifting. The sugar-water bottle warred with the electronic ankle cuff.

When she turned around Blaze was staring hotly at her. Townsend told the boy, "Come over here and greet our neighbor, Miss O'Rourke. It's April, right? You were born when the crocuses come out?"

"No. I wasn't *born* in April, my birthday is in July." She always hated trying to explain it. Her parents had named her April because it "sounded optimistic" to them. Her name was cumbersome because of that confusion.

"Say hello to April," Townsend told Blaze.

"No problem. We've already met," April said. "He was testing his cuff—but I don't think that thing is working." Each time she re-lived the boy's slippery-wet handshake, she felt it beneath the waist.

Townsend turned to Blaze. "You can't just barge in on people whenever you want."

Blaze ignored his father. He patted the sofa and invited the brindle dog onto its soft pillow beside him. The dog curled up next to the boy, resting its nose on its front paws, its eyes darting left and right in a nervous, self-conscious bliss. It feared its good fortune might be a mistake, and it would soon be booted off.

Townsend told Blaze, "Your manners—"

Blaze stood up and walked over to April. "Last name O'Rourke? That's Irish, right? Is that shanty Irish or lace curtain?"

"It's *tweed*," Townsend joked, trying to smooth it over. "You know, she's the college prof, with patches on her elbows."

"She's *tart*-an,'" Blaze said, making it worse. He stood his ground from his mean-streak perch, but he extended his hand.

This time she didn't accept it.

Looking straight into her eyes, he waited.

She wrinkled her nose, Gidget-style, right back at him, unable to stop herself.

Townsend saw the exchange and leaned aside, out of their frozen volley. He seemed amused that she didn't act like a librarian. At that instant a horse entered the back hallway. It came along, clip-clopping, until it stood in the big, wide open living room. A big bay gelding, not the crippled horse but its stable-mate, had nosed open the huge plank slider in the back of the barn. Townsend explained that he hadn't yet replaced the big door panel that hung from a track. It was easily bumped open if it wasn't latched. He said he had ordered new French patio doors to replace the panel. The new doors would frame the open pasture to offer a sweeping view of the fields from inside his concept trophy house. The doors hadn't been shipped.

She patted the horse on its silky cheek. She said, "He's trying to reclaim his pied-à-terre, right?"

The boy said, "That's right. He lost the roof over his head. Just like I did."

"He's got his own barn," Townsend told April.

April assumed Townsend was speaking of a leaky lean-to in back, just one of several ramshackle out-buildings and weanling pens on his Waco back lot.

Townsend led the wayward horse out of the big room, tugging him by the forelock. With the horse banished, the boy had returned to the sofa and put his earphones back on. He leafed through a CD wallet trying to ignore her.

She followed him there and opened her hand. She held her palm level before him, and wiggled her fingers, hoping he would slip her the tiny fuse. "I've got to go to work," she whispered. "I need my brake lights."

Blaze shoved his fist into his pocket and waited.

"You want me to tell your father about this?"

"What is it you're looking for? I forget."

"Very funny. Just give me the fricking fuse," she said.

He handed her the silver-pronged sliver of plastic. The item was warm, almost hot, coming straight from his pocket. She cupped it in her palm, curling her fingers tight. The exchange was gaining a weird aura of some kind, and she didn't want to drag it out.

Blaze got up to open the door of the wood stove. He shoved a split log inside, kicking it deep into the flames with the heel of his boot, without regard for his ankle gizmo. Fire and smoke shot out. He slammed the little door and adjusted the flue knob. Again, he sat down and put his feet directly on top of the opened spine of the big photography book.

April began to understand the boy's little pot holes of mood and his lack of hospitality. He wasn't a willing participant in Townsend's remodeling project. He was under lock and key, a JD outcast forced to rot with his father in the half-built house that as far as she could see had only a hot plate. In one corner she saw a whole pallet of some kind of processed dinners.

Townsend said, "We got these at Job Lot. That's twenty cases of MRE dinners."

"MRE?"

"Meals ready to eat. We've got beef steak, enchilada, chicken tetrazzini, vegetarian manicotti," he read from the menus printed on the sides of the cartons. "Comes with side dish, dessert, crackers, spread—"

"Comes with spread!" Blaze called out from the couch.

April's empty stomach twisted tightly, but she enjoyed the teenager's sarcasm.

"Same as what they get in Iraq," Townsend said, confident in the GI product.

It was quite a bargain, she said, but she found the military dinners to be depressing and the place itself to be an unnerving setting in such close proximity to her pristine house. But Townsend's quip "You look like someone who might have done a little sideways searching" kept ringing in her ears. She started to feel that maybe Townsend's haiku board and his know-it-all explanation of the encroaching grape vine somehow applied to her.

She had moved sideways into her extra-marital affair. And every time she looked at the manure heap, it, too, was creeping *sideways*! Worst of all, she felt that the kid was shoving her across some kind of lateral boundary. One she had never crossed before.

Townsend said, "Take a look at this."

He was standing beside a new wall safe, a sleek rectangle recessed in the new Sheetrock, like a compact hotel vault. It looked like something you might see in Las Vegas, maybe in the original Rat Pack movie, *Ocean's Eleven*.

"I just got this finished. It's nice, isn't it? Remember, you don't talk about it after you leave here. We won't broadcast it. Okay?"

"Of course not," she said. But she wondered why she was in his circle of trust; he hardly knew her. His request, "We won't broadcast it. Okay?" was no different from the provost's routine caveat each time they had sex.

On her way out, she noticed a towering pile of board games, probably souvenirs from Townsend's long haul at Diggs & Snyder. She said, "That's quite a library of games. You could start an old folks' home."

He showed her an original copy of the company's famous game Dumbwaiter. He unfolded the board, the color of an antique map. It was a cross section of a Victorian-era hotel called the Volney, showing individually numbered guest rooms along the top tiers, with the front desk, kitchen, and maids' quarters on the lower squares of the board. "This came before Chutes and Ladders," he told her. "They sort of stole our idea. But this game is more fun. It works on the idea of social class and the scandals of the wealthy."

"I heard of it," she told him.

"A guest wants room service and the kitchen staff has to send it up, square by square, on the dumbwaiter. Players draw menu cards and can order lamb shank. Shirred eggs. Milk toast. Opposing players try to get what they want from downstairs. Everything has to go up on the dumbwaiter. Then things go wrong. According to the dice and the cards a player draws, there might be some complication in the room, or the pulley gets jammed, or there's some backstabber in the kitchen. The guest gets his meal delivered, or he might get an unexpected surprise. He might get *found out.*

"Everyone's cheating somebody. Maybe a rich tycoon has his secretary in the hotel, or downstairs there's a laundress in love with a bell captain. Or someone's bilking someone. Depending on these cards, they can win or get their comeuppances. There are several blistering narratives going on. Each disaster scenario is printed on a card."

"Who invented this game? It sounds so Evelyn Waugh or something."

"A lot of tawdry things happened at the Volney."

She imagined that the Victorian board game might mirror her all-too-common experiences at the Westminster. She didn't want to be reminded. She told Townsend that she was late for work.

At the door, Townsend said, "So tonight you'll be back for drinks? Maybe to break bread?"

"Not if you're fixing that jarhead menu, I won't."

"How about lamb shank, or milk toast?" Townsend smiled. He was glowing with optimism. She was thinking, *What a nice face he has.* His warmth seemed to come from a seasoned authority and baskets of charm. Blaze had returned to his instant messaging with Lucinda. He stared at the screen, stone still. Again April was startled by his ungodly, gorgeous profile, his features both wounded and haughty, like the marbles stolen by Lord Elgin.

Chapter Ten

April's classes were usually a succor to her. She could immerse herself in her students' accelerating struggle, a sometimes comic ordeal as they moped and floundered through their academic maze like Townsend's game of chutes and ladders. She roamed the classroom, encouraging her students to participate in the discussion; with both affectionate scolds and heartfelt praises, she sometimes felt like a dog trainer urging pups through obstacles on an agility course. The trainer trots alongside a pet, gesturing with hand signals and vocalizing commands as the dog slinks through weave poles, climbs teeter-totters, shoots through open tunnels, or barrels over high jumps. Like that, April was a lively, engaging teacher, and with her give-and-take approach she pushed hopeless sloths or reined in the high-strung and jittery. She worked hard, and like Blaze had said, she kept "the rag moving."

That afternoon, she wasn't herself. She didn't pace the classroom but sat at her desk to listen to a young man read his annotation of Conrad's "Youth." Although sensing that the student had indeed been transformed by the discoveries he had made in the text, April could hardly pay attention to his heartfelt presentation.

The student described the fire aboard ship, and the molten anchor chain that had burned a hole through the deck, its sizzling coil slipping into the sea—a dramatic instant in Conrad's piece, with powerful metaphoric meaning. The student expressed genuine awe when describing it. April was miles away; one minute she was in the Westminster Hotel, and the next, she was standing in the gravel driveway face to face with her neighbor in the fearnaught jacket. Or she was daydreaming about Blaze trying to tug her onto her sofa.

She was meeting the provost in an hour. That morning she had already been knocked off balance by her meetings with the two Townsend men. Identical bookends they were not, but in her vanity she allowed herself to feel like a precious codex pinched between them. At last, when the classroom had fallen dead silent, she realized that the boy had finished reading his homework annotation and was waiting for her response.

She told the student, "Excellent job."

His shoulders drooped at her open-ended generalization.

She was in her office when Claudia called back. Her friend complained that the file on Blaze Townsend was a tome, and she couldn't parse it in a crunch. She said that records stated that Blaze came from a disruptive "family constellation" to begin with. His worst battles seemed to erupt with his matriarch until Blaze was sent to the training school.

"There's a note here from Judge Welsh at family court,"

Claudia said. The judge had followed the parents' embittered separation and saw that the problem had not merely been the couple's more than twenty-year age difference, but that Townsend had also been his wife's boss at Diggs & Snyder. The judge had written in his notes, "That prickly distinction is not always easy to absorb into matrimony."

The women laughed.

"That's the problem with husbands, they're hard to *absorb*," Claudia said. Claudia told April that Janice Gallen was now a payroll clerk at Electric Boat in Quonset Point where they manufactured hulls and did most of the outfitting for General Dynamics' Virginia class attack submarines. She earned extra cash taking digital pictures at horse shows. "Reports here say Blaze has a lot of complaints about her."

"Complaints about his mom?" April remembered what Blaze had said about his mother's vicious streak: *Bitch doesn't pass the food-bowl test.*

"These adolescent boys are really vulnerable. They're fighting their own testosterone storms," Claudia said.

She listened to Claudia paw through the print-outs on her desk. "Says here that the client gave several examples of what they call 'covert behavior' by the mother that might have led up to 'overt behavior.'"

"What do they mean by 'covert'?"

"April, I really can't discuss these files with you, you know, because of my professional commitment. It's called duty of confidentiality. I hope you can understand."

"I think I have the picture anyway."

"You did *not* get a *picture* from me!"

"Of course, of course." April had her own pictures. April's father had often passed her in the hallway half dressed, in only his Hanes V-neck, and sometimes without his boxers. And worse, he had often peed and not flushed the toilet, on purpose, as if he wanted her to find the golden water. It was his little secret surprise for her as she dashed into the bathroom to brush her teeth before school. Forced to flush the toilet, she was acknowledging his message. He waited to hear it. She never wanted to sit down and pee unless the bowl was rinsed.

As Claudia backed away from the report about Blaze, April recalled her father when he adjusted her Milwaukee brace. She always fought against these buried memories, and told Claudia, "How can parents act like that!"

April remembered the boy's seething braggadocio when he talked about the MAP channel. This kind of cynicism about sex might be how a kid would react to those who had harmed him.

She didn't believe that Blaze was a reliable narrator. She thought that if there were switchbacks in his story to DSS, Blaze might have been duping them right up to the minute, just as he had tried to dupe her. She asked Claudia, "Can't you just give him a lie detector test? Wouldn't that prove if he's telling the truth?"

Claudia laughed. "A polygraph? That can't be ordered without a court warrant. Without any charges filed, there's no crime."

April could have told Claudia that her car had been stolen.

"And these polygraph tests never work on kids anyway.

Kids are natural liars. Children don't distinguish when they're lying. They *believe* their own stories. It's an automatic safety mechanism. Like baby fawns have those white spots on their ass—they don't try to have spots. Spots *come with*. That's their camouflage. It's natural protection."

April pictured these little spotted fawns, like Bambi, with baby Blaze amidst them.

Claudia said, "Judge Welsh said that Greylock was his last-chance 'shock and awe' sortie inside the academic war zone. After that, no school would have him. He wore out his welcome. His choices were jail or the homestead in Westerly. He went home with Townsend."

A needle was sawing behind her eyes when she got off the phone. April swallowed two Advils. She decided that Blaze had probably watched TV reports about kids' victimization by priests, coaches, and school teachers, and had heard about their subsequent dismissals or defrockings.

Yes, Blaze had accused his own mother about something just to get her de-mommed.

Chapter Eleven

She had expert control over her gag reflex. Her style wasn't rushed or half-hearted, never too studied. Mirhege whispered, "Missy—oh Jesus, you're so into it," his stair-stepping eyebrows froze in pleasure as he flopped back on the bedspread. April finished him, but she was thinking of her young neighbor with the beautiful name. Even after Claudia had explained the boy's suspect history, April couldn't get his *name* off her tongue. His name evoked an exotic melt-in-your-mouth sensation.

Then she thought, wasn't it ridiculous where her mind wandered when she was giving head! And when she wasn't thinking about Blaze, she made shopping lists or worried about where to buy more fuses for her almost religious ordeal with her Camry. Or she recalled the crazy narratives written on the little cards of Townsend's peculiar board game Dumbwaiter. She imagined that her secret trysts at the Westminster would certainly trump the scandals that occurred at the Volney Hotel a century ago. Mirhege never expected that she was lost in thought, tallying up important things. Mirhege was right there, in live time, yet she was thinking of her students' prickly laughter when they chimed, "We *go* to Sin, but you have to *work* at it!"

Yes, she could tell her class, she kept the rag moving at the college and also at the Westminster.

The provost was a casualty. She waited as he drowsed, watching him enter the luxury station of post-blowjob reflection, when men always seemed so babyish. It could tug on her heartstrings if she wasn't on guard. She allowed him a moment to recoup and she plopped into a tub chair beside the bed. She picked up a rocks glass from a tray and flicked off its paper cap. She poured an inch of scotch for herself from the utilitarian L.L. Bean plastic flask that Mirhege always remembered to bring. The flask had a corny Black Watch plaid sleeve, which almost spoiled the freshener effect of the golden therapist.

After a few minutes, Mirhege sat up. He told her, "Pour one for me."

She sloshed a little scotch in a tumbler and handed it to him. And just as she had rehearsed in her mind—a little polite chitchat, and remember to ask about his daughter—she said to the provost, "How's your daughter's harp lessons?"

"Her teacher says she's a natural."

"Of course he'd say that. He wants the job. Not many kids sign up for harp lessons."

When April was still in Providence, she had walked past the provost's house one evening, surprised to see a harp through a first-floor window. The front parlor shades were never drawn and the instrument was in full view, an alarming contraption. Mirhege said his thirteen-year-old daughter took lessons.

April had started to notice the routine. When she passed the house, she saw the young girl sitting in a cage of harp strings, like a little jailbird trapped behind bars. This had annoyed April. The provost wanted his daughter to play the harp when girls at that age listened to teen idols and boy groups. Putting his daughter on a stool before a giant harp in his front parlor window was his attempt to neutralize her sexuality, when the girl had reached her menarche. Seated behind the ridiculous harp grille, she was behind a moat. He was saying to the local boys, "Don't try something with my daughter! She's my little angel."

April often waited until after dark to walk down the sidewalk opposite the provost's big nineteenth-century Georgian house. She looked up at his daughter's big harp in the front window. She felt it her duty as a feminist observer to one day rescue the girl from her prison of wires. April had once asked him, "What's your daughter going to do? Get a job at a dinner theater? Harpist for hire at weddings?"

He told her, "I just want her to grow up to be the kind of woman who—"

"Who what?"

"Who can play a musical instrument," he said. She understood what he meant. He didn't want his daughter to grow up to be a woman like April.

Asking about his daughter now wasn't going to relax him. She charged ahead. "So tell me, do I get the chair job or what?"

"Excuse me?"

"The department slot."

"Not here," he said, "okay, sweetheart? We don't want to talk business when we're visiting."

She wasn't sure if he was using "we" as an intimate or impersonal pronoun. Again, he might have said "we," suggesting the inclusion of his cohort in its floppy little hat.

She told him, "I have to know about the chair appointment. Right now. There's no reason it shouldn't be mine."

He said, "I guess I have to tell you. You're perfect, we know that, but the president has gone in a different direction, April."

This was academic jargon. "Gone in a different direction" was a polite way of saying a sensible decision had been opposed for no good reason. She'd heard it before at retreats when the administration argued against faculty proposals for specific advances in curricula that required more funding or college services.

"You offered it to the newbie?" she said. "He self-published that pamphlet on Joyce, you know. He's a fraud."

"He's highly qualified."

"This is personal," she said. "You just don't want me to have a speck of power. Take out our faculty handbook. It clearly states that if your decision has the purpose or effect of 'unreasonably interfering with an individual's work performance or career advancement, especially if it's between individuals in a hierarchal relationship,' it could be considered sexual harassment. Right, boss?"

"Don't be silly, April. Give him a chance. He's very bright," he told her. Seeing no immediate truce in sight, the provost pulled himself out of bed and padded to the bathroom. She heard him tear open the little box of hotel soap. He cranked the shower tap. He wanted to clean up before heading home to his wife or before returning to his office because April's perfume "clings to him like a tropical vine," he had once told her. She thought she saw him shudder when he said it, as if he had just probed a little mound of maggots with a number 2 pencil.

Yet he had just made love to her.

She had told him, "My perfume is Guerlain. That's French, not tropical. Don't forget, I'm half French."

"Oh right. I know which half," he joked. "But the French colonized the tropics. The French didn't limit themselves to temperate climates. You're proof of that. You're sizzling."

He flattered her, but it always became a lecture. He continued with a condensed history lesson about French capitalism in Vietnam and French Guiana. He rattled off the exotic names of places in the French Virgin Islands and French West Indies—Martinique, Guadeloupe, and Port au Prince. He said he admired the nineteenth- and early-twentieth-century French businessmen for their manufacturing and corporate savvy. In everything, from sugar cane to silk, they were far ahead of American industries.

She was tired of his NPR well of knowledge.

"And the French give exceptional blow jobs," he added after the fact.

She waited to hear him pull the shower curtain across the

rod, a plastic clatter, and then she started to get dressed. He'd be surprised to discover she had left before their usual parting, an annoying ritual, when he kissed her good-bye at the door and always asked her to wait until he'd grabbed the elevator first. Today, she'd be on the street before he toweled off.

She had already penned her farewell note. When she read it again, it was too apologetic. She didn't have to leave a note at all. The fact that he wouldn't support her for the chair's job was the deal breaker. She'd exit without any more fanfare.

But as she stepped into her skirt, something swooped past the window. The room was on the fourteenth floor and faced the east wing of the hotel, above a small courtyard in between. She pulled the curtain back to see a young woman standing at the window of a hotel room opposite theirs. The girl had balled up someone's trousers and dress shirt and was trying to stuff them through the window.

The window track was sticky and the girl was having trouble forcing the vertical slider open. A six-inch slot was wide enough to feed the trousers through. Next, she fed his powder blue oxford. The dressy items tumbled witlessly out the chute, losing their formidable cut and drape. In their liberation, the clothes were plain yard goods sent drifting, textiles set free. April watched them flounce in a stiff wind and coast past her window. The provost wore made-to-measure oxfords, with barrel cuffs and single-needle tailoring. Losing an investment like that would be a crime, but the other girl didn't seem to care what *her* sweetheart had paid for these items. She walked back to collect his socks and wing tips. She reached out the window slot to chuck one, and then its mate. April watched the shoes fall end-over-end like little capsized gondolas. His muted socks fluttered after them.

April was mesmerized by the sideshow. She recognized that there was a lover's quarrel unfolding in the identical hotel room, although she couldn't see *him*. She felt an immediate connection to the girl. Yet April didn't have the courage to toss the provost's shoes. His favorite pair had rich, buttery leather, very elegant and yet deeply hetero. Men's shoes had a strong effect on her. After her boyfriend died, his shoes had been the last erotic tokens she had parted with. She had finally left a box of Riley's shoes at a thrift store in East Providence when she couldn't bear to see his oxfords, Doc Martens, and Nikes piled across the closet floor. The next time she walked past the thrift store, she was alarmed to see her lover's boots lined up in the window, with their tongues tugged forward.

She picked up the provost's gleaming pair and smoothed her palm over their firm leather, their pointy tips. She cupped their weighted heels and felt the little burn of her fetish. Nothing was stopping her from pitching them out the window and she started to imagine it. But it wouldn't prove anything. She had only herself to blame for the mess she found herself in. *You fell in love with your own voice,* she reminded herself as she placed the provost's shoes back where she had found them. The provost had liked to hear her love talk, her dirty whispers or sex instructions, but she had tricked herself with these ridiculous confabulations. And she remembered when the provost had once showed up wearing novelty underpants that his wife had bought him. A scuba diver appliqué was stitched on his jockeys, including little air bubbles. "*Cute*," she had said. That was one item of his clothing April would have loved to fling.

"Mistress, *dis*mistress," she scolded herself as she walked back and forth before the big hotel mirror and finished getting dressed. But she no longer felt so disappointed that her romance was coming to an end. It would be better for both of them, and it had ended without her losing admiration for his scholarship. That was a saving grace, she was thinking.

She saw the provost's wristwatch on the hotel desk, an expensive Rolex knock-off. She slipped the silver stretch-band over her wrist and imagined extending her arm out the window, teasing it over her knuckles. She pictured the provost losing all his clothes, with nothing to wear but his wristwatch. It was an amusing vision. She put the provost's wristwatch back on the desk. She picked up his key case and studied his Sinclair office key, which looked just like her own. He never locked his office at the college, but left its upkeep and security to his assistant. He didn't need his keys. She could shoot them underhand out the window.

Milt would think she'd lost her mind. He'd say, "You've gone East Westerly!" She didn't have the same recklessness or the same ire as the heroine in the window. When the girl came back to lob a wallet and a shiny object, something like an iPhone, into the alley, April felt sorry for her.

April found the provost's billfold in the breast pocket of his jacket, the same olive windowpane plaid that she despised. She resisted an urge to count his cash. It looked like a Presbyterian block of neatly folded bills, enough for a businessman's daily requirements. She saw a photo of his prissy yet homely bride. Prissy *and* homely is a difficult meld but his wife had mastered it! And in a little fold-out window there were photos of his two girls. But again, the goddess next door came back to tease a sport coat through the window slot and it drifted, landing spread-eagled against a ventilation cage three flights below.

April hoped that the girl would not forget to collect the bedclothes and to rip down the wall of opaque drapes, a billowing circus tent. She could drag it all out into the hall, pushing it inside the ice machine closet.

The tyrant-in-question would have nothing to cover up with.

Nothing unless he wrapped himself in the icy vinyl shower curtain.

Mirhege called to her from the shower, "Come in here. *We're* still interested."

April stayed at the window until he came out of the bathroom. Scrubbing himself with a towel, leaving a fleur-de-lis of wet drips on the carpet, he said, "What are you watching?"

"You should see this," she told him.

The girl had jerked the bedside phone from its jack.

She tossed the cheap GE console out the window. Its

ringer warbled once as it bounced off the sill before it tumbled fourteen stories to its gaudy smash up.

"Jesus! Think of the pedestrians—" Mirhege said.

"It's just the empty courtyard—so what?" April revealed her partisan sympathies.

The mystery man turned up at the window. An even older version than Mirhege, he was perhaps the young girl's elderly boss or maybe a university don, someone like the provost—after all, it was a college town. Standing bare-chested, he was shouting at his vixen so that April and the provost could hear everything. "Nancy!" he boomed. "My fucked-up kitten." "You crazy cunt!" and "Baby, please, get my pants!"

Alone without a stitch, he would have to walk into the hall and bang on someone's door to find a sympathetic soul. Perhaps another cheater would be amused and lend him a pair of trousers. At midday few businessmen were in their rooms. "He can use the hotel phone on the console table beside the elevator to call the manager," Mirhege said, in his problem-solving mode. "My cousin will take care of him."

"Yeah, you guys have to stick together." She sided with Nancy, happy to have learned her name.

He said, "I guess I better be careful never to get you so worked up?"

"Too late."

"I mean that girl is borderline. She's at the fucking edge. On the lip!"

"Not your business, I don't think."

"No, *you* are. You're my business."

"I am?" She wanted to believe he meant it. She was glad she had controlled her wicked impulses. Her irritation with him had suddenly subsided. He looked so silly, almost helpless. As he stood naked, with his hands on his hips, his genitals looked like awkward bystanders, and she thought, *Poor thing. How do men walk around with that encumbrance in front of them?*

She told him, "Come here," and she sat down on the bed. She patted the coverlet.

He obeyed. He crept onto the foot of the hotel king and folded into her arms, unaware that she was performing an act of mercy. She gathered her skirt higher and peeled down her panties. He kissed her as if she were someone new. Nancy's outburst across the alley was exciting to him. He took his beautiful time.

Afterwards, he was dozing again.

She didn't leave her Dear John note, or tell him directly that it was the last time. She had straightened her skirt, slipped into her shoes, and was out in the hallway, studying the fire alarm. The directions said "To activate . . ." She wanted to *activate* the fire alarm. She imagined its bleating tone erupting in short, persuasive blasts. Its air-horn pitch almost painful but still comic, would force Nancy's geezer boyfriend to flee without any pants on. It would certainly wake the provost. She didn't pull the lever, not wanting to disturb the other hotel guests.

She was already on the elevator.

The compartment stopped at the tenth floor. The door

opened and a girl got on beside April. It wasn't her heroine, just another loner. The newcomer wore a one-piece outfit of tight pink pleather. Her boots were leopard fur wedgies—as if she were walking on two severed paws. The girl squared a few large bills and stuffed them inside a mini accordion file like a coupon wallet.

April wanted to tell the girl about the feminist tempest she had witnessed. She wanted her elevator companion to appreciate its special significance to *them*. The girl didn't recognize April as her sister, another cartoon concubine just like her, and she had turned away to watch the buttons blink and extinguish as the two women sank floor by floor.

April looked forward to telling Milt about her afternoon. She felt a gentle, warmed-by-the-hearth feeling as the elevator flumed to the lobby.

Chapter Twelve

Janice left the A-frame, taking her leatherette envelope and her travel mug. As she sat down in her minivan, she sloshed some green tea on the seat. She unsnapped the elastics on her pocket file to look inside, making sure the papers were dry. John Two had been browbeating her about the money Townsend owed her. She had told him about Townsend's new safe. *Me and my big mouth*, she thought when John Two said, "Don't come back tonight empty-handed."

She drove to East Westerly and found him outside the barn. Townsend saw her van and said, "Don't park that Woodstock jalopy out here where my customers can see it."

"I don't see any customers," she said.

"That's right. You're scaring them away."

She grabbed her papers from the passenger seat. "You're signing these," she said. "It needs two signatures. I want my cut."

"That's a ten-year CD. I'm not touching it. If you bothered to read the fine print, you'd know that with the good rate an early withdrawal cuts into the principal. So it stays put."

"Forty thousand of that is mine," she said.

"That's right. So I'm just thinking of you, half-pint."

"My lawyer says you sign this or he gets involved."

"That ambulance chaser? You don't need him. What you want is somebody called a financial planner. That would be *me*."

She tipped her face right under his chin. "These CDs and the Exxon Mobil stock? I told you I want to cash out early. It's you who absorbs the penalty, since it was you who forced me to throw in my savings in the first place."

"That's a good story," he said.

"You're just punishing me."

"Not my idea. Janice, you're going to have to hate yourself *by yourself*."

She walked in a little circle, absorbing his zinger. She didn't like it when he psychoanalyzed her. Sometimes he widgeted just the right place, scraping away her self-confidence, and she refused to look in the mirror.

She knew Townsend didn't like John Two. He told her that none of her lay-about fill-ins could add up to what she'd once had with him.

Sometimes she wanted him to intervene, and she wore that *Rescue me* expression, but she'd bite his head off if he asked her, "Is your lip puffy? Are you getting smacked around?"

In arguments Townsend liked to evoke their romantic first date. They had gone to an Italian trattoria on Federal Hill, in Providence, where he knew the waiter. The waiter put them in a private nook that was curtained off. Janice ordered something called baby calf Florentine. Since then, in their many squabbles, he liked to say, "I know you like pounded veal, but stop trying to tenderize me."

Janice said, "I guess family court still doesn't know you got axed at Diggs and Snyder for those under-the-table transactions?"

"You're the one who's famous for your under-the-table transactions every happy hour."

"Exactly what deals did you make? I bet you were involved with those recalls, the little toy trains with lead paint? That's criminal. When DSS finds out you're a cheap-suit, an unfit dad, Blaze gets a state cot again."

"Janice, Diggs &Snyder never made any charges."

"Sure, they're not going to pay their corporate lawyers when they can just fire your ass."

"Don't be a flea, Janice. Or I'll unroll the flypaper."

"The kid will go back to RITS. I guess you don't want him?"

"You can't *sell* him to me, Janice. He's mine."

He climbed into his truck.

Janice watched him roll down the gravel drive and turn onto the road. She looked at the pretty white house next door where she'd spent sixteen years. Its windows looked newly washed, but their hundred-year-old leaded glass still showed that uneven wobble. Not a day went by that she didn't relive little snippets of her family life. No matter how hard she tried to whitewash it, she couldn't cover her tracks. Her mistakes in that house were indelible, like cigarette burns in the linoleum. She and Blaze had once tried to repair the floor covering using

Testors enamel paint that Blaze had bought for his model airplane kits. They mixed the smelly paint and she daubed it on the little burned holes in the linoleum. She couldn't exactly match the splatter pattern, and it got worse the more she messed with it. Everything tumbling too fast in her life seemed to present the same splatter-pattern catch-22.

She was a teen mom for some kind of eternity. Her years in the farmhouse, trapped behind the deformed glass windows, were just a blurry smear of motherhood chores and alcohol.

She was paying for it now.

Chapter Thirteen

Blaze was sitting at the Dell, instant messaging Lucinda. She wrote from her phone, *i want to see you*

> *me too*
> *you coming?*
> *ETA 24*
> *far out*

He heard Janice's voice outside. He went to the window and saw she was walking toward the barn. He went back to his keyboard and pecked the keys, "TBC. L8r." As he typed, he knew it was old school contrived lingo, but Lucinda liked it. He cleared his screen.

In the bathroom he turned on a hot shower full-force. He shoved the slide bolt on the door until it was snug. He sat on the toilet lid and watched the room fill with steam. When Janice couldn't find him in the big, empty room, she knocked on the bathroom door.

"Go away. You better pray I don't open this door," he said.

She said, "Let's have breakfast. I'll make johnnycakes."

"Not now."

She wasn't fazed. To her, he was a mouse that roared. She didn't flicker or sputter. She was an eternal flame. "Come on, honey," she purred.

"Get lost."

"One person goes half-way. She wants the other one to go half."

He couldn't see very far in the scalding mist. The tiny room went white.

"Blaze, open this door. Let's talk."

"You want to talk? Call a radio show."

"Oh, nice."

He got up and held his ear to the door. He pressed his lips to the fresh fir panel, then his whole body. Janice caused a storm of electrical surges and testosterone shocks. She could short out his circuitry until he was dizzy.

He didn't come out of the steam. He listened until he heard her walk away from the door. She started nosing around in the clutter. She'd probably try the combination on the new wall safe, but he heard her banging things around in the mock kitchen. She might have started to make breakfast if Townsend had had the stove connected. When they cooked, they used a hot plate, and even that wasn't plugged in.

Without seeing her son, Janice went home. She walked back to her bedroom. She had not yet made her bed. She was slipping into her old funk, when she didn't bother with household chores. *Better Homes* spotless was for *Women's Day* wives. The tousled sheets would make John Two furious, so she pulled them up and tucked the blanket. It wasn't the same bed she had shared with Townsend. Townsend's antique four-poster had been jury-rigged with screw bolts that stripped the wood, and the frame was always knocking. She had hooked her two eight-pound dumbbells over the headboard to keep it from banging when she had sex with him. She didn't like Blaze listening to their racket, but he'd heard them go at it for years.

At the A-frame, John Two's new bed was modern, with a sturdy bookshelf headboard. There weren't any books in it. So she had put the cast-iron cat on a top shelf, its frozen eyes staring ahead. It was a token she couldn't dismiss. She rationalized that with the cat she would never need to use her neoprene dumbbells as counterweights against Saturday night's routine turbulence in bed.

When Blaze was living at home before his first lock up at RITS, he'd get into shouting matches with his mom. Janice would start it. But she encouraged Blaze to hand it right back to her, witch's tit for witch's tat. He'd fume through the school week, but on weekends she'd take him to horse shows where she photographed contestants, getting parents to sign contracts for eight-by-ten glossies. She asked Blaze to carry her equipment, her film canisters, and her Nikon camera bag with her lens attachments. When she switched to a lightweight digital camera, she made him carry her clipboard with names and e-mail addresses and, of course, the deposit checks.

He stood in the crowd of spectators as Janice went into the field to crouch beside stone walls and water obstacles as the horses pounded through intricate courses. One time a horse wrecked, and for a moment, Blaze couldn't see if Janice had been trampled. Janice bounced up from where she'd dived out of the way. She waited beside the injured rider until an ambulance drove onto the field.

At these upper-crust events they bonded, feeling especially close when they were up against the yuppie tableau of pampered Thoroughbreds, blue-blooded grande dames, and all the Mercedes parked with their trunks popped open for tailgate parties. Some of the wealthy parents treated Janice well, with respect for her professional chores. Most of them acted like she was no better than a carnie, with Blaze as her nobody helper. But if someone was rude to him, she'd let them have it.

He had always wanted her maternal affections whenever she had deigned to act motherly. She'd say, "Oh please, I was just a baby when I had you. We could be brother and sister." He understood this to mean that he had robbed her of her youth and he shouldn't expect her to mother him, nor did she act sisterly. By the time he was fifteen, he was having trouble sorting through her mixed messages. She complained about his father and tried to conspire with Blaze. Together they balked at his patriarchal authority, but in awkward moments she sometimes hinted that she and Blaze shared a more unorthodox bond, more encompassing than just their enslavement to his father, and more inescapable than blood. She seemed to believe that blood was only a farcical social boundary to designs she had about him.

At first Blaze chose not to acknowledge these aberrations. He remained fuzzy on purpose. Her initial invitation was the most unexpected, and therefore it wasn't yet bracketed by his guilty anticipation or by his drowsy afterglow, steeped in self-disgust. He stopped going to horse shows with his mother. Janice's bedroom was somehow intertwined with the spectacle and dangers he had witnessed in the open jumping ring. Beautiful creatures plowing through boundaries at breakneck speed.

The first time it happened, Janice had just survived a routine blow-up with Townsend when they had both been drinking. During a fracas with Townsend she often asked Blaze to defend her opinions. If Blaze weighed in on her side, she'd wait until Townsend drove off, and then she'd reward him. She'd make cup cakes from scratch, order pizza, or allow him to play Internet gun games past midnight.

That night, empty cans of Rolling Rock began to pile up on every available countertop and coffee table; more empties rolled free across the carpet and were kicked into corners. It was a typical "bitchkrieg" installment with the usual verbal back-and-forth that accelerated to destruction of property.

Blaze had seen his mom rip bed-sheets, break bottles, or simply turn her coffee mug upside down, spilling scalding decaf right onto his dad's desk blotter, his sports pages, and one time right onto his tax forms. This time, she took the kitchen shears and snipped off her bangs, revealing her white-white forehead.

She didn't cut off her pony tail. Next, she tore down the living room curtains, spraying drapery tacks, sharp as fish hooks.

No one called the cops. Townsend left on his own when he'd had enough. He often went to the Hilltop Tavern to drink with the last of the stonecutters. Local quarries specialized in monument stone. He often told Blaze that soon these oldsters would no longer be at the Hilltop Tavern but *on* the hilltop beneath their own markers of Westerly red granite. He sometimes took Blaze along with him. He'd buy him a bottomless Coke and give him quarters for the pool table. That night, Blaze stayed with his mom.

After the contest with Townsend, Janice retreated upstairs with a can of beer in a rubber-foam huggie. Blaze was surprised to hear her call to him from her bed. She asked him to bring her another Rolling Rock. "Get two," she said, "I know you like it," her ambrosial instructions rising at the end of each sentence, like the ascending notes of a pan flute.

He climbed the stairs with two cans of beer.

He handed her one beer and she handed back her empty. "Sit here," she said, patting the covers. He noticed her dumbbells hooked over the headboard. "One day, those are going to clonk you," he said.

He sat at the foot of the bed and sipped his beer. He held the empty can she had already drained. She patted her knee and told Blaze, "Why are you way down there? Come here."

He didn't move.

"Your father is an asshole," she said. "We both know that. You can't expect me to wait for him to die."

"Who said he's going to die?"

"That's what I'm saying. Who knows when?"

He held the two cans, one on each knee, and didn't know what to tell her.

"So what am I supposed to do?" she said.

"It's a no-win," he said.

"Exactly! Unless I take my ass elsewhere. Then we see who wins."

"You mean, 'Winning isn't everything, it's the only thing'?" He was just trying to keep up with her, not trying to encourage her.

But she said, "Like they say, one door slams, another door opens."

He never liked these slogans about life's transitional phases, like "window of opportunity" or "in the fullness of time." "Tomorrow is another day" never seemed palliative, but like a new burden. Yet she was trying to tell him she was leaving his dad, plain and simple. She told him that her exodus from marriage wouldn't necessarily change her connection to him.

"I'm fine with it," he said. "No problem."

"I've waited until the right time.

"I guess."

"It's now or never."

"You mean 'Today is yesterday's tomorrow?'"

She smiled. "Put those down over here," she said, pointing to her bedside table.

To arrange the beer cans, he had to move her cigarettes and her oversized chocolate bar that she sampled parsimoniously, making it last several days as she nibbled it from opposite ends, re-wrapping it each time. He lifted her jar of emollient face cream with its greasy lid.

When she sat up against the headboard, he saw she was dressed only in her bra and panties.

"Sit here, next to me," she said.

She lifted the top sheet, a swirl of blue and gold paisleys that made him dizzy.

"Honey," she said, "why are you shivering? Don't freak, you're going to do okay."

"I'm okay."

She said, "It's a no-brainer. The divorce, I mean." She tugged his hand and pulled him off balance. He felt his knees unlock, like when you break down a folding card table, and he tipped into the bed beside her. She shoved him against her pillows, steering his shoulders until he was stretched out full length. Her breath was branny from ale, but her bed itself was an envelope of sweet gardenia. "Whatever happens with your father, don't worry."

"No problem," he said.

"You and me, we've got each other," she said.

"All right."

She started it on her own. He told her, "Wait. Stop—"

She peeled his jeans from his hips. She told him to point his toes so she could tug the tight cuffs. She climbed on top, her hands on his shoulders, her knees pinching his sides. She hovered expertly, her curvy buttocks flared from her tiny waist, as she carefully, gently tucked herself onto him. She said, "Mmm. That's good. Go slow. Like this, right?"

He closed his eyes. He remembered her innocuous powders and the little Matchbox cars. Little toys circled and collided like bumper cars inside his head until he opened his eyes. She inched forward a little and sat back, forward again, and back, in a purposeful, businesslike rhythm. It was a blur to him and then lucid, a blur and then lightning. She finished him.

In the next weeks, if she curled her little finger, it happened again. Like a zombie, his mind numb, he followed her upstairs. He resisted momentarily, until with a swooning, stabbing abdominal wave he sank into her bed. She wanted to prove something to him, or disprove it, and like a junkie who shares her needles, she showed him the routine, she showed him the habit. He was in her spell which was not a conscious regimen or pattern of will, not a brain game, or a scheme of heart. It was fever. All he had to decide to do was to be ready whenever she was.

He tried to avoid being at home alone with her. If Townsend was at the Hilltop, Blaze left the house and stayed out all night, going to parties with wharf rats at the harbor in Point Judith or Narragansett. When fishing crews tied up, mates without families to rush home to stayed on their boats. They spent their pay on pot, pills, and boxed wine. Blaze often slept on a dragger named the *Sea Flea* and was adopted by its crew when they recognized a little of themselves in him. They'd send Blaze on foot to get a sack of grinders, or to get take-out from Ming Garden, and he didn't go hungry. At home, he stopped taking showers. His long, thick hair got dirty, so he wore it in a heavy rope down his back. Townsend walked past the living room couch and tugged his pony-tail, telling him, "You're getting a little rank. You in a Pigpen contest?"

Blaze didn't read *Peanuts* cartoons and didn't know the reference. Townsend said that his son's open holes in the cultural literacy made him feel ancient.

"Hey Fu Manchu, you should shave," he told Blaze.

But if Blaze stood at the sink, Janice came up behind him and wrapped her arms around his waist. Blaze told his dad, "We need to fix that lock on the bathroom door."

Townsend said, "What are you so shy about?"

"It needs a lock."

"We're not selling tickets for what you do in there." Townsend recognized it was a teenager thing, undue bashfulness about his bodily changes. Townsend replaced the old hardware with a privacy knob that had a spring lock.

During this time, Blaze started to have bad dreams. He had repetitive, interlocking dreams, night after night, what a MSW therapist would later explain was a phenomenon called nested nightmares, a condition that is commonly suffered by incest victims. *His tongue is trailing like a kite streamer or an empty sausage casing; she's sucked it out of his mouth in one of her long, devouring kisses that turns him inside out.*

He's holding her hips and shoves it in. Or he fucks her tit-pussy, rubbing his dick between fleshy pillows. He shoots across her face.

In his nightmare fugues, the dreams started with sex but soon became violent. *He clutches her throat, pressing his thumb into her galloping jugular, cinching her wind-pipe shut. She bucks under him. Her eyes protrude, her tears bright red pearls.*

Now he's got his dad's drywall knife; its double serrated edge cuts back and forth, without having to lift the blade off.

He didn't understand what was happening to him. Feeling guilty about his ugly night visions, he felt worse when his science teacher talked about "nature versus nurture." The teacher explained that children, just like wolf pups, gained their preconditioned traits and predilections while they were still in the womb. Their nasty, predatory instincts were the result of corkscrew DNA strands and had nothing to do with conditions they were born into. They were self-made monsters. "You can't tame a wolf," the teacher said. Blaze interpreted this to mean that he was born with these DNA maps and that his violent thoughts about his mom were self-generated and were his own fault. Yet the teacher also explained that other scientists had opposing theories. Runts and misfits could overcome genetic frailties if they were mothered by super-moms.

A student asked, "What's a super-mom?"

"She'll go to all lengths to bond with her child. It's called attachment parenting. These super-moms even sleep with their kids in something called 'a family bed,'" the teacher said. "The jury's still out on what kind of backlash that can have. Kids should have their own beds."

Blaze listened to the teacher's lecture on wolf pups and super-moms with anxiety. Soon after his visits with Janice had escalated, Blaze was first arrested. He didn't exhibit the typical aggressions of an Oedipus complex. He didn't confront Townsend directly or want to attack his father.

Society would pay.

He met other kids with a similar ax to grind, and he found succor within that brotherhood and its constantly morphing pack mentality. Most were amateur operators, hoisters and spongers who stole from their own kin or lifted tip jars from counter clerks. Their combined resumes included everything from serious drug trafficking operations, meth kitchens, incidental stabbings, hobby bomb shops, weapons clubs, car jackings, and date rapes to minor transgressions like fist fights, finder's-fee flea markets, spelunking for CD decks, and all kinds of teenage grift and amateur skirt-chasing disasters. Family violence included verbal attacks on moms and grannies, waving guns on back porches, breakfast-table hold ups, dinner-fork stabbings, sibling conflicts, father beatings, baby shaking, and self-inflicted wounds. One final insult to society got these boys nicked and sent away to the training school just in time, and their worst nightmare: the silver toilet. Lock up at RITS, the ACI, or Cedar Junction. One judge looked at Blaze and warned him, "Pretty boys are fish food."

Blaze had earned a respectable sheet with two bits at RITS. He had first been apprehended in junior high school for possession of three tabs of ecstasy. He had liked the absurd ring to the charge, "possession of ecstasy," and he tormented Janice, repeating it in sing-song when she drove him to appointments with his probation officer Dick Yarborough. Then it was a meth charge. Blaze didn't have his own kitchen, but he had met an older fiend named Baxter who cooked a potent crank recipe in his double-wide out in Hopkinton. Baxter sent Blaze to every CVS and Rite Aid to buy pseudo ephedrine tablets, both Sudafed and Mini Thin tabs, right before a law was passed forcing stores to keep these items behind the counter, where customers had to sign for them and show ID. Store security officers had their feelers out when they saw Baxter and soon they recognized Blaze.

Baxter was always checking his pager, and once Blaze drove with Baxter to meet his shadow people at the Wal-Mart parking lot. It was always the same slackers and a few rural moms with a carload of toddlers and babies who waited long afternoons until he and Baxter rolled in. One skinny mom was just a NASCAR T-shirt draped on a mop handle. She had advanced meth mouth, her rotten teeth like broken kernels of un-popped popcorn. Blaze hated to see the female form diminished into a bag of sticks.

Alongside working pharmacy, Baxter sometimes drove Blaze around in search of raised mailbox flags where people had left outgoing mail for the carrier. Baxter said he could wash personal checks with acetone. After seeing how it was done, Blaze told Townsend that he should get their mail delivered to a P.O. Box in town, but he didn't explain why. Townsend told him, "Hey dummy, we're RFD. That's rural *free* delivery, so why would we pay rent for a post office box?"

"So no one can steal our mail."

"They can pay my bills, if that's what they want."

Baxter started to follow UPS trucks into suburban developments. He and Blaze cruised gated neighborhoods where McMansions were left unsupervised during the daylight hours. The first time out they stole a brand-new Mac Pro system, complete with a twenty-one inch monitor and an HP LaserJet printer. The system had been left on the doorstep of a big house in Warwick. The homeowner had left an invitation in the form of a signed note to the UPS driver taped to the front door: "Leave Apple boxes on porch. Thanks!"

"You're welcome, fuckwit!" Baxter said as they collected the boxes and put them in his truck. Baxter sold the whole Mac package for a fraction of its real worth, but free money has that crisp cash feel when it's turned around in an afternoon.

Baxter took Blaze into an empty trophy house in Kingston. Blaze said, "What's to steal? There's nothing here. It's cleaned out."

Baxter got to work. He showed Blaze how to remove all the polished hardware from everything—drawer pulls, door hinges, towel bars. They took the handles off the kitchen cabinets and bath vanities, including the shiny baroque spigots from the sunken tub.

Going room to room, as Blaze removed privacy knobs, the heavy Christian doors glared at him with big empty eye holes. With everything dismantled, they took their booty in a mesh laundry bag and walked into a place called the Salvage Connoisseur back in Warwick to get cash, no questions asked.

Deconstructing someone's showplace gave Blaze an edgy feeling. Baxter had told him they could make even more cash ripping out copper wiring, but Blaze didn't like doing demolition. Stealing doorknobs didn't feel like a sin; they could be replaced. Tearing into the pretty cabbage rose wall covering and gouging the powdery gypsum had a whole other feeling.

Janice prized her cabbage rose wallpaper.

It wasn't his outings with Baxter that had rolled out the mini-max carpet. Blaze "borrowed" a Kawasaki crotch rocket, and the very next week he put the Arctic Cat snowmobile at the bottom of the frozen pond.

At the court house, with his mom standing beside him, Blaze listened as the arresting officer narrated the story. He said, "Your Honor, the pattern here is, with Blaze Townsend, if he can sit on it for five seconds, it's gone."

Scolded for running the snowmobile into the pond, the family court judge said that he knew what was happening to rural families in South County. The tensions of contemporary society were reaching farther and farther into remote communities. Tight farm families were splitting up. And in Westerly, families who had once worked in the quarries sawing granite or for a century had done lobstering from boats so old they had welded patches on top of welded patches, had introduced a whole new generation who weren't finding work in these traditional occupations. Kids might swim in the quarries every summer, but they had never sawed granite. Townsend himself had left his father's sheep farm to go white collar at Diggs & Snyder, and later Janice went to work full-time at Electric Boat. The judge said, "Rural teens turn to rot like a turnip crop left too long in the mud. Kids go bad if they aren't dug up, scrubbed, and shipped out."

After Blaze swiped the Arctic Cat the judge asked him, "Where do we go from here? Why are we back at square one?"

"It's his O-D-D," Janice said like a broken record.

The judge said, "Don't you have any responsibility to your boy?"

"What about him?" Janice looked at Townsend, who stood on the other side of the aisle. Neither parent had any answers for the judge.

Once again, Blaze was dug, scrubbed and shipped.

When Blaze was certain Janice had finally left the barn, he cranked the shower off. He emerged from the bathroom dripping in misty sweat. He tried to instant message Lucinda, but she wasn't answering. His father was gone, and when his new neighbor, too, had buzzed away in her Camry, Blaze went outside, into the open air.

He surveyed the sweep of property, the tractors lined up like grand prizes at some kind of redneck convention. He understood his situation. Without high school he wouldn't have college. Without college he wouldn't get a job that didn't involve lifting and hauling, digging or pounding, shingling or painting primer. He'd be delivering propane, pumping septic tanks, or collecting garbage. If he was lucky, he'd join a crew framing houses, but using nail guns always gave him a queasy flip in his stomach. A friend of his got a job pressure-washing houses. That machine was scary too, like a hydro knife. If used on its highest setting, the one for blast-cleaning concrete, it could slice off your leg like a chain saw, his friend had told him.

Not that Blaze wanted a desk job. But he understood it didn't look good for him.

Chapter Fourteen

Bravo, April," Milt said when she told him about her final soiree with the provost at the Westminster.

She brushed her hands together in the age-old pantomime of *That's that!*

"A defenestration of Men's Wearhouse best buys? It's priceless. I would have paid for a ticket to see it. It's not exactly Simone de Beauvoir or Betty Friedan," Milt teased her, "but maybe in the same league as *I Shot Andy Warhol*."

Whatever Milt said, she still admired what she had seen. The girl named Nancy was her new hero.

Happy to have returned to her office, she invited Milt to sit down in her extra chair. He curled his legs underneath him, like a proprietary house cat. She was glad to have a cheering squad but today she didn't want criticism.

Milt often read her e-mail dispatches from the provost and he had started to call Mirhege "Perv-pro," as her lover's e-mails had become increasingly crude. One recent note had said, "I can't walk by the Westminster without wanting to sniff your scent on my fingers, baby—"

Milt squeaked, "Lordy—that's filthy!"

"It's so fifth grade, like a middle school brat."

She had clicked delete. Milt grabbed her mouse and went back for a second helping. He dug the e-mail out of her trash file to read it again. He reminded her that the normal recovery process described in a brochure for someone grieving the loss of a loved one should be to "adopt a pet" and "eat healthful snacks," and should not be to hook up with a married man.

Milt was happy she had finally taken action. "The provost is toast!" he said.

Her e-mail chimed and Milt stood behind her chair, thinking it would be a wounded tirade from Mirhege about the heave-ho at the hotel. She elbowed Milt, not wanting him to horn in on her victory. But the message wasn't from the provost. It was an e-mail from Endless Pools. A splashy video announced a yearly pre-summer sales campaign.

"I keep getting these. It's kind of weird."

"After the accident, didn't Endless Pools send you a sympathy letter? Damage control from their PR department?"

"It never stops!"

"Don't think about it anymore. Today's a red-letter day. Perv-pro got his pink slip."

"It doesn't solve anything," she said. "I mean, since Riley's gone, what's the difference if I roll around in the golden gutter with the provost, or with the crazy farmer next door, or whoever. Who cares if I keep it or give it away!"

"More of your guilt game, April, you're a broken record. It's self-destructive." Milt tried to be sympathetic but he himself had never taken responsibility for Riley's accident. Milt had invited Riley to swim at his health club, where Riley had drowned.

It started with a car wreck.

April often dialed Riley to see if he was gridlocked on the Southeast Expressway. There was a big window of time between the moment he left his office and when he arrived home. She had her suspicions about this stolen time, despite the contract she had made with him never to question his extracurricular hobbies.

The day she called Riley, she heard him say, "Oh shit, here's my exit—" He zipped across two lanes to take the ramp and slammed into the breakaway stanchion that supported the exit sign. The impact kicked the pole free, but the big green fiberglass sheet broke loose and sliced down onto the roof of Riley's little Nissan. The car skidded to a stop beneath the wild, impromptu awning.

Riley was a little banged-up. A passenger in the car had also been taken to the hospital to get stitches for a nasty cut across the forehead. April learned that the young man in the passenger seat was a programmer at the same start-up where Riley worked. In the emergency room, Riley told her, "It just sort of happened. I didn't see it coming."

She thought he was talking about missing his freeway exit. Of course, he was saying much more.

Riley suffered a fractured thumb which the doctors had fixed with a tiny metal pin and a few screws. Even with his injured thumb he could work at his keyboard and use his mouse. He had a welt across his rib cage where the seat belt had grabbed him, a diagonal red stripe like a beauty contestant's sash, and he also had back pain. The doctor prescribed physical therapy for Riley's minor back problem and he started swimming in an Endless Pool at Blackstone Rehab Hospital.

The trough-shaped pool had a strong current that churned at a fast five thousand gallons a minute. Riley enjoyed the work-out in the forceful surge of water. The Endless Pool was sometimes used to prepare swimmers for the grueling conditions they encountered attempting the English Channel. The water could be iced to equal the wintry thermal conditions that diehards faced on that frigid swim.

Riley went to rehab daily to swim in the Endless Pool, enjoying its frothy breakers. April blamed herself for having distracted him on his cell phone, making him drive off the road into the sign pole. Scientists have distinguished different vision centers of the brain. One area responds to external visual stimuli in the elementary way that an insect's eye captures light, color, movement. But the second vision center prompts subjective visualization. These subjective visualizations interfere with what a driver is seeing out the windshield. At the time of the accident, April was arguing with Riley about a late fee on a credit card bill. She had not mailed the monthly payment before its due date. A credit card statement with a nasty late fee would have been the mental picture Riley was seeing as he was driving, or perhaps he saw the new built-in dishwasher, the purchase in question. Because of her telephone call he had missed familiar visual cues. "If Riley ignored his insect eye," she told Milt, "it was my fault."

Since Riley's death, April had stopped using the dishwasher.

She washed her kitchen utensils, her one dinner plate, and her single coffee mug in a sink full of suds. The sparkling stainless steel dishwasher sat untouched. Milt tried to convince April to use the appliance. He said, "Come on girl, you can't be in *dish*pair forever."

April didn't follow suggestions described in bereavement pamphlets, brochures that even had recipes, cut in half, for "sudden singles" and widowers. Her grief had peppery layers and extra tendrils of revengeful fantasy.

Riley was buried in Portland, Oregon where his mother lived. He had come east to escape his mother's nosy interference, but she was getting him back. His mother had always been ticklish about his relationships with women, and April shouldn't feel singled out, Riley had said. When they agreed not to get married April believed it was because they shared a progressive ideology about the social convention, but his mother was behind it. April learned that Riley had often made side trips to visit his mom, taking along male friends. His mother was never critical of them. Riley went into the ground in a cemetery only a few hundred yards from his homestead. His mother told April that she could see his marker from her bedroom window.

April had purchased Riley's casket. She had accompanied it and Riley's body all the way to Oregon. Flying American Airlines, she was booked into business class, but before boarding, she had to do paper-work to have his body shipped in the pressurized luggage compartment. At the shipping desk in a chilly hangar, she saw a Great Dane bitch in a kennel crate. The dog's owner made awkward chit-chat, exchanging pleasantries. A dog was "live cargo," but Riley's casket would be loaded in the same compartment. When the dog's owner heard of it, he complained to the airline agent. He said that the dog's sense of smell was so acute that, if placed beside the deceased "passenger," the Great Dane might be put in distress. He wanted Riley's casket and the dog crate to be isolated from one another.

Milt didn't attend the funeral. He was giving a paper at Temple University, his alma mater, and couldn't get out of it. April was surprised to see that a group of Riley's techie colleagues and gamer friends arrived to pay their respects. April had met only two or three of them, but they were all socially awkward. These young men routinely hid behind monitors in remote locations, so Riley's friendships with them had been invisible. His membership in the nerdy cluster of elite game designers, programmers, coders, graphic artists, and writers had spawned some of their worst arguments before they finally came to their "agreement." Riley was free to sample the full menu of these geniuses, regardless of gender. April had felt she had no other option if she wanted to hold on to him. She found solace in her intense mothering impulses and homemaking regimens, which Riley appreciated. He was patient with her relentless story about her near-miss pregnancy and her brush with a "stone baby." He let her mother *him*. She decorated their condo, she cooked, sewed buttons, protected him, and he told her she was the hub of their little family.

Their conflict occurred when two of Riley's associates lured him to work with them on contract jobs for DreamWorks Interactive, creating new video games based on blockbuster movies. Riley helped design games for the Jurassic Park franchise and worked on the digital sequels to super hero feature films. The money was good, but Riley's hours were almost 24-7, a schedule of accelerating deadlines that were never actually met but extended week by week to meet the designers' new whims and constantly morphing criteria.

He was invited to join the team at a development studio called Ion Storm, a start-up in Austin, Texas founded by the same talent who had created the best selling "Doom" series.

April didn't want to leave New England.

After Vassar, she didn't get accepted to the better doctorate programs at Columbia or Yale, like so many of her Vassar classmates, and she settled for a state school in Indiana. After her years in the middle of nowhere, she promised herself that she'd never leave the East Coast again. She and Riley knocked heads about the pros and cons of Austin, and she pleaded with him not to take the job. Finally, Riley promised he wouldn't force her to go with him. He'd stay with her.

Two of Riley's brethren who had made the move to Austin became overnight super stars. They were cult heroes to core gamers and often signed autographs at techie conventions, cyber fairs, and electronics flea markets. They were invited to the annual Ziff Davis Electronic Gaming Summit in Napa, as guests of honor. As they developed better computer games, they e-mailed each new component to Riley, on a daily basis, to get his feedback. They loved his ideas and had credited him in the packaging notes.

Riley remained close to them, although these liaisons and bonds had been formed in the ether. He sometimes traveled to game conferences with his fellow believers, but when April saw Riley's mother enfolded by these men at the funeral, she understood that Riley had brought the boys home to his mother on previous occasions. April was the outsider.

At Riley's burial, the ceremony was unexpectedly delayed. The cemetery director pulled Riley's father aside to discuss the situation. He explained that there had been a terrible "oversight." The coffin could not be lowered into the grave.

The hole was too small.

April had purchased an *oversized* coffin. Almost a foot too long. The error had just been discovered. Not until after the service could gravediggers finish the job and Riley be put to rest. His mother blamed April. She complained that April had bought the coffin from a wholesale supply company.

When Riley's body had finally been interred in Portland, and April returned to Rhode Island, she had no gravesite to visit. April was robbed of the healing ritual of standing before a marker with the parentheses of irrefutable dates carved in granite that would have helped her accept the truth.

April knew of a shrine she could visit, and she often went there with Milt. School kept her busy weekdays, but weekends were too elastic. Milt would be bleary from a Friday-night liaison, pouring a beaker of Mylanta and swallowing aspirin when April called him Saturday morning and begged him to go with her for a drive.

As a teen, April's father had often said, "Hey, let's go motoring," the way other dads might say "Let's go bowling" or "Let's go to the movies." Her father thought that old-fashioned words like "motoring" romanticized the ho-hum activities he preferred to organized sports and feature films. He told her to sit beside him on the bench seat and not to hug the window. He treated her like a queen. She thought her trips with him were special until he had squeezed her knee, a little too high. Once, she found a pretty glove in the front seat. April recognized the fluffy mohair mitten. It belonged to her father's secretary. She had felt an instant wave of jealousy, but then she was relieved. This little mitten would be the defining image of her parents' break-up. After years of her father's attentions, with the mitten April was absolved. The break-up had nothing to do with her.

On their Saturday drives, April asked Milt to take a particular stretch of highway on Route 114, just to stop at a sentimental grotto in the small town of Warren. The sacred spot was called the

Playhouse Cottage, a tiny summer house where she and Riley had spent a week early in their romance. The cottage got its name from a local community theater group that had converted an American Tourister suitcase factory into a rustic summer stock venue. The original American Tourister neon sign was still operating, and it blinked like a talisman of their romantic getaway. Although Riley didn't want to enter into a traditional marriage pledge, he wanted them to be a couple. It was there, sitting with him beneath the rose arbor and neon sign that Riley had told her he had turned down the job at Ion Storm.

"You're annoying me with this sentimental shit," Milt had once said, when they stopped at the honeymoon shack.

She turned off the ignition.

She told Milt, "This is my rule. Whenever we pass this place we have to stop or it's a jinx." The tiny house had held everything that was clean and perfect in her world of Riley. She could see its interior when she closed her eyes. Its rattan chairs and wicker loveseat, the bed with its white-on-white dust ruffle, the antique hutch with its willow ware china, charming plates, cups and bowls that were rose-colored and not the ordinary blue ware.

She stared at the shrine.

Milt turned in his seat. "Riley didn't mean to hurt you."

Milt always acted like he had the inside track on Riley. He wanted to soothe April's anxieties by explaining too much. He wasn't condescending to April, but Milt felt he had the right. Milt was the last person to see Riley alive.

The week before Riley died, April had asked him, "Can you swim in that pool with those pins in your thumb?"

"The bone heals into the screws," he told her.

"No kidding?"

"The bone grows into it."

It became a sex joke between them. Making love, she'd tell him to be careful with his sore back and injured hand, but he fucked her and told her, "Don't worry, baby, *the bone grows into it.*"

As he regained his strength, Riley had asked his physical therapist to increase the Endless Pool's acceleration. His therapist warned him that he wasn't practicing for the Olympics, he should slow down. But he liked the strongest current and his back improved.

When Riley's insurance wouldn't pay for more PT at the rehab pool, Milt invited him to use the Endless Pool at his health club. He could come as his guest. "We'll say you're *mine*. And no one will bother you."

Riley was addicted to the regimen.

One morning, April walked into the kitchen surprised to find Milt already at the breakfast table, with Riley still in his pjs.

Milt told Riley, "Hurry up. Move your ass or you'll miss your ride in the Milt-Mobile." April thought Milt was referring to his new Prius hybrid. Then Milt leaned over and whispered something to Riley. She saw a wave of pleasure flutter across Riley's features, a shivery smile as if Milt had told him a tidbit of delicious gossip.

"You shouldn't be swimming every day," April told Riley.

"Why not?" Milt said, wholly comfortable when he challenged her authority, whether it was at a faculty meeting or in her own kitchen.

"Because he has torn ligaments. And a broken thumb," she said.

"That pin? It's okay. The bone grows into it," Milt said. He smiled at Riley.

She didn't think Riley had told anyone about their secret sex prod, but Milt had exhibited a kind of propriety when he recited the silly quip. And before the men left, Milt said, "April, can we have some towels? The ones at the club are too thin, almost transparent."

"Like the Shroud of Turin,'" Riley said.

The men waited.

She came back with only one towel. Milt said, "Never mind. I'll use Riley's."

"Sure. He'll use my towel," Riley said.

Later that morning she was in her office expecting to meet with the parent of a student who had recently changed his major from pre-law to a major in English. The student's father was alarmed and wanted to discuss job opportunities available to his son with only a degree in literature. She was ready for the face-off. The knock at her door wasn't the concerned parent but a man from Milt's health club and Detective John Primiano from the district attorney's office. The men told her that Riley had been found unconscious in the pool at Milt's club. She didn't know what they were talking about. They said that Riley was submerged in the shallow tank, with its current turned up full force. Once he was discovered, staff members could not revive him

The detective said, "It might not be an actual drowning we've got here. For a drowning, EMTs always do a Heimlich before performing chest compressions and CPR. They said that the Heimlich didn't produce any aspirated water. Foam in the airways. Middle-ear hemorrhage. Shoulder girdle bruises. These occur in a drowning, but your husband had an odd mark."

"That's from his seat belt," she told the detective. She suddenly felt that the mark had been an omen. When the bruise didn't fade, it had been a supernatural warning. Why had they ignored it?

Finally, the detective's words poked through.

They were telling her Riley was dead.

She remembered what Riley had told her that morning, the last time she'd seen him alive. He had joked about the Shroud of Turin. A shroud joke! In hindsight that, too, was a scary omen. She dabbed her eyes as the health club director told the investigator about Riley's exercise routine in the pool.

He said, "Over-did it," deleting the pronoun. It was as if he was talking about binge-eating, drinking too much, or a day in the outdoors without enough sunscreen. The lopped-off pronoun was especially painful to her. Riley was unreferenced. She had lost him. *Riley was gone.*

Days later, April was still in her bathrobe at noon when Detective Primiano dropped by the house. She had just washed her hair and it was dripping onto her shoulders, making the fabric cling. She said she had a new pot of coffee and she showed the detective into the living room. He took a chair and she handed him an oversized coffee mug.

He explained that he had initiated an investigation into her boyfriend's death.

"An investigation?" she said. "You don't mean anything criminal, do you?"

"His autopsy report states that your boyfriend didn't die from drowning."

"I know. They said it was a ruptured intracranial aneurysm."

"That's right. It seems to be natural causes. But his blood work showed evidence of amyl nitrite."

"It showed what?"

"It's sometimes called poppers, TNT, snappers, or bullet on the street, a drug often used for heightened sexual arousal," the detective explained without looking up.

"I've heard of it, I guess."

"So, did you and your boyfriend use poppers on occasion? Maybe that morning?"

She felt her face and throat blooming with heat. She didn't expect that the conversation would be an examination of her intimate life with Riley.

Primiano said, "You never tried it? It wasn't your thing?"

She didn't wish to be asked about "her thing," or about any details regarding the specific, all-too-complex ladder of fantasy, tone, and physical manipulation Riley had used to bring her to orgasm. She felt her damp robe plastered to her curves and was relieved that the detective didn't steal glances at her.

Primiano said, "Amyl nitrite is more popular with gay men."

April was overcome with a sensation she had sometimes felt when waiting for a train. She stood at the lip of the platform, leaning over the empty track, craning her neck to search for the approaching locomotive. Something huge and chugging, dangerous but still unseen, was coming around the bend.

She said, "We aren't into drugs. I mean, we *weren't* into them."

The detective sipped his coffee. He said that the medical examiner had requested that Riley's stomach should be pumped and the contents examined.

"They never told me that they pumped his stomach. Why did they do that?"

Primiano looked at April's collar bone as he continued. "The medical examiner found semen in Riley's stomach contents."

She steepled her hands and stared at them.

"He died of natural causes, right?" she said.

"That's right."

"So why are you concerned about this?"

He said, "We were hoping to identify whoever might have been at the club with him. Can you think of someone?"

"It must have been swarming with members."

"The department has got a little sheet on your boyfriend. Not much. He was picked up twice at the scenic rest stop on I-195, you know the one? It's a cruising spot. He was issued a couple warnings for loitering, but he was arrested only once. He ever tell you about it?"

"Arrested for loitering?"

"He paid a fine. Nothing much. The profile says he had some kind of active interest."

She looked at the detective. He was telling her that they had proof Riley had been "active" in a lifestyle that didn't include her. There was paperwork!

She had already asked Milt, "Did you have sex with Riley? How many times?"

Milt had said, "Time will say nothing but I told you so / Time only knows the price we have to pay / If I could tell you I would let you know."

"You think Auden can get you out of this?" she said.

"I just hope you'll forgive us, April. Forgive and forget."

"I can forgive Auden, I guess."

Milt said, "I don't know who Riley was with that morning. I had my nine o'clock class. It could have been anybody in the pool with him—" Milt judged her for her blind faith in Riley, for her Pollyanna defense mechanisms, but she had been Riley's real lover. In their sex play, he had often fantasized both ways, and if he had actually practiced these fantasy scenes in real life, he had always made her feel she was privy to his loosely veiled substratum. She wasn't left out.

The detective said, "Sorry to spring this on you."

"He's dead. I have to accept it." Death was the greatest betrayal, not sex. He had called her the *hub*. But with the official news about Riley's autopsy, something had slithered into her chest cavity, something icy, weaving and threading between her ribs. It was an invasive feeling she experienced whenever the establishment intruded in her private life. The detective watched her. He was an old hand at giving bad news, like a white collar, or an older sister. His professional restraint was generous, and she was grateful to him. Other men looked at her differently, like a cupcake left on the plate that shouldn't go wasted. She tugged the lapels of her bathrobe tighter.

Chapter Fifteen

At the end of any typical day at Sinclair, April dragged herself home with a little more stuffing spilled out of her. It was worse after April's lunch hour with the provost, and she wondered if people noticed she looked ruffled. She wondered if *he* had noticed. Maybe he didn't quite recognize she had dumped him when she left without any good-byes. He might have thought she was just running late. She had made her decision. Not only had she left him for good, but she had called Betty Clark in Academic Affairs to complain about his intrusion in the process of her application for the chair's position. She hadn't directly called it sexual harassment, but with her preliminary complaint to Betty Clark, he would get a whole new picture of her unabashed commitment to self-preservation. Her decision to make a complaint was nerve-wracking. She felt its aftermath humming through her body. It happens after your adrenaline spikes and then falls away. Her limbs felt like taffy.

On her way home, April stopped at Whole Foods. An ambulance was parked right beside the market's automatic doors. April walked into the building to see a crowd gathered around a woman who had collapsed. Then April saw Janice Gallen standing to one side in the produce section, behind a pyramid of melons. April walked up to her.

"Looks bad," Janice said. "A heart attack, I guess."

The EMTs had brought the defibrillator.

"That's somebody's mother," Janice said.

"Probably."

"Your mother still around?" Janice said.

April said, "She moved to Jacksonville when my father passed away. She's at one of those 'cruise ship' retirement homes. You know, three meals, hair salon, shuffleboard, water aerobics, bingo, everything you want."

"Is that assisted living?"

"Oh, it's got that too. When and if."

"My mom's gone."

April said, "Oh, really? I'm sorry to hear that." She pretended not to know. Janice wouldn't want April's two cents. So April was surprised when Janice said, "I found my mother dead. She was frozen. Her arm was sticking up in the air. Rigor mortis or something. I was just a kid."

"She was frozen?"

"She was drunk. She fell outside the house and didn't get up. It was after a heavy snow storm. Did you ever see blue snow?"

April said, "I don't think so."

"If you kicked your boot into a drift, it made this bright Windex blue tunnel."

"Blue snow? Was it toxic waste or something?" Ever since the sludge pile, April was seeing toxic threats in everything.

"No, it's not toxic. They say it's when light passes through ice. Sometimes the red light is absorbed while the blue is transmitted. It's the build-up of all the blue wavelengths. Wet snow gets compacted and the color is intense."

Hearing Janice's elaborate explanation, April recognized that Blaze got his tendency for wordy ramblings from his mom's side of the family.

"I thought my mom's death had something to do with the blue snow. If we hadn't had that storm, maybe she wouldn't have died."

April was enamored with Janice's story, finding it wrought with poetic resonance and metaphoric sadness: "the build-up of all the blue wavelengths." April believed that her whole life, if she thought about it, was nothing but the build-up of blue wavelengths.

Despite her first impressions of Janice, despite all the nasty reports from outsiders and jabs from her son, April sort of fell for Janice Gallen, right there and then. Janice didn't seem to recognize her story's symbolic threads or charged sentiments. She didn't romanticize the blue snow episode. That was April's weakness.

They watched the EMTs lift the ailing woman onto a gurney. She was wheeled through the automatic store doors. They weren't really doors at all, but a modern system of opposing air currents that kept the cold and rain outside, as forceful as the dryers at a car wash.

Janice moved down the aisle with her shopping basket. She waved to April, and turned the corner.

For the next couple of days, April tried to follow her normal routine at the college, and she was careful to avoid the provost. At the end of each day, she was happy to return home, almost pleased to see the black mountain of sludge. Her little ongoing tussle with Townsend was a comforting distraction. Townsend's SLEEP, CREEP, LEAP. signboard had started to feel like a WELCOME HOME sign, but she had not yet decided to accept his invitation for a drink. When she had visited the barn, she recognized that Blaze wasn't happy mixing it up with his father as a third wheel.

Returning from Sinclair, she collected letters from her mailbox in front of the house. Bolted to a tilted post, the oversized rural mailbox was roomy enough for a laying hen and her brood. It was her mailbox now, but Townsend had asked her if he could still use it until he got a new box of his own. Every day she had to sort through Townsend's bills, catalogues, flyers, his *Westerly Times*. She'd discover items that Townsend didn't seem to want to claim. He'd leave the same dunning notice, addressed to him, inside the box as if he wanted the mail carrier to take it back or as if he hoped April would absorb it.

She lugged her mail and a stack of mid-term papers into the house. She dumped her keys and her student papers on the kitchen table. She took off her coat, unwinding her scarf, letting it drop in a circle around her feet.

In her stack of mail she found a brown paper bag with two poems in it and a glass medallion the size of a coaster, fastened to a string. It was a bird-safe ornament for her window, to ward off the kamikaze grackles that she had found so nerve-wracking. The little gift was charming. Like his hummingbird hat, the bauble supported her desire to believe Blaze was a decent kid, and innocent of the misdeeds attributed to him.

She wasn't prepared to see yet another side of him when she unfolded the first poem he had sent:

> *I don't care who died today.*
> *There's not a single reason*
> *to list the deaths today.*
> *I could follow death like a woman*
> *into the subway where death*
> *is just a headline, where boys light*
> *freezing derelicts on fire.*

And, the next poem was even more startling.

> *Who will be the lover of that woman on the bench?*
> *If she wants to hurt someone, she can use me.*
> *Did she mean it, or is she trying to be unforgettable.*
> *If she wants to use someone, she can hurt me.*
> *I always sigh when I see a girl like this;*
> *I don't know where it comes from, and I don't know*
> *where it goes.*

The poems disturbed her by their distinct language and by the *tone* of their content. She remembered what a politician had said, "You campaign in poetry, but you govern in prose." These lines seemed beyond a teenager's grasp and she was certain he had copied them. The subway reference was a give-away. But as a teacher she knew that students often romanticized urban lore and might write about the city even when they hadn't stepped outside their suburban homes. Because she didn't immediately recognize the poet he had plagiarized, she allowed herself to think that maybe the kid was, in fact, some kind of polymath.

She centered the glass ornament on her window lock and was relieved to think she wouldn't hear the sudden thump of a bird crashing into the glass. The wildlife would be spared, thanks to her young neighbor, who was some kind of baby environmentalist, another charming characteristic for a teen boy and a nice complement to his artsy side, even if he'd copied the poems.

He would want to hear her critique, and of course he expected only praise, but she was relieved not to run into him that evening. She didn't want to have to accuse him of plagiarism.

The next afternoon she came home from Sinclair unprepared to find another offbeat gift from Blaze when she walked into her kitchen.

Tethered to one leg of the dinette table was a miniature horse.

It was one of the beautiful creatures she had seen at the spread down the street, one of the animals she had first believed were carousel cast offs, but that were, in fact, healthy livestock. The snowy white colt was just as startled as she was. Its explosive mane was a tousled skein of silk as it shook its head. It swished its long tail, swatting the refrigerator. The creature was so small that it didn't come up to her waist. But its eyes were huge, full-sized spheres as it looked at her with a strange beseeching expression, like, *You and I know this is not going to work!*

Blaze was trying hard to impress her. By giving her ornaments and poems, and he had even been collecting her trash for her, emptying her garbage bin outside, she had noticed—it was as if Blaze had adopted the role of her amanuensis—and now the little horse. She untied the nylon lead from the table leg and pulled the horse's diminutive halter, trying to lead it outside. It was skittish at the doorway and halted at the ledge of her stoop but finally jumped down both stairs at once, in one shuddering leap. It started to trot down the drive, until she sawed the rope to control it.

Townsend returned the little horse to the yuppie farmette up the road. The owners had not yet discovered that Blaze had "borrowed" it, and there was no harm done. Blaze told his father, "You said she'd mentioned those ponies, and maybe wants one. They've got a herd over there, and two mares are in foal again. Bad as rabbits. Besides, I was going to pay for it."

April told Townsend, "Do I have to get my locks changed?" The boy's crazy displays of affection, coupled with his mom's dreamy tale of blue snow, only further complicated her feelings about Blaze and his family. She was getting indoctrinated in a complicated dynamic that seemed dangerous but hard to resist.

That afternoon, April received an e-mail with a YouTube video link. She feared it would be a promotional campaign from Endless Pools. They had specs for both economy packages and luxury models. They sold the EPWIDE for "breaststrokers with a pronounced frog kick" and the EPDEEP for "chest-deep aquatic exercise and water-running."

And for installation in a tight space they offered a model called the EPSHORT.

April hated to be reminded that Riley had died in one of these contraptions at Milt's club. When she clicked on the play icon, her hands became clammy, and she was breathing too fast, sipping air faster than she exhaled. She remembered reading that the Hindu word for "breath" was the same as the word for "soul." Whenever she had panic symptoms and had trouble getting her breath she imagined that it meant that her very soul was suffocating, struggling for air.

She was surprised to see that it wasn't an Endless Pools ad on the screen, but a dimly lit bedroom, like in a Motel 6 with typical cheap furnishings. The camera panned 180 degrees to the motel bed. She expected to see a couple engaged in sex. She was ready to see two men going at it in feverish, jerky motions and hear a soundtrack that captured happy purring sounds and pleasure yelps coming from the man who was lying prone.

With Riley on top.

Instead, she saw Riley seated at a little table with three other men. The table was draped with a bright paper tablecloth. Each man wore a shiny paper cone hat on his head like the kind you might purchase at a party supply store. The table was littered with foil blow outs, party poppers, and other cardboard favors. An unnaturally pink sheet cake was centered before one of the men, its candles freshly lighted. The group was laughing, cheering, and singing the sickly first phrases of "Auld Lang Syne" as together they encouraged the guest of honor to enact the familiar rite. The center of their attentions, a young man with dewy eyes and a big grin, obediently blew out the candles in three exacting, individual puffs. Then Riley instantly kissed him. Deeply. The tender, long-lasting kiss was more upsetting to April than if the video had been the outright pornography she had expected.

She watched the brief video until it blacked out. She was dizzy. It was as if she suffered from what they call reverse seasickness or mal de débarquement syndrome, a medical condition often experienced by travelers when they return to land after a sea cruise.

April didn't recognize Riley's twinkie or his other companions but for one detail. They were younger than him. She didn't understand if one of these youths had sent the video to her in anger or in solidarity. Maybe one of these men had been sending her the mysterious e-mails and had written the alarming note, "I want to meet you!" She didn't know the connection that was implied, or what they wanted. She watched the video again. Their tone-deaf serenade. The pink cake. The kiss.

In order to calm down, she forced herself to grade papers for the rest of the afternoon. She was careful to line edit text, making recommendations, rewriting awkward sentences, and reorganizing paragraphs. She tried to crowd her head with her students' banal ideas, but it was difficult after seeing Riley at the joyous motel party.

She never wanted to take Milt's advice or adopt his brusque techniques. He graded student papers by merely writing along the margins "MEGO," for "My eyes glaze over!" and "FUBR," for "Fucked up beyond recognition."

April would never be so insulting, no matter how bad the work, and she believed she could teach more successfully by praising her students as often as she used necessary criticism. If a student wrote a strong section, she was sure to mark it with a compliment, and she avoided scribbling happy faces alongside a good paragraph, as lazy teachers might.

Her charity was soon used up, and she shoved her school work aside. She shuffled her papers to find the poems Blaze had written; she read them again. For some reason, the poems were comforting. Even if he had stolen them, he had somehow put his mark on the lines by writing them out for her.

She heard someone outside the house trying to start up one of Townsend's mini tractors and she was pleased that he might be making a dent in the bio-sludge pile. She went to the window to see the Bobcat, but its little saddle seat was empty. If Townsend or Blaze had tried, in earnest, to begin moving the sludge to the flagpole, he'd been too late to start the job. It was getting dark. Where the pile had been gouged, the grunge was steaming, proof of how the hill cooked from the inside out. Another nor'easter might just topple it, spreading it across her front lawn like rank chocolate frosting. At the window, she searched the pasture for Townsend's horses. She often looked for them, finding solace in the pastoral vision. She saw them in the north corner of the field. Flurries had started up again, dusting their rumps and withers. She wanted it to snow hard. She hoped to get the chance to see for herself the blue snow Janice had described.

Her monitor chimed, announcing an e-mail. April expected to finally get an angry phone call or an e-mail message from the provost. He would want to have the final word. She almost welcomed a little tirade from him now. He might use a snippet from the King James Bible, a paragraph from *Madame Bovary*, or a line from Blake's *Proverbs of Hell*, such as "Improvement makes strait roads; but the crooked roads without Improvement are roads of Genius" or "The fox provides for himself, but God provides for the lion." He often tried to entice her into a reversal of feeling by using bon mots from the canon. When she opened the message in her Outlook Express, it wasn't an e-mail from her wounded lover, whom she had left so unceremoniously in the hotel room.

She saw the sender's name said "Marlboro Coffin Supply Company," a casket manufacturer in Pawtucket, but it wasn't where she'd bought Riley's box. The subject line said, "We have to talk," but there was no message attached. The macabre e-mail address was chilling. It wasn't as straightforward a threat as one she had read about in a novel when a stalker's e-mail address had been *revengeisnear@imhidden.com*, but she was confused by the introduction of a middleman without any further explanation other than the subject line.

She wondered if a disgruntled student or even the "at risk" kid next door had somehow learned about her boyfriend's death, but she didn't believe they would have had any access to the homemade sheet cake video. That was an inside job. Whoever it was who tried to harass her, he seemed to be taking pleasure in his angle of attack by using a coffin supply e-mail address. She started to think it must be one of Riley's business friends; these techie nerds were often hired to create websites, and Marlboro Coffin Supply must have been an unwitting accomplice.

She didn't think her stalker knew her personally; the previous note, "I want to meet you!" seemed to suggest she didn't know him at all. She did have one troubled student at Sinclair, a privileged brat named Taylor Moffett. He had charged into her office that very afternoon to complain about his grade. "I don't get the point of Emily Dickinson," he had said. Milt had had his own minor fracas with the same hothead in the fall semester. Milt called this student the Beautiful Boy. April thought that it was to his credit that Milt didn't actually cruise the campus for prospects, but he liked to survey the bullocks and lambs. He critiqued them, ranked them; he christened them with nicknames. He made his guesstimates, often just to get a rise out of April. She could see he was right about the Beautiful Boy. He was a looker. His sharp features were symmetrical, his face unmarked by any heavy-lifting mental tasks, no worries, no frail penumbra of typical teen dread or nervous self-analysis. Unlike Blaze, whose glower was charged by an innate interior angst, the student looked clean and stupid, like a daisy. But that afternoon the daisy had shown up in a fretful state. He asked her, "Can I talk to you?"

"Of course, what can I help you with?"

"I want you to change my grade in here. I need an A," he said. "Or I'm going upstairs to Dr. Mirhege." She didn't think the student knew anything about her relationship with the provost but was simply threatening to go upstairs to complain to her administrative superior.

The fly in the ointment was that the boy's grandfather had been a major donor to Sinclair's capital campaign. The business-man had paid for an expansive new classroom high-rise on campus called the Moffett Building. Students were assigned to rooms called M205 or M416, and the like. Professors had been encouraged to be conscious of the student's connections when assessing his academic status. Some teachers softened their critiques, plumped up his test scores, and excused his late papers.

April compared the Beautiful Boy with her young neighbor. She preferred the tarnished sneer and fierce eyes of Townsend's kid. That was something she could work with. Like the Beautiful Boy, Blaze, too, was handsome, but he wasn't a poseur. His face revealed his real predicament. It wasn't a veneer. Blaze always seemed to be hatching his thoughts at a dangerous velocity; his tumbling conjectures and conclusions were genuine eruptions. She had come to think of the car-jacking in its primal form, as a display of his outsider authenticity. Of course, she knew she was romanticizing.

She tried to sympathize with the Beautiful Boy as he searched for the right rabbit suit to wear to please his overbearing grandfather, but she didn't change his grade.

She wanted to tell Milt about the motel birthday party video. Maybe he would recognize the young men. She could ask him to come over and watch it with her. Something held her back. Instead, she called him and said, "I know he's your pet, but do you think the Beautiful Boy could have sent me these Endless Pools e-mails?"

"Did he really say, 'I don't get the point of Emily Dickinson'?"

"Yes, he did."

"I could turn him around, don't you think? With a little mentoring—"

"Shit, is that all you can think about? I'm being stalked!"

She changed the subject to talk about the manure pile. "Did you know there's a hazmat pamphlet that says bio-sludge gives people nerve damage? It might contain chromium and arsenic—" Blaze had told her that he got dizzy trying to move the stuff.

"Your nerves do seem rattled," Milt said. "Are they buzzing, tingling? Any headaches? Numbness?"

"When I say I have headaches I'm not just using an idiom. I'm talking about a real slicing steel band."

Her headaches from the sludge pile were a smoke screen she used when she couldn't describe the real problem. Riley's death had been like a tailings dam disaster, when the very ground she walked on had liquefied under the crust. She had lost her footing. In its slurry she had started her messy affair with Mirhege.

Milt joked, "People have their baggage April, but you have *a real mountain of shit.*"

The sludge pile wasn't just a metaphor; it had become a prop or theatrical machination in a midlife drama. And the curtain was rising.

Chapter Sixteen

Single Woman Found Buried in Blue Snow Bank
An East Westerly woman was discovered during highway
cleanup of Sunday's major blizzard. Her body temperature
was measured at a near fatal 92.4. Hypothermia is often a
killer, but doctors believe she will pull through. . . .

The sun was going down. Grading papers had not been enough of a distraction, and April had watched the motel video several times hoping overkill would numb its initial insult. It had the opposite effect. The night would be long. Her insomnia typically unfurled like a tight papyrus scroll that stretches open for miles. Night presented an unedited narrative. It was night without end stops, night without margins, night without space breaks, and night without any help from the old reliable *Manual of Style* that she kept handy, on her bookshelf.

She was standing in front of her refrigerator trying to find something to eat when she heard someone outside. She went to the window and was surprised to see a figure standing halfway up her front walk. Blaze was lurking outside. She'd tell him it was rude to peep at her. Then she saw it wasn't the kid. The young man was a stranger. He stood on her front path, frozen to one square of blue stone, hands in his pockets, as if he couldn't decide to come to the door. He was small-framed and of average height, probably in his twenties, and he was dressed in that familiar sloppy, nerdy way Riley had dressed, part mountain gear, part outlet-store designer seconds. In fact he was wearing one of Riley's political T-shirts. It was a shirt that had always raised eyebrows and had made April embarrassed every time Riley had worn it in public. The shirt said MILITANT ATHIEST with a sub caption that shouted OUT OF THE CLOSET!

It wasn't something you'd find on the racks at J. Crew, and not at Abercrombie. Riley had had fun wearing it. April wasn't a believer and she didn't care that the shirt was anti-God, but the shirt had made her uncomfortable. She had come to realize that by parading the announcement "Out of the closet," Riley had worn the shirt with pride, rejecting both God and woman!

April didn't remember finding Riley's shirt when she packed up his clothes and miscellany for the Salvation Army bin. It might be Riley's shirt that the man was wearing.

She had been surprised to find another of Riley's T-shirts on the floor of the laundry room where she'd left it to add to her next wash. When she retrieved it to begin a new load, the shirt fell apart in her hands, a tangle of moist shreds. A bottle of bleach had overturned, leaking a puddle on the linoleum. The shirt had completely dissolved. Finding the shirt, eaten up, seemed to mock everything she had lost.

The prowler looked familiar. He might be the sheet cake boy or one of the others in the motel video, but she couldn't be sure. When she went to the front door to confront him, it took all her nerve to twist the dead bolt. When she stepped onto the front stoop, her shady visitor was gone.

"Militant atheist, my foot," she mumbled to herself. In the deepening twilight, she was shaky, but she forced herself to walk around the house to find him. She was in the back garden, in its eerie gloaming, when she heard an engine revving and a car rolling away on the gravel drive.

She went back inside and stood in her kitchen. She decided to finally accept Townsend's invitation for drinks.

She didn't want to be alone in her house.

If she asked for Townsend's advice about the e-mail stalker, she didn't know how she would broach the subject. Now that a prowler had surfaced, she was relieved that his son wasn't involved. She wanted to see Blaze again. She was still a little wary of his oddball presentations, but she was grateful to him for giving her the boost she had needed for her go/no-go with Mirhege earlier that week. That was something to celebrate.

On her way to the door, she stopped in front of the cameo mirror. Her lipstick was smeared as if she had just been forcefully kissed. She didn't know how she had smudged her mouth. She feared that her interior collapse was somehow visible, her weaknesses surfacing in her features, like in Dorian Gray's portrait. She reapplied her lipstick. She tugged her fingers through her tangled hair and squared her shoulders.

Yes, she could use a drink.

She grabbed her jacket, but before she went over to the barn she searched her kitchen drawer for her retractable self-locking tape measure. Looking for ammunition, she went outside and hooked the tape on the window well, just as Townsend had done. She paced over to the mound, tugging its stiff band. In the murky twilight she tried to read the numbers. The tape read eighteen feet, five inches, when earlier the pile had been twenty feet from her door.

The pile had expanded since Townsend had taken the measurement.

She marched over to her neighbor's place. She knocked twice on the big trophy door, and Townsend's dogs started barking. Townsend pulled the door open.

He stood there with a smoky martini glass filled to the brim. Lemon twists swirled in his glass like little tropical fish. She recognized the habit. Her own mother, a booze artist herself, never dumped her glass when she went for refills, and by dinner time she carried around a tumbler of olives, salty artifacts of her evening's decline. It was a way she could tabulate how many re-fills she'd allowed herself. When April's father complained that her mother was drinking too much, April watched her mother become secretive. She allowed herself one olive—at a time—so that April's father lost track of how many drinks she mixed.

Townsend's lemon peels kick-started April's anxieties about her mom. He saw April's worried look and told her, "I know. We didn't get far with the Bobcat. It's on my to-do list."

"That pile is edging closer. You have to do something."

"Come in, we'll talk about it. I'll make you a drink."

"Look," she said. "I just came over to say I'm not kidding. That muck has to go." But in fact, she wanted to keep bartering. Her argument with Townsend had gained a homey predictability that she found comforting, especially after her day's events and the stalker's visit which had authenticated the seriousness of his obsession with her, whatever it was.

She smelled Townsend's dinner scorching. She saw a pan of refried beans smoking on the hot plate. A drink would be good, but she hoped that Townsend wouldn't expect her to stay for supper. He might offer her those beans or an indigestible MRE platter from his pallet of bargain GI cuisine. Instead, he mixed a martini, but without a silver shaker. He used a dime-store highball glass full of ice cubes. He stirred the gin until it was chilled and with his fingers he plucked out the ice cubes unceremoniously, but in fact, it seemed all too ceremonious. The tall glass was more than half full of Beefeater. She didn't see a vermouth bottle anywhere. He liked his martinis bone dry. He took a chilled glass from the freezer and poured her some of the concoction.

He saw her watching him. "No vermouth. Sorry."

"That's okay," she said.

"A well-stocked bar should always have it," Townsend said.

"Yeah," Blaze called from the sofa, "you missed your chance to get her tipsy."

So, he'd been listening to their patter. April smiled at Blaze, but he looked away again. She told Townsend, "No, really. Just the gin is fine." She was certain that Townsend had poured more than she bargained for. She shouldn't get drunk when she was outnumbered.

She took a sip. "Ouch," she said. The glass was chipped. A drop of blood bloomed on her bottom lip.

He said, "Shit. Is that blood?"

She daubed her lip with the back of her wrist until he shook out his handkerchief. "Not serious," she said. The little cut chugged for a few seconds as she patted his handkerchief against her mouth and scrubbed it across her bottom teeth.

"This is no way to start out," Townsend said. He found her a new glass and filled it to the lip.

Blaze and Townsend watched her closely, relieved that she didn't seem upset. And she couldn't resist looking back and forth between the boy and his father. They both had an attractive dimple on the exact same side of their faces. They were alike in many ways. One is the copycat, the other is the mold. The father is often the razor-sharp prescient one, but he doesn't necessarily see his shadow life in his son, and therefore Blaze was, in fact, way ahead of *him.*

Her two neighbors exaggerated her current dilemma, her "midlife crisis," as she tried to straddle youth and old age. She was turning forty, and while Blaze helped to distract her from the march of time, Townsend's demeanor showed a venerable allure and made growing older seem almost intriguing.

Her sudden maternal impulse for Blaze was acceptable, but she felt uncomfortable when it was spiked by something gnawingly sexual. She was all mothers and lovers. Milt often said she was man crazy. "Speak for yourself," she said. But it wasn't her fault that she felt this confusion in the presence of her neighbors. There had been so many prods. The boy had licked his palm when shaking hands with her. And Townsend was just so damn likable. She'd tell Milt, "It's just so fucking hetero over there."

"They removed his cuff today," Townsend said. "It was giving him chilblains."

Blaze stood up. He tugged the knee of his pant leg and rotated his ankle so she could see it was gone.

"Really?" she said.

"His hearing has been postponed as well. The other parties can't make the date. They're backing out of their weasel hole."

"Our Miss Nancy, you mean," Blaze said, with blistering hatred for the effeminate opponent he was talking about.

"So Yarborough says the cuff comes off. He's been wearing it three months already."

"No shintok!" Blaze said.

She said to Blaze, "Congratulations."

"He's his own man now," Townsend said.

The cuff hadn't kept him out of her house, or from getting behind the wheel, or from stealing ponies like a horse thief, but now that he was free to walk around she was suddenly alarmed. She tried to calm down and said, "Is that hot plate still on? You better move your dinner off the burner."

She walked over to the hotplate and lifted the frying pan. She didn't know where to put it. The makeshift countertop was plywood and she didn't want to burn a circle. Townsend gave her an oversized pot holder. She saw it wasn't a pot holder, but one of those Red Sox thumbs-up victory mitts they sell at the ball park.

"Go Sox," she said, resting the pan on top.

Townsend laughed at her caustic tidbits.

Blaze, too, looked happy.

They stood over the dinner relic, a gluey mess. The burning pan was searing the comic foam-rubber hand. But a cold rush of air blew into the room.

April said, "Oh no, the horse. He's at it again!" She expected to see the lonesome gelding nosing open the panel slider, but Janice Gallen and the pipe fitter walked into the barn.

Janice was wearing wraparound sunglasses, although the sun was down. She was dressed in an oversized one-piece khaki flight suit, like something smoke jumpers wear to dive out of air-planes into a forest fire. She looked lost in it. "You making dinner? Smells scorched," she said.

John Two saw the frying pan. "You should microwave those beans so they don't stick to your pan." He peered into the crusted goo. "I think I could eat a boot first."

Townsend said, "That isn't exactly dinner yet."

"I think that was dinner in sixty-four," John Two said.

April watched Blaze straighten, seeming to gain another couple inches. It was the same phenomenon as when cats fluff up or a dog raises its hackles. His face changed from chilly to frozen to permafrost. Janice grinned at him, a smile of warning, not of warmth. Her body language said, *Don't start something.* On second thought, she blew him a little, starchy kiss, as if to make up for her mixed messages by sending more of them.

Townsend told Janice, "You here for quality control on my bean burritos? You want to complain about my cooking?" He looked at the manila folders she was holding crooked inside her elbow, the way a hostess holds laminated dinner menus. He recognized his own handwriting scrawled across the tabs. The folders were stuffed with banking items, CD notes, and oversized sheets of watermarked stock certificates.

He leaned closer to his ex to study her face. April saw it too. There was a swollen fig under Janice's right eye that her sunglasses didn't cover up. "What happened to you?" he said. "That's quite a shiner."

"I was taking pictures at the 4-H horseshow at the indoor stadium in Warwick. I tripped on the cavaletti."

"Cavaletti?"

"Those little fences for the kiddie class."

Townsend nodded, impressed by her story. Janice could always fetch a lie out of thin air.

April wondered if she was wearing the one-piece suit to cover up other bruises.

Janice told Townsend, "You haven't got your stove hooked up? DSS should hear about these living conditions. Unless you listen to me—"

Then Blaze told his mom, "Who invited you?"

Janice looked at April. "They invite you to put on the feedbag? I hope you brought your little purple pill."

"Well, actually—"

"That's right," Blaze told his mother, "she's invited. Not you."

"She's kind of old for you, don't you think?" Janice said, hitching her elbow at April.

Blaze said, "That Bible Belt Betsy wasn't my age. You didn't care about her."

Janice didn't acknowledge that she had recently met April at the supermarket or that she had spilled her story about the blue snow. She told Blaze, "I didn't think there's one Special Ed teacher left who'll come near you. She'll be down for the count soon enough."

April told Janice, "Look, don't *third person* me."

"Well, are you here to tutor him? Good luck," Janice said. Her jealousy was visible even with her sunglasses on. She hadn't expected to find April at the barn and didn't want the outsider to fog her mission.

Blaze waited for the cat fight with a cold grin

April said, "I might help him with his GED. You have a problem with that?"

"Relax, I've got it," Townsend said. He burned into Janice. "Looks like you want a bank teller? This drive-through window is closed."

"I need your signatures," Janice said. "You can't keep giving me the brush-off."

"These aren't mature."

"Mature? That's you, geezer. Forget Fidelity and Charles Schwab."

"Forget Fidelity" was a pun Townsend might have utilized to accuse Janice of shacking up with John Two, and John Boss before him, but he told her, "We'll sit down with Ed Miller again, want to? He'll explain our investments to you in small, one syllable words."

"Just give me what's in that safe. I'll take my half."

Townsend looked over at Blaze, wondering if he had told Janice about the wall safe and was playing both sides.

Janice said, "I'll take it in fifties, twenties, whatever you've got in that front loader. That'll be just fine."

John Two sat down on the scuffed leather couch. He called over to April, asking her to help him work the remote. She didn't know how to operate the futuristic, streamlined gizmo any more than he did. "Which is the on button? No, that's the DVD, but where's the cable?" John Two asked her.

"It's a dish," she said.

"Okay, which one is that?"

Janice was saying, "You give me my money or I'm going to Judge Welsh. You tricked me into it when we were married—"

"Oh, I remember. 'In sickness and in wealth.'"

No one noticed Blaze had left.

Townsend told Janice, "Look, half-pint, you'll have your cash in the fullness of time. It's earning, not sitting still."

Beyond their bickering, and the chaotic blare of John Two flipping through the satellite TV selections—they heard something. Like African bees in a tin can, it was the Bobcat mini excavator at full throttle.

"That's perfect," Townsend said.

"He's got the tractor?" Janice said. "Oh shit."

"You always stir him up. Don't you know that yet?" Townsend said. He peeled away from his ex and walked to the front door. The dogs bounded after Townsend and quivered at his heels, hungry for a prowl in the dark. April saw her chance to leave. She followed Townsend outside through the tunnel of yellow fiberglass. The sharp night air was a relief. Then she smelled the manure pile.

Blaze had already dumped at least two buckets of sludge onto the windshield of John Two's GMC Jimmy, and he was going back for a new load. The muck was steaming.

Blaze hunched in the saddle seat, swinging around again, sitting pretty in the Bobcat's 360-degree cab rotation, with the boom extended, bucket high. It wasn't as forbidding as live TV of Waco, when the ATF attacked the Branch Davidian compound with dozers, but April saw the connection. The mural was edgy, not slapstick, as Blaze steered the mini excavator towards the Jimmy, backlit by a glittery moon.

John Two came up to Townsend. "That Bobcat's got pry force, don't it?" he yelled, his fists planted on his hips. "He can tip my truck if he wants to. So I'm going to have to stop him."

Townsend told him, "He's not using its pry force, he's just scooping mulch. We can pull your truck over there—" He pointed to the spigot lost in darkness on one side of the barn. "We'll hose it off."

Blaze wasn't finished. He made a three-point turn and was heading back to the mountain to get another daub of the hazmat gurry when John Two tugged him off the saddle. The tractor kept rolling into the hill of sludge.

Wind-milling his arms and spinning his fists in a crazy egg-beater mannerism, Blaze was teasing his opponent to take the first swing.

John Two grabbed Blaze by the shoulders, no second thoughts, and head-butted him in the face.

Blaze took it in the nose, and April thought she heard the bridge of it snap like a Popsicle stick. As Blaze staggered backward, she could almost see the little cartoon birds circling his noggin. But he straightened up and sprang forward again.

Janice ran between the two of them. "Leave him alone!" she told her boyfriend. John Two flung her aside like an empty grain sack, and April saw how fragile she was, skinny as a waif in her tomboy flight suit. Townsend got into it and grabbed his son. Hooking the boy in the crook of his arm, he wheeled him around a half turn and shoved him hard in the direction of the barn. Blaze stumbled a few yards, crashing into April. Blaze told her, "Shit—sorry—get out of my way!" and stomped through the aisle of Easter fluff insulation, slamming the trophy door.

She hoped his nose wasn't broken. Men got their faces rearranged and they often ended up looking like under-card contenders. That would be a shame. As April edged down the driveway, Townsend crowded beside her, his breath on her collar. She smelled the juniper as he talked. She had never finished her own drink. It would have helped a lot.

He said, "I didn't know that they would show up. Blaze gets kind of moody with Janice. That ape she's bedding down with is bad news. She knows it too."

"He's unique," April said.

"Don't worry, princess, it's not your problem."

She wasn't listening to his explanation. "Since when do you call me that?"

"What?"

"*Princess.*"

"My invention, I guess."

Every man who called her corny pet names believed it was his privilege.

"Well, please don't," she said.

He looked back at Janice once or twice, to make sure she wasn't getting more flak for coming to the boy's defense. John Two was already hosing his truck. Townsend walked abreast of April, talking nonstop. "Just so you know, moving the pile might be a bad idea, it might have a worse effect. It could stir up some noxious odor if I move it, you know? It will reek."

"That's not supposed to be *if.*"

"Calm down, contessa. Loosen your bun."

She kept walking.

"I'm telling you I'm a hundred per cent sorry about tonight," he said.

"Tonight is over," she said.

He stood in front of her.

He wants to kiss me, she thought. She stepped back and tipped her face, ready for it.

"I'm not trying to rush you," he said. "But just so you know—you're my new project."

She couldn't decide if he was flirting with her or trying to act fatherly. Then she recognized that he might be trying to get Janice's attention; a spark of jealousy might ignite dead embers. April shoved him away, surprised to feel his rock hard pectorals under his thin shirt. In the melee, he hadn't grabbed a jacket. She trudged to her house, following the desire line across the tiny knoll of grass that separated their properties. She knew he watched her, so she was careful not to slam the door when she entered her kitchen. Once inside she whipped around to pull down the window shade. To her embarrassment, the shade snapped up again, its tight roll spinning.

Chapter Seventeen

After the free-for-all at the barn, Townsend had gone to the Hilltop, but Blaze stayed home. He was holding an ice tray against the bridge of his nose, deciding what to do next.

April was in her kitchen heating a plate of leftovers in her microwave when a car turned into her drive. She thought it might be a new delivery of sludge, but it was still too early for the midnight dump truck. She heard tires spinning, then silence, then spinning again. She went to the window. It was the provost's Audi, its wheels making a trough in the fuming hill. He had tried to turn around in her driveway. He didn't see the gullies of slop until he had backed into it.

She watched the provost climb out of his Audi, lifting his feet in awkward stork steps to avoid the muck.

The taillights flickered twice as he clicked his door locks.

She recognized his window-pane plaid jacket but was surprised to see he carried a supermarket bouquet of daisies, their flopping stars bouncing over his fist as he tiptoed through the mud.

First Blaze had used the age-old tactic, bringing flowers, and now it was Mirhege. Then she realized the provost was at the back door and she would have to deal with him face-to-face. She remembered the episode at the hotel when she had watched the girl throwing her lover's clothes out the window. At the time, she had noticed sharp tines cemented to the window ledges outside both their rooms, to keep pigeons from roosting. These rows of teeth looked like the serrated fronds of a Venus fly-trap, and both she and the young woman were trapped behind them.

Mirhege ceremoniously wiped his feet on the jute mat and walked into the kitchen. He handed her the bouquet and said, "An aspirin keeps them fresh."

"Did you come here to give me housekeeping tips?"

He got right to the point and said, "If you submit a complaint about the decision about your application for chair, you know, maybe you'd like to be transferred to Continuing Ed and meet your classes on weekends. Or we can schedule your first class at the crack of dawn. You'll have to meet them every day at eight a.m. And you're not a morning person."

The college's Continuing Education Department was where Sinclair farmed out dead-weight professors, teachers who had poor student evaluations and who never published a speck in "the periodicals of the day." CE was a ring of hell with a faculty of has-beens and oldsters forced to teach oversized classes, at odd hours, before they finally retired or just gave out. In fact, CE classes were held at a different campus, in an unsightly building far off in East Providence. "You'll be at the night school. I can arrange it," Mirhege said, "if you force me to."

"Are you threatening me? I can do the same to you," she said.

The kitchen door banged open. Blaze waltzed into the house. The microwave beeped as he walked past it and he jumped.

"That's just my dinner," she told him.

Mirhege said, "Oh, I see you're expecting company? Is this one of our own?"

Blaze was amused to be mistaken for a college freshman, but he looked at the daisies on the kitchen table. "Question is—where's he from? eHarmony.com?"

She told Blaze, "He's from Sinclair."

Mirhege looked at Blaze, whose shirt was covered in blood. "Looks like he needs first aid. You running a walk-in clinic?"

Blaze said, "If you're looking for the Liquor Mart, that's a mile down the road. Or if you want that wrinkle bar, it's in Warwick Neck."

The provost, using his familiar tactic of mix-and-match pronouns, asked Blaze, "Why are we bloody?"

"He was in a fist fight," April said.

"I guess he's bothering you?" Blaze said, looking directly into her eyes. He would force *her* to force the unsanctioned visitor to leave.

She turned to Mirhege. "Just what are you doing here?"

He told April, "I wanted to see you."

Blaze said, "You want my dad's Dallas cheerleader DVDs, 'as seen on TV'? I'll lend them to you."

"This is my boss at the college," she warned Blaze. She rolled her eyes, letting him know she wasn't exactly fond of the intruder.

"I bet he sightsees online," Blaze told her. "Girls beware!"

"And what's your screen name?" Mirhege said, "Hopeless Case? Bitter Fruit? Born to Raise Hell, something like that?"

"Yawn," Blaze said.

She watched them shoot freestyle like middle school brats, but she was relieved to see that neither one seemed sinister enough to be the Endless Pools nut.

Mirhege looked at her with crumpled eyebrows.

He said, "Let's talk, okay? About your issues."

"Jesus," April said. April told Blaze, "You. Wait. Here." She pulled out a kitchen chair. He sat down at the dinette table as if he expected her to serve him a bowl of Froot Loops. Instead, he unscrewed the cap of her salt cellar and poured out a startling white hill dead center on a place mat. April didn't care about that, but she wasn't too happy to go into the parlor with the provost.

She sank into a wing chair. Mirhege crouched beside her and grabbed her hand. "I'll do better," he said. "We'll take more trips together. I've got that thing in Seattle next month. We'll have dinner in the Needle, want to?"

She imagined sitting with the provost in Seattle's garish tourist trap. She almost smiled. She told Mirhege, "Let's call it quits." Her voice sounded falsely serene like a canned explanation from customer service or an automated recording of a current bank balance.

He said, "Baby, this is just a bad patch—" He tried to kiss her hand but she closed her fist.

"It's so over," she told him. She liked saying the melodramatic qualifier, "*so* over," used by coeds describing victorious break-ups with their boyfriends.

He said, "It's over? Then 'I am a man whom Fortune hath cruelly scratched.'"

She tried not to laugh.

"'And, like a dew-drop from the lion's mane, be shook to air'?"

"Oh, please," she told him.

He stood up. "Remember, April, 'We pardon to the extent that we love.'"

She was tired of his literary bargaining chips. His ability to quote substantial instances from famous texts had finally lost its pleasure for her, despite her original respect for his groundbreaking essay on Frank O'Hara and Coleridge. "Just get the fuck out," she said.

A kitchen drawer crashed to the floor. Blaze appeared in the archway slicing the air with the long carbon prong of a sharpening steel. He jabbed the air with it like it was a fishgig or a fencing foil. He smiled in a wide white slice.

"Mr. Mirhege was just leaving," she told him.

Blaze said, "That's right. He's gone already. He wasn't even here." He started to herd the provost out of the parlor, crowding him like a cutting horse or a Border collie.

"Since when did you start babysitting these misfits?" the provost asked.

Blaze listened to his prissy scold, still smiling, but his jaw was locked.

Mirhege watched the boy's signals. He recognized that Blaze was in a stand-up mode and shouldn't be tested any further. So without another borrowed quotation, Mirhege worked his way to the back door, where he turned around again. "If you're moonlighting in remedial cases, that's a violation of your contract."

"Oh spare me your ball-less threats," she said.

"I'm saying, if you're tutoring these dropouts, the department will have to know about it."

"Betty Clark will fill you in on my plans for you."

Blaze stepped up to Mirhege with the sharpening steel, prodding him lightly in a pudge above his belt buckle.

April watched Mirhege. His eyes were different now, as if he didn't hope to firm up their plans for a trip to the Needle, or to schedule an appointment at the Westminster. The look on his face revealed a history of damage, a serial struggle worse than she could ever know. Absently, he brushed off his shoulders as if he felt its talons pinching.

Blaze broke the spell of their wordless glances with two upward jabs of the poker. He plucked at the provost's jacket lapel and popped off a button of his oxford. It skittered across the linoleum.

They each watched the button until it stopped rolling, a little symbol with a distinct meaning for each of them. The provost trotted out the kitchen door and down the driveway to his car. Blaze pitched the wad of unwanted daisies after him and the blooms sailed apart in mid-air.

April watched from the back stoop as the provost rocked his car back and forth, squirting fans of sludge.

As he drove away, April crabbed her fingers in quick repetitions, in the rote farewell offered by flight attendants going off duty after a bumpy ride. Blaze stood nested behind her, his chin resting on top of her head, totem-pole style.

Chapter Eighteen

With Mirhege dismissed, Blaze felt confident he could return to the little sofa in April's parlor. He toed the heels of his shoes until his Nikes flipped across the floor, but his socks came off with his sneakers

When she walked into the room, April was surprised to see his bare feet propped on the coffee table.

Blaze said, "That guy's not really your type—"

"My real boyfriend died a couple years ago. Didn't your dad say?" She watched his expression.

"No, he didn't tell me about that, but he said you have freckles. Where *are* these freckles? I don't see any."

She refused to follow him.

"So, you didn't report me to the cops?" he said.

"I still might."

He smiled, staring at his naked feet.

She said, "So you're out of that cuff? That's a first step, right? You don't want to go backwards."

"ELMO sucks, but I'm still on probation."

"You mean that electronic monitoring? But you still have to report to the PO, right?"

"I will until I don't."

"You'll get a job, I guess. You need to keep busy."

"*We* should get busy," he said.

"Well, don't you play guitar or something? What happened to your band All Smiles?"

"Broke up. We made a CD. It turned out really nice. Five songs. Absolute power violence. The shortest song is thirty seconds long."

April tried to imagine what kind of music Blaze might have played. All she could remember was the annoying "Smells like Teen Spirit" refrain.

He grimaced, as if he had heard it too. "Band is defunct. My mother sank the boat, anyway."

She thought he meant Janice had quashed his dreams to be a musician but he said, "*All Smiles* is at the bottom of Chapman Pond."

He wasn't going to narrate the story of the *All Smiles* disaster to April. He saw something else that reminded him of his mother. On a bookshelf in the corner of April's parlor was a tiny object. "Where did you find that?" he asked.

"The Flower Bug? It's always been here."

"I guess it belonged to me," he said.

"You want it back?"

He walked over to the shelf and picked up the little Matchbox car. Reclaiming the amusing teetotum had opened a trap door for him. He rubbed its little wheels back and forth on the palm of his hand. He saw Janice Gallen in a shimmering mirror, a stuttering holograph that blinded him from within.

He trails Janice up the steep stairs. He's holding her hips, and at the landing he's nipping the back of her neck. In her bedroom she turns on a lamp and peels off her sweater. She folds back the checkerboard quilt and reveals her paisley sheets. She pushes him down onto the sateen and tugs his boots free. She rolls his waistband over his hips and teases off his pant legs inside out, revealing the pockets' floppy ears. She has a little trouble when his pencil jeans snag his feet.

"Are you all right?" April said. He turned around and grabbed April's hand. He pulled her down beside him on the sofa. She didn't resist. She wedged her embroidered pillows behind her head and leaned back against the sofa's beautiful curved arm. She felt exhausted. In a nice way.

He showed her the little car. "It's cute, huh?"

"I really kind of love it," she said.

Blaze started to unbutton her blouse.

"Hey," she said.

She let him shove its silk sleeves down her arms and pull them off her wrists inside out. He tugged her camisole over her head. April didn't assist him, but she no longer protested. After her difficult visit with the provost, she didn't seem to care about *losing her mind*, at that very instant.

She sank deeper into the sofa. She didn't blanch or complain. She lifted her hips as Blaze removed her slacks; the slippery acetate lining of her trouser legs made it all too easy.

She heard Coleridge in the silence. *"Her gentle limbs did she undress / And lay down in her loveliness."*

Her body was pale as snow. Blaze sensed a potential thaw as he rolled the little car slowly in circles over her smooth belly, ascending up to her collar-bone. She closed her eyes and tipped her chin. He followed his own map across her slopes and curves, but she said, "What are you doing?"

He dipped the car between her breasts, tugging its wheels, tiny as the provost's collar buttons, up and over her nipples. The toy lost its metal chill and moved in a little river of warmth across her skin. She was more than twice his age. Sensations she'd felt with Riley filtered in, but she forgot about Riley. Mirhege wasn't even in the wings. Blaze buzzed the car farther, into the off-road frizz. She grabbed his hand. She said, "Stop. Stop it right now."

He tried to kiss her and plowed his chin against her cheek giving her a proprietary whisker burn. With his kiss, he fed her eternal emptiness with his own seductive bottomlessness.

She told herself, *I can't be his mother's rival*, but she felt their abyssal secrets twinned. The perverse and the beautiful entwined her ideas. Blaze seemed to obey *her* louche impulses, and without any instruction from her, he was taking responsibility.

She brushed the trinket to the floor. She shoved him off the narrow couch. "Go home," she said. She retrieved her blouse and covered up. She couldn't make love to him and live with herself.

He said, "I know you want more. Come on—"

"Please go."

"Oh, nice. Don't go away mad, just go?"

He had every reason to blame her, and for an instant she almost changed her mind so he wouldn't accuse her. April always had trouble assessing moral stickiness. She thought of more Coleridge lines: *"Her girded vests / Grew tight beneath her heaving breasts / He who on the cross did groan / Might wash away her sins unknown!"* She wanted to tell him, "You have a right to be angry at *someone*. That someone can be *me*, I don't mind." That was just like the provost's didactic smooth talk. She had learned to recognize his breezy, slithery tones behind his intellectual jargon. And her father, too. Once, when she had refused to jump from a diving board, her father stood neck deep in the water and said, "Don't be scared, April. It stands to reason that people with the greatest love of life will have the greatest fear of death." She didn't want to get in the water with him. But he said, "I'm right here, sweetheart. I'll catch you. No one is watching."

She told Blaze, "Go ahead, you can hate me. But not for the same reason that you hate your mom."

Blaze was surprised to hear April bring his mom into it. She seemed to know that Janice was somewhere in between.

He collected his shoes and came back. "You sure you want me to go?"

April said, "Yes. Go. Or I call the cops."

Chapter Nineteen

Blaze walked through the dark, a little stung. He tried to understand how Janice had nixed it when she wasn't even in the room. His secret had spawned a perennial backlash that he'd forever have to deal with, female to female. Somehow, April had the dope on him.

He was almost at the barn door when April came out on her back stoop. She called to him, "Wait!"

Blaze froze.

She said, "I have an idea. Let's go for a drive. Want to?"

He was pleased to see April was changing her mind. But he hated how girls always dribbled out the proceedings. Even Lucinda was back and forth. Of all the women he'd known, only Janice would get right to the point. Janice wasn't a pencil sharpener. You didn't need a mood ring to see what Janice wanted.

April came out to her car. He walked over and sat down in the passenger seat of the Camry, unsure if April's invitation was a change of heart or trickery. So far, her teases were a crock. So he said, "If we're going for a drive, I'm behind the wheel."

She said, "You want to drive? That's all right with me." They got out of their seats and circled the car to trade places. As Blaze went around, he thumped the hood once in a little burst of glee which he regretted exposing.

Before he sat down, she handed him the little fuse. He leaned under the seat and inserted the sacred sliver, teeth first.

"That dohab sprayed your fender with mud," he told her.

"That what?"

"Your friend. Dropped on head at birth."

He needled her with slang, but he seemed glad to be driving again. He peeled onto the county road and smirked when she told him to slow down. "Don't boss me. I own you," he said.

"Use your brights." And she said, "It's forty here," as the road signs ripped past. "Do Not Pass," she read the next sign.

These banal observations were made by driving instructors, high school coaches, and guidance counselors.

"Use both hands on the wheel!"

He enjoyed her scolds. Each time she criticized him, he tried to tamp down the corners of his smile. When he tipped his head back she asked, "Is your nose still bleeding?"

He looked at his face in the rearview to see how bad it was.

"Watch the road!' she said.

"I see it."

They got onto the interstate and she told him, "This is sixty-five!"

"Smother has the word 'mother.'"

"Cruiser up ahead!" she warned him.

"So where are we going?" he said.

She could have told him about the girl named Nancy at the Westminster Hotel, about how the girl had inspired her to take control of the situation she was facing. Blaze wouldn't understand her battle for a promotion at Sinclair or the glass-ceiling metaphor, although he might identify with the provost's young daughter trapped behind the harp grille. She said, "There's this girl being abused by her father. We're going to rescue her."

"No shit?"

Blaze opened the moon-roof shade until the night above was revealed. He glimpsed the constellations smearing overhead and said, "Most of those pricks of light aren't really stars, they're navstar contraptions."

She said, "'A star, a star is falling / Out of the glittering sky! / The star of Love! I watch it / Sink in the depths and die.'"

Blaze didn't recognize the Longfellow, but he was impressed by its cynicism.

He said, "You ever hear the chicken song?"

"Is it punk rock?"

"Not. It's by the Red Clay Ramblers. It's a folksong about a pickaninny at a spelling bee." He didn't wait any longer and started to sing the nonsense rhyme at a crazy, accelerating tempo.

> "C—that's the way to begin
> H—that's the next letter in
> I—that is the third

C—time to season up the bird!
K—I'm fitting in
E—getting near the end
C-H-I-C-K-E-N
That is the way to spell chicken!"

The sunny little ragtime tune was instantly enthralling. His unfettered performance was authentic and didn't seem like one of his mean gimmicks. She was a little stunned. Everything challenged her first impression of him.

"That is the way to spell chicken? Does it mean 'that's the way the cookie crumbles'?"

"It translates Do it. Get to it. Don't fuck it up."

"Got it," she said. She told him to get off the highway at the very next Providence exit.

April knew that they should quit before worse things could happen. She stood to one side and watched Blaze jimmy the window. He unlatched the screen, letting it flop to one side. He lifted the sticky sash and climbed in head first, greeted by Peck's pointy nose in his face. The setter circled him, excited by the game unfolding. It wagged its ropey tail, uncurling its long tongue, pink as rubber. It slobbered Blaze with indiscriminate kisses.

"Not guard dogs, are we?" Blaze told the setter as he led it to the front door. It bounded out onto the front steps. April squeezed past the dog to get inside and Blaze shut the big door. They tiptoed across the plush carpet in the quiet living room. Suddenly, the setter was at the same window Blazed had jimmied, on the other side.

The house was quiet except for a pedestal clock's scratchy metallic repetitions.

They stood beside the six-foot harp, a monstrosity even in the darkened room. It was like finding a gilded giraffe. It looked forbiddingly official, almost regal when backlit by only the hall sconce. Its tall column rose above April's head, swept across a harmonic arch, then curved down a sweeping sound board. Its upright form was an off-kilter triangle, fabulous and awkward.

Mirhege had once told her that the harp had thirty-six strings made of different-gauge wires, each made of gut, nylon or metal core. He had explained the difficulty of stringing the harp and had complained of the expense of keeping it tuned. He said they paid the music teacher extra cash to do the repetitive chore, although learning to tune the harp, by herself, was a major component of his daughter's weekly practice schedule. He said, "She hates it, but one day she'll be glad I made her take lessons." April thought it was bad enough that he forced his girl to play the harp, but asking her to keep it tuned was just added torture. Harps could get out of tune within a single day from variations in humidity when the heat went on and off. Harps need constant tuning. "Just like you," he had teased her during their foreplay. And he had some-times joked, "My bass string needs more tension." April had never liked it when his daughter's world was brought into bed with them.

The girl was her rationalization. "She's about your age. Maybe younger," April whispered to Blaze.

"Oh yeah?"

April said, "Shouldn't she be playing electric guitar, maybe bass or something? I don't think Courtney Love plays the harp in that old hit 'Like a Virgin.'"

"That's Madonna, you know."

"Mirhege doesn't know the difference between virgins and whores."

"But you do, I guess?" he said.

April fished in her pocket for the wire snips she'd brought with her. A tenured faculty member at a respectable institution shouldn't be involved in what she was about to do. She remembered Mirehege's observations about Frank O'Hara's essay "Personism." O'Hara says that in writing poetry, "You just go on your nerve. If someone's chasing you down the street with a knife you *just* run, you don't turn around and shout, 'Give it up! I was a track star for Mineola Prep."

"Okay. We are doing this for the girl," she told Blaze. But she had a moment of doubt as when she had wanted to set off the fire alarm at the Westminster Hotel and luckily had thought better of it.

Seeing her freeze up, Blaze said, "Let me do it," with increasing excitement. He seemed in awe of April's wacky plan and wanted to commandeer the operation, to get the most from it. He took the snips from her.

"Wait," she said, "be careful. Cover your face, or a wire

might blind you." Hooding his face with one hand to protect his eyes, he clipped the first string where it was anchored to the soundboard. The long bass string popped loose in bewildered freedom, the way heavy-gauge fishing line snaps and flounces after a battle with a striper.

He snipped the next string, and the next. Each crisp cut made ascending thudding notes as the strings bounced free and wormed left and right. He didn't stop.

The harp was almost denuded, its severed strings lying in crazy cork screws across the carpet, when the provost stepped into the room. Mirhege faced the boy. The scene was embarrassing, both familiar and taboo, as the harp strings shivered and spiraled like spermatozoon tails between the two rivals. Blaze said, "Hey, Pops."

April was interested to see that the provost, standing in his striped pajamas, didn't look at all like a Rat Pack leading man but instead looked like the dated Disney dad Fred MacMurray.

She told him, "Your daughter. She'll thank me. She won't have to sit in front of this thing."

Mirhege told April, "I guess you think you're some kind of Pixanne?"

April was pleased that her impish scheme might have spared the girl. "You can't force her to play the harp."

"You'll see what I can force you to do."

"You don't scare me."

"This is good, April. It'll prove my argument when I go into Academic Affairs and talk to Betty Clark tomorrow about your mental health. You're lucky I don't call the white coats right now."

"A butterfly net has room for two," she said. She remembered Scott and Zelda Fitzgerald. In literary circles, it was always "Scott and Zelda." His name always came first. It wasn't until Zelda went nuts that she grabbed more attention and took center stage.

Blaze was smiling. A woman's fury was a delicious spectacle. Cutting harp strings had never been in his diary of misdemeanors. Her ingenious plan made his affronts to society seem run-of-the-mill. Leave it to a girl to come up with it. He felt privileged to be invited in.

"A medical leave isn't so bad," Mirhege told April. "In the bin, they teach you to make pot holders. Remember Miss Selby? She had six weeks in OT at Butler Hospital. She came back with some pretty decoupage boxes that she handed around."

April said, "Is that a threat? In our faculty handbook it states that 'quid pro quo sexual harassment' arises in the context of an authority relationship, as in the case of a supervisor and a subordinate. It's called a 'power differential,' remember that? Or don't you read your own policies? It says I can make a complaint. I guess you want that hearing convened?"

Mirhege said, "I can't believe you'd take that angle, April. It's beneath you."

"Let's see. You're saying who's beneath whom?"

Mirhege sat down in a Windsor chair and crossed his legs. One of his leather slippers gaped, and he tugged it back on.

Blaze plopped onto the opposing divan.

Pivoting in a circle between the two, April waited for one of them to call it a night. They heard someone upstairs padding down the hallway. His wife peered over the tight balcony rail, turned, and ducked back into her bedroom. His pretty daughter remained. The girl leaned over the rail, letting her hair slide loose in a dramatic fan. She seemed more curious to see Blaze than to see that her golden harp was fatally plucked clean. Blaze waved at her and slowly inched open his beautiful smile. His grin made the girl shiver and turn away, her long hair floating behind her. But again, she whipped around. She came back to the balcony and leaned out, balanced on her hip bones. She took another gander at the harp as if she did not yet understand what had happened. She gasped. "Awesome!" she said. "You guys did that? You are the greatest! Thanks!"

"You're welcome," April said. She imagined her Vassar classmates who had gone on to become pro bono lawyers for abused wives and rape victims, and others who saved abortion clinics from closing their doors, and still others who supervised all-girl sports teams, all of them nodding their heads in approval of the feminist triumph of the dismembered harp.

Mirhege told April, "I'll have your ass for this."

"Daddy, stop!" the girl said.

"Yeah, lighten up, boss," Blaze said, smiling at the girl.

Mirhege said, "Okay. Let's say we understand each other, want to?"

"You mean a truce?" April said.

"Immunity to all," he said.

Blaze said, "That's the way to spell chicken—"

April turned to Blaze, who had stretched out on the sofa. "Get your shoes off the toile."

He stood up.

The provost walked them to the door. If he was worried about explaining the harp to Sarah, he could tell his wife that April's bizarre behavior was due to her having been denied the promotion and the chair's stipend. He would say that the boy accomplice was an insufferable delinquent on the yellow brick road to the ACI. Sarah shouldn't concern herself with them. But the harp would remain in the living room despite its disrepair. It would still look great in the front window, even better now, with "no strings attached," if Mirhege meant what he'd said, and was calling a truce.

But in the brief time it took Blaze to complete their prank, the family pet had disappeared into the night.

It was early morning when Blaze drove April home.

"I can't believe we did that," she said. "I must be crazy. I've lost it," she said.

"It was excellent. No question about it. See, April? That's the way to spell chicken!"

She started giggling uncontrollably about the severed strings, talking in metaphors about how she had snipped her tethers. Blaze liked girls' laughter, but April's laugh was weird. At first, she laughed reticently, in slowly ascending octaves, like a choir girl practicing scales in the vestibule of a church. Then she exploded with belly-deep cackles just like a mad woman locked in a bell tower. But when he parked in her driveway, she had regained her composure. She said, "Thanks for your help. You'll never know how much I appreciate it." He walked her to the door but she wouldn't let him come into the house. "Thanks," she said trying to disentangle from him. She looked tinier than he remembered; her face wasn't up to his breast pocket. He had a peculiar feeling that he was shooting up taller and taller, tipping out of her reach like one of those bean-stalks that disappears into the clouds, and he wanted her to hold on to him.

But he saw that she was leaving him on the stoop. "Good night," she said.

"Oh, come on—"

"Bye," she said.

He knew the drill. A prick tease. She's just too beautiful and pure, gets what she wants and disappears, the way a snowflake melts in the palm of his hand. "*Goodbye?* Yeah. Boner nochy," he said.

Chapter Twenty

Townsend was asleep on the scuffed leather couch, propped up in a sitting position to manage his acid reflux, just as his doctor suggested. The door of the woodstove was wide open with a just a few red coals burning. Blaze fed it a few logs before slamming the door shut, wrenching the handle tight. He adjusted the flue. His father didn't move as Blaze threw a blanket on top of him, tucking it under his chin. He retrieved an empty martini glass, its leftover lemon peels tangled like twistties. He looked at April's place out the window. Her bedroom light was still on, and then he watched it snuff out.

He saw himself in the pedestal mirror. A cold twin stared back. He flipped the heavy panel upside down, until the mirror faced the window.

Each day, the ELMO corral had squeezed tighter. He still felt it now, even without the cuff. He started to see that the barn was no different from every lock-up and ding wing he'd been in. That night, kissing April, he hadn't once thought of Lucinda, but he thought of her now. He was probably going to run.

He checked the wall safe. Sometimes Townsend left it open a crack, when sorting his papers or recounting his haul with his burster. But the vault was locked. Townsend had written the numbers with a Sharpie inside the tongue of one of his Timberland nubucks. It would be easy for Blaze to open the safe, but his dad was still wearing the boots. The boots never came off.

At the couch he crouched over his father's boots. He tried to untie the laces, but his dad shifted his legs and mumbled. He was talking to Janice in his dream. That alone—a one-to-one with the missus—might wake him.

Blaze remembered Baxter saying he had a cache of Lunesta, the yuppie sleep aid. Blaze thought that maybe he could add a little pharmacy to Townsend's bottle of Beefeater to get a hold of that tongue! Blaze would take it slow and find his strategy. He wasn't blind to the fact that for the last few years he'd always been on the lam, running away from home or making the one-two from the system. His dad said he was "doing life on the installment plan" and DSS called him an "environmental refugee." The truth was he had no place to be. He had nowhere to go but the wilderness of his own mind. And whenever he pulled up stakes, he was always on the Jersey side.

On his last day at Greylock, Blaze had made his final plans to dust the teen tank. He hated it even more than the other schools Janice had sent him to because of its annoying green doctrine. No one had to tell him how to love planet Earth. He'd grown up in East Westerly, where it was bleak but gorgeous terrain, endless oak and maple sticks, swamps, and meadows, like a bottom-rung national park.

To get out of Greylock he would have to hike up Little Hen. He studied the hill's vertical rise and followed its ridge trying to find a notch. He'd have to approximate a point where it dipped and that's where he would summit to make his descent down the other side. A coyote trail or weasel path crisscrossed the campus and he'd follow that. But Little Hen repelled visitors; it didn't attract hikers and weekend climbers. It wasn't mapped or listed in the Appalachian Trail brochures. No one wanted to climb Little Hen. That fucking green waffle was a hundred per cent New England jungle.

Janice Gallen was already living with her second new boyfriend in the claustrophobic hippie haven. Townsend had told Blaze that she might own the A-frame house, but she didn't own the land it was built on. The land belonged to the wacky commune. "Does that make any sense?" Townsend said. He told Blaze that in his mom's neighborhood, everyone was squatting. Blaze speculated that if Janice didn't buy the land she was perched on, maybe she had ideas about coming back to *them*. Townsend told him she was becoming a statistic in that battered wife syndrome, since he'd seen her banged up for no good reason. He told Blaze that John Two was a hothead who negotiated with his "little head," but when that failed, he used his bulk to communicate. Blaze had seen it first hand, the time he had planed the wrong end of the door.

For Blaze, "the wrong end of the door" wasn't just a metaphor, but had become the "logic" of his existence.

During his two bitter months at Greylock, Blaze had been miserable. He hated the work-study routine. Every morning started with chore duty. That morning, he'd swept the stairwells and was hauling trash barrels as usual. His routine began with the sun. Monotony's fiery blob.

To carry the trash barrels outside, Blaze had to weave his way through a knot of homeboy clientele who liked to congregate in the mud room by the back door. Amateur stick up artists. Firebugs. Country-boy car-jackers. Rust-Oleum Rothkos and lowly bird dogs. A whole wad of MINS and CHINS were standing between him and the exit.

At Greylock, Blaze had plenty of shock capital to deliver to his audience, but he had no desire to exchange hate mail or climb the rigging with his inferiors. He was above it. He left that to Rick O'Donnell, the biggest me-most. O'Donnell was always trying to ignite a fuse, crank the electric-start, and topple someone's dominoes.

O'Donnell wouldn't move out of the way for Blaze. Blaze shifted the trash container and waited. He said, "Asshole parade."

O'Donnell wouldn't budge.

Blaze pushed the boy with the big trash can, the way a circus clown wearing a hoop barrel bounces into his fellow clowns to knock them around. When O'Donnell fought back, Blaze dropped the bin and slammed his fist into O'Donnell's front teeth, directly wiping the sneer off. He picked up his trash can and walked through a huddle of his astonished fan club.

Blaze worked with another kid named Newton. At Greylock, new kids were partnered up with long-timers who were supposed to act as mentors. His new charge had a waspy name that sounded too nerdy, so Blaze changed one syllable to assert his ownership: Newty was born.

As Newty sorted trash, Blaze looked at the hill in question. Little Hen. He understood how it got its name. It looked like a fat pullet sitting on its brood. If only it would get up and waddle out of his path, because it was going to be a bitch to fight his way up and down its pitch pine bowers with its booby-traps and wall-to-wall prickers.

Newty's mom kept sending him books and glossies. Along with brainy periodicals like *Scientific American*, techie manuals, college brochures, and vegan cook books, she sent a big, heavy *Encyclopedia of Dogs* with color pictures of every breed. The staff rifled through everyone's mail before handing it over, searching for contraband concealed in envelope seams. All candy was unwrapped. Shampoo bottles were decanted. Dental floss was removed from its little box, and anything that could act as a container for dust, pills or weed was opened and discarded. No hardcover books were allowed, and even paperbacks were sliced open so a shiv couldn't be smuggled onto campus hidden in its spine. Even the Living Bible was ripped from its covers. Newty's *Encyclopedia of Dogs* was presented to him that day in two separate halves, its binding sawed right down the middle.

Newty gave Blaze one half of the dog book and they went to sit on the stairs together. They perched a few risers apart so they wouldn't crowd one another. Enraptured, in their own worlds, they cradled the maimed encyclopedia halves and paged through the glossy color pictures with descriptions of every breed under the sun. Dogs meant everything.

Blaze showed Newty a local advertising weekly called the "Berkshires I Wanna" that he had dug out of a trash barrel. The paper had a double-page ad for the SPCA adopt-a-pet program. The page showed pictures of shelter dogs. Each photo came with a caption and a name chosen to explain a dog's particular issues or behavior problems. One dog was called Chewy and the caption said, "He is known to eat shoes and to gnaw the bottom rungs of chairs." Another dog was called Bonkers, its eyes wide, and ears pricked at opposing angles, giving him a wild look. "Needs an extra firm-hand and obedience training."

"Like us," Blaze said.

"Word," Newty said, using the lazy expression Blaze often heard from his peers. Whenever they said "word" it seemed to prove they were robbed of their voices, they were dumb fucks, and couldn't think of anything better to say. Blaze never used the expression.

Rick O'Donnell showed up, his upper lip swollen. He avoided Blaze and stood directly before Newty. He said, "I guess you're his new bitch? I say you come with me."

"Ignore," Blaze told Newty.

"Word," Newty said.

"Hey. Dead serious," O'Donnell said.

"You're not serious, but you're tragic," Blaze said.

O'Donnell said, "Oh yeah? We'll see about that." He went up the stairs at his own deliberate pace. He climbed one riser, then another, and disappeared higher.

Unwilling to part with Blaze, Newty said, "How many schools have you been to?"

"Lost count."

"Ditto. I'm here 'cause I killed a dog," Newty said.

"You did not," Blaze said, "kill a dog."

Newty smiled. "Shit, I couldn't hurt a *dog*. It's my mom. My mom is afraid of me."

"Oh yeah?"

"I showed her a gun."

"No kidding?"

"Put it in her face."

Blaze said, "Moms don't like guns. But my mom has her own gun." The fact still bothered him. When he was living at the A-frame he had asked Janice for some spending money. She sent him to look in her bureau, where she kept some cash hidden from John Two. In her top drawer he was alarmed to find a little pistol sitting on top of a nest of her panties. It looked surprisingly toy-like, a tiny piece made of matte stainless with a rubber grip.

"Where the fuck did you get this?" he asked Janice.

"I picked it up at the Powder Horn. Four hundred dollars."

"Jesus Christ."

"It's a Taurus CIA."

"It's a what?"

"Their CIA. 'Carry-it-anywhere' model. It's a .38 with a two-inch barrel. Be careful."

"It's loaded?"

"It's got five rounds."

"You got your permit?" he said.

"At the police station. It's a two-hour lesson with Officer Friendly and then a multiple-choice quiz."

"You have a 'license to carry?' This is ridiculous," he said. "You won't leave that prick but you get a weapon?"

"Look. It's for when I get Alzheimer's. You won't have to change my diapers."

Newty said, "Your mom has a gun? No shit? So, she let you shoot cans?"

"Never."

"Moms are cunts," Newty said.

"Word." Blaze gave in.

Encouraged, Newty recited a malicious rhyme to entertain Blaze. "I one my mother. I two my mother. I three my mother. I four my mother. I five my mother. I six my mother. I seven my mother. I *ate* my mother!"

Blaze was impressed. He had never heard that one before.

Newty kept going and recited:

"Go get the axe, there's a hair on baby's chin.
A boy's best friend is his mother, his mother!
She hit him with a shingle and made his fanny tingle.

Walking down the lane, with his britches full of pain,
A boy's best friend is his mother, his mother!"

Blaze understood the sexual connotations in the nonsense rhyme and his stomach fell away. Blaze thought that Newty might have had the same Janice-type situation at home, but Blaze soon learned about Newty's story. His dad had died in the South Tower. Blaze knew of only one other kid who'd lost someone on 9/11. A girl at Westerly High had had a sister who'd been a prep cook chopping vegetables and stirring soup at Windows on the World. Newty didn't talk about his dad, or try to get sympathy. He had his own claim to fame. He was a gluer. He didn't huff glue; his forte was vandalizing pets and property with adhesives. Epoxies, Gorilla Glue, old-fashioned liquid cement, and veneering adhesives. He was supposed to have been an expert with wicked instant glues that cured in less than five seconds.

Blaze finally said, "Did you glue that little girl to her trike? You smeared Liquid Hide on her banana seat?"

"That's bullshit."

"I figured." But Blaze had believed the story.

Newty said, "I'm late for CMA." Some residents went to AA meetings, but Newty attended Crystal Meth Anonymous. He had all the mannerisms of a meth fiend in recovery. He was always bobbed as in discombobulated. He furiously scratched both elbows at once in a repetitive mannerism. He talked without taking any breaths.

He stood up. "You coming?" he asked Blaze.

"No, I clean toilets this afternoon." But talking to Newty had made the mom problem bite into him.

Except for occasional field trips, and their supervised daily outdoor chores, Greylock residents were under twenty-four-hour lock-up. The campus wasn't fenced; there was no concertina wire or chain-link mazes like he saw every day at Rhode Island Training School. Even without razor wire, Greylock was "hardware secure," and it wasn't just the honor system. The front drive had a security gate, and the whole place was throbbing with motion sensors and surveillance cams.

After eight p.m. unit doors were locked for the evening count. At night, monitoring of the perimeter wasn't a hundred per cent secure since the Superwatt floods didn't fully sweep the woods and meadows. Blaze could sprint across the back field where it melted into shadow; he'd have a good head start in his ascent up and over Little Hen. Staff just won't believe he's that desperate to try it in the pitch dark. Then he'd grab a ride with a trucker on the Mass Pike. Long haul sultans always tried to impress him with their radio talk, using CB handles like Pussy Hawk or Box Stretcher, but one way or another he'd get to Hartford where Lucinda had just started a new hitch with her granny.

Thinking about his perfect fade he felt a weird sensation in his testicles. His sack tightened and he had a sickening flip-flop in his abdomen. It was the same feeling he experienced whenever he walked across a bridge above a freeway, with cars speeding underneath him. He felt his balls shrink and his stomach drop away each time he visualized his AWOL route, as if he were already moving.

Yes, he was going out.

He knew it would be like a *Survivor* episode getting across that wilderness, through thorny olive and dense pines caked with snow. There had been another six inches overnight. The crust melted a little during the day, but then it refroze, so every step was going to be like punching through Sheetrock.

That evening Newty had asked Blaze to proofread the letter he was writing to the notorious high school shooter Kip Kinkel who was in lock-up at McLaren School for Boys or he had been moved to Oregon State Correctional. Newty had both addresses and didn't know where to send it. He said he'd write *two* letters. Newty was obsessed with the Columbine tragedy and talked with fanatic reverence for those trench coat killers, but those boys had died, and he couldn't write letters to them. Blaze had always had more sympathy for the shooters than for their victims, but he wasn't into it like Newty was. Newty said, "Do I tell Kinkel I was a gluer? Break the ice? Or maybe that's too too."

"Too too? For a killer? Why don't you forget about writing to Kinkel? Give up. It's lame. Besides, they won't deliver letters to him, coming from you." He tried to convince Newty to drop the pen pal routine. It wasn't going to help Newty sanitize his sheet if he kept doing wacko things like writing to the high school shooter.

After dinner, he went looking for him, but when he entered Newty's unit, it was empty. Everyone was downstairs watching an Elvis movie on the big-screen TV. Blaze watched it for an hour. It wasn't like *Girls Gone Wild*; instead, there were chicks in dowdy retro bikinis and bras made from two hairy halves of a coconut. After a while, he left to find Newty. When Blaze didn't see him in the unit, he searched the open pod of showers.

Nothing but mold growing.

Then, in a tight corner beneath the window, where the spy cam didn't swivel, he saw it.

O'Donnell had his pants shoved down and he was trying to bang Kinkel's pen pal. Newty was making the plank for him but it wasn't consensual. He saw that O'Donnell was holding a forbidden Seki-Cut fixed blade in one fist as he hunched over Newty, his busy hips throbbing like a wasp abdomen.

Blaze came up behind them and grabbed the Seki-Cut from the predator's fingers. For an instant, he admired its nicely balanced burl handle, weighing it in his hand. He sawed the knife through O'Donnell's left ear. In one dexterous swipe, the ear came off, like a spongy morel from a tree stump.

Newty rolled free and tried to stand up. O'Donnell sat back on his heels, rubbing his ear to look for blood. There isn't much blood when an ear comes off. "I want my knife, you cunt!"

Newty told Blaze, "Give *me* the knife. He's mine."

"Shut up," Blaze said.

Blaze shoved the pared flesh portion into his pocket and kept the knife. He saw O'Donnell's ear crater and told him, "Now you've got a pussy hole. You can listen to your dick as you fuck yourself."

He strolled away from the tousled couple. Newty called after him, "Are you going out? Going now? Take me!"

Blaze didn't answer. Soon O'Donnell would be getting doctored, and screws would be looking for Blaze. He visualized the long and winding road of shrinks, bench bitches, DSS dicks and disgruntled court clerks that lay in wait for him. In the stairwell, he dodged two staffers. On his way out, he left the little tab of flesh, white as tripe, on the banister, taking a moment to center it on the newel post. In less than an hour the ear would be necrotized and couldn't be reattached.

He was outside. In five, he was deep into the snowy fields behind the Greylock campus, careful to travel the black apron of the hay field where the floods didn't hit. Blaze worked his way onto the scary back side of Little Hen. Pine branches slapped his face with their cold white arms; his boots got packed, clumps of snow slithered down his neck and stuffed his jacket cuffs. Half way to the top, Little Hen was winning. He got his second wind when he thought of Lucinda or pictured Janice waiting in her fluffy slippers. He kept climbing the Mountain of Love. He was over the hill before the school's security boyos had belted up with Maglites and lanterns, before they had put on their snow boots and Yaktrax ice cleats, before the hippie cook had filled thermoses with spiced tea and double-dark hot chocolate for their party-mood posse.

He waited on an embankment outside the Pittsfield/Lee toll-booths at I-90, hoping to get a ride. He tried to sneak past the kiosks, but the Mass Pike disciplinarians watched from their cubes with space heaters purring. He was freezing to death and thought about going back. Instead, he tried to climb straight onto the overpass, but the hill was steep. He kept slipping back each time he scrambled a few feet higher.

Two cruisers pulled onto the berm beneath him. Their floods lit up the white snow bank like a drive-in picture screen. He was the new overnight sensation they'd heard about on their radio calls. Blaze pitched O'Donnell's blade into the scrub where it skittered across the cold pack like an ice skate. He threw up his hands, as ordered. He pivoted, back and front, to show them he had nothing. Troopers asked him to sit down, right where he was. "On your buttocks!" Then they told him to slide down the snow bank, like it was a laundry chute. They prized their polished knee-high boots and they weren't going to ruin their shine by climbing in the snow after him.

Chapter Twenty-One

In the morning, before getting out of bed, without her first cup of coffee, April savored the sweet pick-me-up of her victorious revenge story of the previous day. With the de-wired harp, she was dissevered from Mirhege, once and for all. She tried not to think that her actions were unlawful deeds that an outsider might call criminal. And she didn't want to factor in Blaze, or their time on her French settee.

She bolted out of bed. Her night with the teenager was a big mistake. She would have no more contact with him. "Distance!" she said to herself. "I will distance myself."

Then she thought she heard his voice. He was outside her window. When she looked outside, she was surprised to see him in the driveway playing Wiffle ball with a couple of youngsters. Two little boys had arrived with their father. The customer was talking to Townsend beside a truck-bed full of pea stone. While the men discussed a landscaping project, Blaze had been enlisted to amuse the little boys.

Blaze showed patience with the kids. He called to one,

"Watch the ball!" as he pitched underhand grapefruits. Blaze was hardly past Wiffle ball age himself. He lobbed another one with delicate precision, and the little boy finally connected. The dinger sailed over Blaze's shoulder, and as Blaze whipped around he saw April watching from her upstairs window. Still undressed, she pulled the curtain across, pinching it under her chin.

Blaze waved to her, showing his charged, exotic smile, but she ducked away.

When she peeked out again, she saw him facing her empty window. His shoulders slumped, wounded.

She booted up her computer to find a message from the college. Dean of Academic Affairs, Betty Clark, wanted her to call the office to make an appointment. Betty Clark was the heavy at the college, the administrator delegated to impose disciplinary actions against her own staff. April wondered if the Beautiful Boy had made a complaint about his grade, or if Mirhege had decided against calling a truce. Perhaps he had acted on his threat of forcing April to take medical leave or had suggested she be reassigned to Continuing Ed. Whatever Betty Clark wanted to discuss, April knew it might be sticky.

Also waiting in her in box, was a new e-mail from the mortuary supply house.

The subject line was the familiar Endless Pools motto, "Swim at Home!" It had a video link. She clicked on the paper clip, her heart pounding. With a few mouse strokes, her QuickTime player started streaming a flash video in full color on her screen.

The tight little pool is churning fast, a mist rising from its rolling wavelets. The heated water in the tank collides with the cool air temperature within the tony glass block pool enclosure, creating a lifting fog. The scene is almost Londonesque, a Jack the Ripper setting. The camera zooms in on the empty pool. Churning in the water, there's something colorful. Riley's T-shirt surfaces and floats forward—a flat square—before it's sluiced under again.

It wasn't exactly a pool-house snuff shot, but that was the impression she got. Before she could drink it in, the video blacked out.

The clip lasted only ten seconds; she watched it four more times. The sudsing, highly forced current, the empty jersey floating, tumbling, agitating, before it disappears at the end of the pool.

Someone had thrown Riley's shirt in the water. She imagined it might have been the sheet cake boy. She couldn't understand what he meant to say, except that his message was mean. Something about the video reminded her of Nancy's outburst at the Westminster. A lover's clothing is supposed to be metaphoric of something. The T-shirt was ridiculous. Riley had always dressed down. He ignored *GQ*'s yearly top picks and he never read the Sunday Style section like Milt often did.

That's one reason why she liked Townsend in his stained and lumpy fearnaught jacket. His manliness seemed to shine through his modest, unglamorous attire, and that aspect of his character had become, surprisingly, a promising comfort to her.

Riley had had many associates who might have sent the

link. In Boston, he'd worked at Blue Fang and at Floodgate Entertainment. Then he went with a start-up called Back Bay Interactive and another place called Godzilla Bytes. He did all kinds of contract work and was not just a computer geek, he was a genius. He knew everybody.

Milt had said, "Harassment is hard to prove in court. It's often subjective." And years before, April had once been involved in a harassment complaint when she received a disturbing letter. Before earning her PhD, she had been an English teacher at a high school in Providence. A student had written her a threatening note. The student had said that if she didn't give him the grade he wanted she "would end up like Steinbeck's red pony," referring to a text she had taught that winter.

Her principal asked, "What's with this pony? I don't get the reference."

"Steinbeck's pony had its throat cut," she explained to the administrator.

"A book about a pony getting killed? Maybe that shouldn't be in the curriculum."

But this had happened before all the school shootings, and the administration didn't do anything about it.

April telephoned the secretary for the Dean of Academic Affairs to arrange her meeting with Betty Clark. "I won't be on campus until next week," she told the assistant.

"The dean can see you at three o'clock, today."

"Not possible," April said.

"I've been told it's urgent. Let's not put it off, Miss O'Rourke."

April was surprised by the secretary's awkward tone, her formality rimmed with mock pity and condescension. The provost must have come into the dean's office to discuss the necessity that April be encouraged to take medical leave. April told the assistant, "Like I said, I won't be back on campus until next week." She hung up the telephone.

The meeting with Betty Clark was a tempest in a teapot, she told herself. It would resolve itself if Mirhege knew what was good for him.

Seeing the video clip of the pool made April curious about where it had been shot. After Riley's death April had wanted to visit Fox Point Health Club to see where Riley had died. She knew that people routinely visited sites where their loved ones had been lost. Family members of the plane crash victims of TWA Flight 800 took a boat out into Long Island Sound to throw wreaths in the water. And thousands returned to Ground Zero. All over the country, on interstates and county roads there were hand-made crosses and vases of plastic flowers to commemorate the exact pin dot where people had died in wrecks. There should be a law against it! April believed that these jury-rigged memorials just rubbed it in. She pictured Riley's coffin that wouldn't fit into the ground until the hole was enlarged. She decided that it was finally time for her to go visit the pool.

Townsend was standing with a gas can beside one of his huge tractors when April went outside to get in her Camry.

The dozer sat like a docile Jurassic Park monster between the sludge pile and her car.

"Where you headed?" Townsend said. "You going to the college?"

She told him she didn't teach on Fridays. Then she thought that she might like some company if she was going to visit the Fox Point Health Club.

"I have some errands," she said.

"Anything fun?" He was showing his charm-glow grin.

He looked at her face. She was flushed. She was gnawing her bottom lip in a nervous, distracted way as if she couldn't keep her thoughts from crawling all over her.

"Want to tell me about it?" he said.

"Tell you what?"

"Just start from the beginning."

"Okay."

Townsend agreed to drive to Providence with April if she'd let him take her for a drink afterward. He had already decided what his plans might be. He'd take April to the Sand Bar, right on the water. He knew that the sweat bees at the Hilltop would swarm her if he walked in there with such a pretty thing. And on Friday nights Janice left Electric Boat for happy hour at the Sand Bar, where she could get two-for-one. His plan might include running into her.

First they went into the barn so he could wash up. "Just a second while I borrow the porcelain," he told her. As he used the bathroom and changed his dirty clothes, April waited on the scuffed leather sofa. Blaze wasn't in the barn, but his Dell was lit, its screen saver scrolling. Still photographs from the sixties alternated—the famous Kent State shooting, the glorious FUCK THE DRAFT poster that showed a kid igniting his draft card, and a photograph of Jane Fonda in skintight jeans standing huddled with GIs somewhere in jungle land. April couldn't decide if it was Blaze who had chosen the familiar anti-war mural or if it was Townsend. Townsend was, in fact, in an age group for whom Vietnam had mattered. Blaze might have Googled the images just to irritate his dad, who, after all, was buying jarhead ready-to-eat meals as if he was a patriot.

He came back dressed in a sport jacket and creased trousers, remnants of his Diggs & Snyder getup. His slacks had a hanger mark across the knees as if he hadn't worn them in some time. He was still in his Timberlands. "Were you ever in 'Nam?" she asked him, realizing too late that she was being too blunt.

He said, "Two tours. Gulf of Tonkin emergency, and back again after that."

"You're a vet?"

"Ancient history," he said.

She admired his modesty about it. Townsend didn't have war-vet bumper stickers on his truck or the show-off license plate.

They stared at Hanoi Jane on the Dell. "There's the Fondette," he said. "She was amazing. Then she married Turner and we saw what she's made of."

"I liked her in *Klute*."

"For me, it was *Barbarella*." He asked April, "Hey, have you seen Blaze? He was a little pissy this morning. He took off."

"I saw him playing Wiffle ball."

"He ducked out on those kids."

She pictured his wounded face that morning when she didn't wave back to him. "I haven't seen him. Not lately," she told him.

"Ready to go?" he said.

Townsend grabbed her in another bear hug. She tried to protest, using her faux-librarian freeze-up, turning her face away.

"I'm going to get you really drunk," he said.

"A modest hope."

"For starters."

"Like I said," she told him, "we have a little errand to do. Can we go somewhere first?"

"Oh, *we're* going somewhere, don't worry," he said like a dead-sure rooster.

Townsend wanted to drive and she agreed to climb into his truck. Sitting beside him in the tall cab, she felt like a child taking her first ride in a school bus. And she was surprised when Townsend didn't shoot up I-95. He told her he wanted to hit Newport first to look at some stone lions at a salvage company, if that was all right with her. So they took the bridges.

A little nervous to be alone with him, she turned on the radio, pressing the scan button until she found a call-in show. The topic was the Massachusetts same sex marriage rulings. The caller was slinging hateful accusations about gay couples trying to wed, but he had a speech impediment. He was calling it "thame thex." He said the mangled phrase repeatedly in an accelerating rant until April realized it was a set piece of some kind. The right-wing host was encouraging the caller, and trying to be cute. She punched the dial.

Townsend said, "So what's eating you?"

She told him about the e-mails she had been getting.

"Who from?"

"A sick-o," she said. Then, before she thought twice, she blurted out details of her finale with Mirhege, leaving out any mention of Blaze chasing the provost off her stoop. Instead, she told him about the tussle she'd watched in the hotel suite next door. Townsend enjoyed the story. He asked her, "So the girl just left him there in his altogether?"

"That's right."

"Nothing but his birthday suit?"

"That's the picture," she said.

"The brush-off in the old hotel."

"He probably deserved it."

"There's nothing that juicy in Dumbwaiter, believe me. Not in Plaza Suite, either."

"That girl deserves credit."

"I hope I never get on the wrong side of you."

"What side do you think you're on now?"

He tipped his head and smiled. "You sure that girl you're talking about wasn't really *you* throwing clothes out the window? The old 'I have a friend who. . .'"

"I wish I had the same courage. He's threatening to demote me," she said.

"He can do that?" He was thinking about his own problems at Diggs & Snyder, as if his dismissal from his corporate job somehow matched her looming circumstances. He said, "You sound like you've been having a rough time."

"Not as if you don't have your share with Janice Gallen?"

"She'll be crawling back. Inching on her belly, like a little garter snake. But I have to give her a little time to sow her oats, have her second childhood, because you know, she never had it the first time around. She got pregnant. My fault."

"Aren't you too good to be true?"

"Janice was a kid with a summer job. It wasn't supposed to happen the way it did."

"A summer job? She got jobbed, all right," April said.

"That's what I'm saying."

"She wants your money, right?"

"Money is owed, she's correct about that. And she's got other chits."

April could see that he was still in love with his bride. Yet he was genuinely concerned about April. He had listened intently as she described her recent problems with the provost and the Endless Pools nut. "Things can stack up," he told her.

She said, "Oh, I'm not really complaining. I've got a pretty good set up. You know, I'm a college professor!"

"That and a token will get you a ride on the subway."

"Ouch," she said. But she realized that he was right.

Her achievements weren't very impressive. She remembered listening to the speaker at her graduation from Vassar, a famous scholar who had told the graduating class, "Today, as you get your degree, think of it like this: In *Moby-Dick*, Captain Ahab nails a gold piece into a mast pole, promising the crew of the *Pequod* that the mate who first sights the white whale will win the precious coin. Today, graduates, with your degree you have won the coin, but you haven't yet caught the whale!"

Townsend told her, "Your problem is, you're just a little high-strung."

She said, "I hate that expression." She didn't tell him what therapists had always told her: she had a problem in her relationships with men, because of her father.

April enjoyed taking the bridges across Narragansett Bay, hopping from Jamestown to Newport. *God, it's a terrific country, she thought, when the Army Corps of Engineers can connect islands just by building these silvery arches.* They stopped in Newport so Townsend could look at the salvaged stone lions. He wanted to add lawn ornaments to his landscaping operation. They walked through a menagerie of chipped cement statues, griffins and big cats, some Romanesque and others that were more garish, like the upright Chinese lions she'd seen at a restaurant called Tiki Port. Townsend didn't want them, and he and April were on their way again. She wondered if going to the junkyard had just been a ruse to take her on a long drive.

They were on Route 138 when the traffic slowed. They approached a police car with flashing lights. A sign on the front bumper of the cruiser said WIDE LOAD. It was a public safety escort, with cruisers in front of and behind the procession, because a house was being moved. As they passed the official cortege, April saw a tiny white bungalow on a flatbed trailer. It was secured on a pallet, braced with two-by-fours at all four corners and across its front door. Its windows were crisscrossed with fir strips and its chimney framed by plywood. The cottage looked like a big gift box ready to be Fed Exed. April often saw antique houses being relocated. Historic New England dwellings, when put in danger from urban expansion, were sometimes reclaimed and moved to better sites. It could have been any one of these eighteenth-century antiques, but it was the Playhouse shrine, lock, stock and barrel! She tried to get a better look at the trussed-up abode, but the procession was going thirty miles an hour in the opposite direction.

"Turn around! Turn around!" she told Townsend. "Follow that house!"

"Are you kidding?"

"Turn this frickin' truck around. I've got to make sure I'm not seeing things."

He told her, "You aren't seeing things. That *was* a house going down the road."

She said, "I know it's a house. Jesus."

"You didn't imagine it. You aren't going crazy."

She looked at him. She wondered if everyone thought she was a lunatic. The provost, the detective, her friend Milt, who, although he loved her, eternally thought she was a moon bat.

She didn't want her new sidekick climbing on board.

"I just want to see if it's *my* house. . . ."

Townsend turned into a Mobil station and let the truck idle. "Are you saying that you recognize that house? What gives?"

She said, "Christ, what else can happen now? It's just so ironic."

"Every day opens a new window of irony."

"You can't possibly understand this mess I'm in. When will it end?"

"Any day soon that doesn't end in *y*," he said.

His relentless babble was beginning to wear thin. His one-man cheering squad became a thorn in her side. The traffic had snarled behind the flatbed trailer, and they weren't going to get close enough for a genuine inspection. She told him, "Okay. Don't follow the house." She thought they could verify what she had seen if they went to the suitcase factory to see if the cottage was missing.

In twenty minutes they arrived at the blinking valise beside the old American Tourister complex. When Townsend pulled into the parking space where the Playhouse Cottage had been, the little shrine was missing. Even the quaint picket fence had been extracted from its post holes, its sections piled in a neat stack. The dismantled fence was an in-your-face metaphor for the dramatic undoing of all of April's domestic dreams.

She saw the empty foundation. It wasn't a full basement but just a crawl space of jumbled cement blocks. Nearby, a machine operator tended to a big yellow crane that had been used to lift the little house onto the flatbed trailer. He was collapsing its telescopic boom and securing its hoisting block into a tight elbow. They watched as its outrigger feet retracted, like a big grasshopper lifting all six of its tarsi. "Where are they taking that house?" April asked the worker.

"Jamestown. They're closing the Mount Hope Bridge to all traffic for it to go over. It'll be a circus."

April imagined her little house crossing the suspension bridge and sinking down the other side. Townsend could see her thoughts shift in painful little winces of her mouth and stabbings across her brow. Janice had a similar expression when the world seemed to be against her. He asked April, "Was this the place where you were born or something?"

"Our honeymoon cottage. That's what it was."

"No kidding? Well, someone must have heard about your love nest and wants to give it a second chance. But not beside a suitcase factory."

"Very funny," she said.

He told her, "My honeymoon with Janice? We went to a motel called the Cuddle and Bubble. Tahitian hot tub in every room."

"Those tubs always look like you should be stomping grapes."

"The one we got didn't have hot water. Heater was out. That was a sign, don't you think?"

She wasn't smiling. "I missed *all* the signs," she said, thinking of Riley and those anybodies Milt had talked about.

Her eyes were just pupils and whites, without any iris. She looked like a startled heroine in a classic late night *Movie Loft* horror flick. "Are you feeling all right?" he asked. "Come on, Princess, cheer up," he said.

She rubbed the palms of her hands down her face. "Slap me out of it," she told him.

He leaned over to kiss her, but she shoved him back in his seat.

"I said *slap* me. It's a figure of speech." She realized she was asking too much of him. "You want to get a Coke?" she said.

"A Coke would be good. Just to tide us over."

"Coke is the answer," she said.

At the Fox Point Health Club, there wasn't any parking. Townsend pulled up beside a loading annex. April promised they'd get back before the truck was towed. She collected their empty Big Gulp containers and tossed them in a trash barrel as they walked into the posh exercise palace. And at the big front desk, a wide crescent of granite, there were several white platters of freshly sliced honeydew, mango, and papaya. The complimentary fruit slices were arranged in aromatic rows and spirals. "Help yourself," the attendant told April.

Townsend popped a wedge of fruit into his mouth. "Lots-o'-tropics," he said, grinning. "You want some mango?"

"No, thanks," April said. She never ate fruit from salad bars or accepted unwrapped candies from dishes left out in the foyers of restaurants. A study had examined the contents of restaurants' candy bowls, and in chemical tests, traces of urine were commonly found on the mints. She believed that men never washed their hands after zipping up.

She was introduced to the director of the club. With professional sympathy he told her, "I'm so sorry for your loss."

He spoke in the same obsequious but self-possessed manner as the funeral director who had sold her Riley's oversized coffin. Funeral directors were salesmen, plain and simple. They could be on a car lot, or selling furs from the back of a van. "It looks good on him," wasn't something they might actually say about the sleek, high-end mahogany coffins for sale, but she felt it was a similar pitch. The salesman had used the words "dignified" and "watertight" in the same sentence. Nowadays, environmentally conscious people were choosing to be buried without coffins, in "green" linen wrappings. She remembered Riley's last words to her, when he had complained about the towels being as thin as the Shroud of Turin. Her face was white.

Townsend said, "You okay?"

She told the director, "I'd like to see the pool where my boyfriend died, is that all right?"

They followed the director down a corridor, past a large open floor of Nautilus equipment, where several bulked-up men and stringy-looking women were engaged in loyal one-to-ones with their favorite weight machines. She tried to match faces with the faces at the party table in the Motel 6 video, but she didn't recognize anyone.

The Endless Pool was segregated from the other activities. She asked the club's director about their life guard policy. He told her that the Endless Pool was considered a therapy unit, like a Jacuzzi, and had no supervision. It was only three feet deep, after all. Detective Primiano had told April that the coroner had said that no one could have prevented Riley's death. His brain had had a weak blood vessel. She had read for herself about Riley's aneurism. "Over strenuous exercise, including sexual activity, can be a factor leading to cerebrovascular events, and to a potentially fatal bleed."

She thought that Riley could have died just as easily making love to her. If that had happened she wouldn't be in the spot she was in now—in the position of trying to learn how to hate him.

The pool was built into a private enclosure made of puckered stone blocks.

"That's tumbled marble," the director told them with pride. "They put the tiles in a barrel like a clothes dryer and they get tumbled until the edges are irregular."

"The edges are irregular," Townsend said, enjoying his double entendre about the queer club.

The waist-high pool looked like a lobster tank. At the fish market, Riley had always insisted on having eye-to-eye contact with the creatures, before he finally picked out the ones he wanted. He said that whenever buying lobsters, the pity fest was a prerequisite to the dinner party.

The water was still, not a ripple. She saw a lime-green circle on the bottom of the tank, an elastic scrunchie someone had lost from her hair when swimming. The director grabbed a pole and scooped it out.

Townsend said, "So this thing can really move the water, right?"

"Five thousand gallons a minute. It's got a sixteen-inch propeller inside that casing, driven by a hydraulic motor. The current shoots down the center and circles back through these two side benches." He touched a switch and the water started to move.

April climbed up on a small deck at the opposite end of the pool as the director unlocked a panel and lifted it so that Townsend could examine the motor. Men love motors. And with this one at full throttle, Townsend seemed impressed. April felt numb standing so near the tumbling current. She pictured Riley swimming the butterfly stroke. She saw his hips rising and sinking as he kicked in sync with each rotation of his shoulders. The butterfly stroke was indeed a lewd motion, derivative of fucking. She saw his pretty bottom in his skintight Speedo, a tease to anyone watching. Then she saw his lank body crushed against the gunnels of the pool—in death, or right before death, in his orgasmic afterglow.

She felt a bitter determination rising out of nowhere. Her impulse was instant, dizzy, like when someone snatches a bracelet from a jewelry counter or decides to barrel through a red light. She spread her arms wide and collapsed forward into the churning current.

She belly flopped. The current instantly shoved her back to one end. She was happy to feel so helpless in the water. Its scarves of cool silver wrapped around her shoulders and sucked between her legs. Since Riley's death she had never felt this close to him. But Townsend jumped into the pool feet first to help her. He tugged her to one side of the trough where they didn't have to fight the forced river. The club director turned off the motor, and the men pulled April out.

"What happened to you?" Townsend said.

"I guess I got light-headed."

"You fainted?"

"Not really, I don't know," she said. "I just slipped, I guess." But she knew why she was soaking. She had longed to do it. It was some kind of reverse baptism, that purged her angry ideas about Riley, and she actually felt much better.

The health club had a bank of industrial-size dryers, and Townsend's and April's clothes were tumbling. In the laundry room, April sat in a plastic barrel chair wrapped in a terry robe. Townsend stood beside her with only a towel snugged around his hips. His physique was attractive for a man his age, still chiseled. He reminded April of Burt Lancaster on the beach with the Brit actress Deborah Kerr in Hollywood's old chestnut *From Here to Eternity*. She knew it was a corny idea, but she let it fill her head.

They watched their clothes spinning. A young man who worked at the club brought her a cup of hot tea. She recognized his face. He wasn't the sheet cake boy. He might be one of the others she'd seen with Riley in the motel video. She said, "Hey. Wait a minute. Did you know Riley?"

He told her, "Did I know him? No."

"But you must have known Riley."

"It's club policy not to enter into social relationships with clients."

"That's the *policy*, you say?" She believed he protested too much. "Did Riley have a special friend here?"

"Milt Phelps might know. Milt has lots of friends. He knows everybody."

April was thinking, *Yeah, everybody, the anonymous hordes.* She didn't want Riley lumped in with them. She said, "Milt's got quite a Rolodex. A fat one." She didn't wince when she recognized her double entendre. It was an accident or an accident on purpose.

Chapter Twenty-Two

Their clothes were dry but their shoes were soggy. Townsend's work boots squished with each mushy step and April's fur slip-ons were like sponges. Her socks were still wet. In the truck, Townsend offered April his fearnaught jacket. It reeked of English Leather after shave. "You wear English Leather?" she said. "That's so retro."

"I hate that word," he said.

Still in their wet shoes, he took her to the Sand Bar, a seedy little spot with charm galore. He didn't see Janice's van in the parking lot, but he was certain she'd show up. He'd wait as long as he needed to wait. He told April, "I hope Blaze gets home to feed the horses their oats."

They walked into the down scale bistro where local families were eating bowls of spaghetti and sharing carafes of house red. The bitter scent of powdered garlic hung in the air, and she hoped he wouldn't try to buy her dinner. "Oh boy, I think I'd rather have oats," she joked. They didn't sit down in the restaurant but kept walking until they were in the waterfront lounge. There was a wood stove at the far end of the bar, and he asked two patrons to move off their stools near the fire. "We're sopping wet," he said. They obliged and he told them, "I'll buy you a round."

April sat in the chair nearest to the fire and slipped out of her seeping boots. He placed them on the hearth. He plastered her damp socks on the stove's hood, and the white tubes hissed. But he didn't remove his wet Timberlands. They sat at the bar, a comfortable crescent, with rows of bottles to stare at. Behind the bar, a wall of mirrored tiles oozed grout. A few of the tiles were missing. The mirror was decorated with blinking seed lights, but then April realized it wasn't twinkle lights but just a reflection of harbor lamps on the finger piers outside. Yes, it was a magical place and she understood why men might come here to woo their dates.

Townsend wasn't rushing it. He studied a dish of cocktail nuts that a bartender had shoved in front of him as if the nuts could tell him his next move. Then he stared straight ahead at the mirrored tiles behind the bottles, looking at the harbor as if trying to pinpoint a particular vessel. Townsend said, "He's probably at the pier with his buddies. The *Sea Flea* came in tonight."

"You mean Blaze is out there somewhere? Tonight?" she said.

"They tie up, offload their catch, get paid, but they waste some of it right here."

"They waste their pay?"

"A few run home to their wives. But these boys are loners. When the skipper figures percentages, he doles it out in cash.

They're never happy to be on shore until they're peabodied. You know, until they get sozzled. Plowed."

He talked about fishermen's bad habits but she could tell he was worried about his son who hadn't returned to the house all day. She tried not to feel responsible for Blaze going free-range. *He's a delinquent*, she told herself. She knew she should never have enlisted him in her vandalism scheme, or let him drive the little car across her collar bone. She should have reported him for swiping her Camry. That would have nipped it in the bud.

Like he had promised, Townsend ordered a new round for the exiled couple who had relinquished their chairs. Then he told the bartender, "I'll have my usual. And she'll have a Nervous Breakdown."

"I'll have what?"

"Vodka and Chambord black raspberry liqueur. That's a Nervous Breakdown."

"Very funny," she said.

Townsend said to the bartender, "Okay, no Breakdown. We'll both have a Suicide Pact. You'll like it, April. Just sip it until you are sure. It's a one-way decision."

"Are you going to keep this up?" she said.

Then the gin started coming. Refills materialized before April noticed, and soon she was getting drunk. Again she felt the symptoms of mal de débarquement syndrome and she pinched the lip of the bar when she felt she was sliding off her stool.

After two martinis he talked to her like a lover; after his third he couldn't stopper his corny homespun vernacular. "Where'd you get those bee-stung lips?" he said, tracing her mouth with his finger tip. That was good, old-fashioned lovemaking, and she fell for it.

He went on to say, "After today, I see that you're a girl with a lot of problems. That's more than one monkey on your back, it's a three ring."

"Why don't you just speak your mind," she said, a little miffed by his summary. "You didn't have to come with me."

"I wouldn't have missed it," he said, trying to appease her one minute then zinging her again with, "You could have paragraphs in Wikipedia under 'Lovely Loonies' or 'Cutie-Pie Crackpots.'" He kept looking at the doorway.

Then Janice showed up. Wearing her oversized sun glasses, she only called attention to her splotches. Under her thick face powder her bruises looked like the blue-stamped fell on a leg of lamb. She wiggled between their two chairs to give the bartender her order. "Captain Morgan," she said. April thought that the order wasn't for a novice but that Janice could be schooled in more-ladylike cocktails. April's mom used to say, "You're not an adult without the Beefeater." Janice could have told April that Captain Morgan was the fastest route to the same destination.

Janice told Townsend, "I thought you agreed, this is my place not yours. It's not a free zone."

"You don't own it," he said.

She said, "What's wrong with the Hilltop?" She knew what was wrong with it. Its geezer clientele wore mullets and muttonchops. The men dressed in flannel-lined overalls with rumpled knees and never removed their woolen hats with those silly ear flaps.

"Hello to you, too," April said, leaning forward to assert her rightful station at the bar rail. She was Townsend's drinking partner and didn't want Janice to create a scene.

When Janice faced her, April was startled to see she had symmetrical shiners under her sunglasses. "Good God," April said. "You know, there's something called a restraining order."

Townsend patted her hand, trying to keep April in line. He told Janice, "What's with the Ray-Bans? What the hell is going on? I'm not going to stand by—"

Janice said, "As if I'm talking to you."

He knew she was there just to show him the damage. He said to her, "John Two at it again? You want a grizzly bear or a real man?"

"You think you know one?"

April said, "Rhode Island has a mandatory-arrest law. All she has to do is report him."

Janice said, "Save it."

"No, really, they'll pick him up if you call them."

"Who asked you?"

April knew that battered wife syndrome breaks down a woman's self-confidence and self-respect. The woman has an irrational belief that the abuser is omnipresent and omniscient.

She believes that the violence is *her* fault. Although April was drunk, or *because* she was drunk, she cleaved to her feminist schooling at Vassar and it flooded back to her. April had attended college there long after its late seventies hey-day, but she'd had the full survey, starting with *The Feminine Mystique* and *The Female Eunuch*. These texts were ideological and rhetorical, and there had not yet been direct discourse on wife beaters until Farrah Fawcett in *The Burning Bed*. April remembered her fiery instructors saying that women should support one another, band together, and "take back the night!" These chestnuts seemed stale and unhelpful, so she told Townsend, "She needs our help."

"Don't worry your pretty little head. It's not your monkey," he said.

The doctrine would say it was the same monkey for all women. She and her sisters lugged it around, and no man, including Townsend, would ever take responsibility. Janice should have witnessed what April had seen outside her hotel window. Maybe Nancy's performance would get through to her.

Instead, April told Janice, "There's a shelter. I think it's called Independence House."

Janice told April, "Does your mother know you're out?"

"You should leave that monster."

"I guess you think *you're* doing better? Not what I hear about you."

"What do you hear?"

"Crawl back in your jar of formaldehyde."

Pinched between, Townsend was both sideswiped and cornered. He froze. Janice searched his face, expecting something to happen, as if watching the fuse on a bottle rocket that turns out to be a dud. She didn't want him to defend her from April, but seemed giddy that she'd dumped her dirty laundry in front of them. April wasn't important to her. April was a side salad that could be bussed as they cleared the table.

Finally Townsend told April, "*You* stay here." He pulled Janice away and they disappeared into the noisy kitchen, walking through the wrong side of a swinging door, dodging a disgruntled waiter.

Despite the kitchen warfare, she could hear Townsend's voice rising and falling from within the busy clatter. His speech was muffled, but his words, although incomprehensible, expressed an undeniable tenderness.

April understood that Janice's choice to live with a batterer was a manifestation of her self-hatred. April's Vassar instructor had once explained that battered women believe that the whip is atonement for their innate weaknesses and crimes. In a short time, Janice marched past again. She joined her Electric Boat brethren at a table across the room, no worse for wear. But Townsend didn't return. April didn't think he'd found any resolution with the anti-missus and perhaps he was trying to collect himself after his disappointing intervention.

In ten minutes she realized he might be upset with *her*. In another ten minutes she understood he wasn't coming back.

The bartender asked if she wanted another drink, and

she was too embarrassed to decline. As the bartender filled a shaker, Janice sat down on the stool beside her.

"You think you know everything? You've got all the answers? Let me tell you, there can't be a nail-in-your-foot rumor without a busybody like you."

April said, "What rumor? You're wearing a sandwich sign that says he beats you up."

"You know, they burned a witch in Salem for being nosy about her neighbors. They put kindling in her pussy, rubbed lard on her nipples and lit them up like birthday candles."

April said, "*I'm* a witch? Your son says you don't pass the food-bowl test."

They locked eyes for an instant but turned to face the mirror behind the bar. Just then, two of the mirrored tiles peeled away from the wall and fell from their reflection as they watched. Another square bent forward, arrested for a second in its gluey caulk before it flopped to the floor. The rest of the silvery checkerboard came down, each tile popping loose, noisy as a sudden downpour splashing against the stainless steel sinks and the shelves of bottles.

The women shrieked, their laughter erupting from disbelief and awe. When April turned to Janice, overwhelmed by a feeling of instant camaraderie, Janice was gritting her teeth. Janice refused to acknowledge that any bond had formed between them, christened by shattered glass.

The bartender crunched over the broken shards to shake their hands. "Congratulations, girls. It was just a matter of time," he said. "We were losing them one by one."

"It's the humidity," Janice said. "You're right on the water here." She used the chitchat to escape April. She walked back to her table.

Townsend sat down beside April. The bartender saluted him with a dust pan. "Let's get out of here," Townsend said. He left another twenty on the bar mat and took out his truck keys. He steered April to the door. He had her almost outside before she realized she was in her bare feet. She padded back to the wood stove to collect her boots. She had to peel her socks, stiff as cardboard, from the stove top.

Chapter Twenty-Three

*Mirror Explodes at Local Tavern, Women
Patrons Almost Sliced to Ribbons!*

Townsend parked the Tundra outside April's kitchen door and helped her slither out of the passenger seat. The barn was completely dark and she wondered if Blaze had come home. Then she saw Townsend was her new problem. *As if the older man is any less complicated!* she thought. She figured she was twenty-something years older than Blaze and Townsend had twenty-five years on her, a whole silver anniversary. She tried to do the math in her head but she was soaked in gin. Besides, she didn't want an exact equation, *this* equals *that*, nor did she want to try to discern if the glass is half empty or half full, or to try to remember if it's fifty dimes or forty quarters to a roll. She was losing her self-respect either way. It had started at the Westminster, or even sooner than that, when Riley had found solace in his "thame thex" partners. That is, until he had cheated on her with the busiest suitor, that indefatigable swordsman, Death.

Townsend walked her inside. She twisted out of his arms and stumbled through the living room and up the stairs. He waited at the bottom until she turned around. "Well," she said, "are you coming?"

He climbed the steep antique risers, one creaky step and the next. She stood on the landing and said, "You know what you're doing, I hope."

"I guess we'll find out," Townsend said.

She went to turn on her bedroom lamp. Its pink light warmed the room just the way she liked. She saw the little flower car where she'd arranged it on her bedside table, an exciting little artifact that she refused to part with. She brushed it into a drawer.

"You should talk to Blaze," she said.

"About what?"

She didn't want him asking her questions. She wasn't an innocent bystander despite her fussy instincts about right and wrong.

"Let's leave him out of this. That's my one request," he said.

He refused to discuss Blaze. She remembered what he had said about his precious board game: "*Blanks* are important," he had explained, when describing the occasional empty rooms in the Volney Hotel. He was in denial. He put up walls. "Okay, just bury your head in the sand, or at the Sand Bar," she said.

"I see what you're doing," he said. "You're playing us off one another." He was already tossing her extra pillows and shams right and left, trying to clear a place for them. She had covered her bed with throw pillows, velvet boudoir wedges, damask-weave bolsters, neck rolls, and gusseted eider down cubes, to make it seem inviting, and not off-putting. She'd been fooling herself. It was a *tragic* sight.

"I'm not here to argue," he said. "No use blamestorming."

She told him, "So what do you want?"

"Everything. In due order. A little at a time."

"What do you mean 'everything'?"

He said, "If not everything, one thing. More than once."

His words were exciting. No more peppy anecdotes, ant wacky jargon or Jack Benny schlock. He didn't turn on the hokey charm. He knew what kind of woman he was dealing with.

Cold words made her hot.

She was putty. He made love to her for an hour, without a moment wasted. Mirhege had never found her triggers without April's instructions, but Townsend didn't need coaching or any feedback. She didn't try to fight it. She melted from the waist down, until her dirty thoughts fell out of the cupboard.

As she fell asleep in his arms, his mild snoring was sooth-ing, like a pleasant sound machine. She realized how she had missed that testosterone white noise since Riley was gone. In the middle of the night, Townsend decided he should go home. He told her that if Blaze had come back, he didn't want him left to himself. He leaned across to kiss her, but she had already popped out of bed. She found her robe and cinched it tight, using its hem discretely to wipe her moist inner thigh. She piled her tangled hair on her head and pinned it, a little embarrassed, as if her messy mop broadcasted to all that she'd had indiscretions with her next-door neighbor. Townsend stepped into his trousers. He couldn't find his boots. He got down on his hands and knees to bat her dust ruffle aside, looking under her four-poster. "Hey, you see my shoes?"

"Those work boots?"

"That's right."

"I don't have your boots."

"They can't just walk away."

He padded around the bedroom, looking in every corner. "I didn't take them off downstairs, did I?" he said.

"Well, they're not here," she said. "That's weird."

He told her, "In Dumbwaiter, Lord So-and-So leaves his loafers outside his hotel room door overnight to get polished, but they get stolen."

"He's got microfilm hidden in the insole, right?" she said.

"In 1910? Not exactly. Maybe a passport or something."

"Like a love note or a treasure map?" Suddenly she, too, wanted to find help from the narrative cards in the amusing Victorian game that Townsend referenced each time he didn't know what else to say. She needed a scapegoat, something formulaic, like you'd find in a sweet and savage romance novel. Nothing could compete with what was happening now.

Townsend sat down on the edge of her bed.

She said, "I guess we know who took the boots?"

"Yeah. Guess who."

Chapter Twenty-Four

Blaze wasn't lounging on the *Sea Flea* that afternoon, like Townsend said. He had spent the day with his street pal, Baxter, after he had had a tiff instant messaging Lucinda. She asked him to move into a private chat room. When he logged in, he was surprised to see he wasn't alone with her.

Blaze used the screen name Disneyviolence. In the old days, when Blaze was in middle school the AOL spies didn't like its threatening tone. They said it stirred up trouble and AOL had tried to kick him out. Blaze knew that AOL was so over, but he still liked the screen name dissing corporate Hollywood. Right under Lucinda's screen name, Malibubarbie, an intruder popped up. Someone named Biggerboat was talking with her too, trying to cockblock him. Lucinda told Blaze that her friend's name came from his favorite shark movie. In fact, she was telling Blaze that Biggerboat was taking her to an IMAX movie that afternoon. Blaze imagined Lucinda snuggled with the rival in the steep tiers of an IMAX theater, in those high-rise seats that make girls dizzy if they aren't holding on tight to their boyfriends.

DISNEYVIOLENCE: Luce, whoz this insect f'ker?

MALIBUBARBIE: my manager at Target

BIGGERBOAT: i have the keys to her cash drawer

DISNEYVIOLENCE: i'd step off if i were you

BIGGERBOAT: don't write a check your ass can't cash

MALIBUBARBIE: hey guys, i'm outie if you don't chill

DISNEYVIOLENCE: pls wait for me

MALIBUBARBIE: you expect me to wait for you? what am I supposed to do fri nites?

BIGGERBOAT: build it and they will come, lol

MALIBUBARBIE: Janice said you have a STD?

DISNEYVIOLENCE: no way

MALIBUBARBIE: Janice said so

DISNEYVIOLENCE: she lies.

BIGGERBOAT: baby, 86 this sickdick

DISNEYVIOLENCE: Boat fucker, go back to Gilligan's Island if you want to live

BIGGERBOAT: what? hahaha

DISNEYVIOLENCE: Luce get rid of this dude

MALIBUBARBIE: too late i can't wait for you forever

MALIBUBARBIE: sorry

BIGGERBOAT: gee 96 tears for u peace :-)

Lucinda had encouraged their fisking. She liked watching them flame, but Blaze understood that Lucinda was hooked up with the crasher. The private chat room was an ambush she had used to let Biggerboat do the dirty work and break the news to him. It was an instant-message Dear John. He saw they were trying to poof him.

Blaze wasn't sure Janice had called Lucinda, but if Janice had sensed he was ready to take off, she would try to poison the well. He didn't put it past her. He was wounded and fuming when Townsend's Droid started buzzing. When caller ID said J. GALLEN he didn't pick up. He waited. Then he listened to her message. He wasn't prepared to hear her voice. Instead of her two familiar modes, her bitching or her cooing, she sounded frantic. "I've already missed three days at work. That fuck took my battery. Van is dead. I need a ride somewhere. Someone come get me. Please. This is no shit!"

If Janice needed a car, she didn't say where she wanted to go.

Blaze didn't have wheels, so he hitched to Baxter's place. If he decided to help Janice, Baxter might have a loaner or what he called his "buybacks," vehicles he collected when someone ran a tab. Outside his double-wide trailer it looked like a car lot.

Baxter had started an irrigation business, although he had not yet begun to visit his clients' properties to turn on their sprinkler systems and reset their clocks. The green-up-your-lawn rat race didn't start until May. So Baxter was still cooking meth. When Blaze arrived, he was surprised to see Baxter's usual crew of serious tweakers—who talked a mile a minute, scratching their crank bugs and peeling their scabs—involved in a kiddie party.

Baxter's six-year-old girl was visiting for the day and the

dopers were helping her make a papier-mâché tortoise for her school project. The little girl was covered in pasty white goo as everyone dipped strips of wet newsprint in a tub and smoothed them onto a big, lumpy shape. The tortoise began to take form, and Blaze was happy to help. He pinched the mushy wads and fashioned the pulp to create its bulbous head, making sure to give it a pointy beak. He liked getting his hands into the sweet-smelling paste.

As they let the turtle dry before a fan, Blaze shared some meth and smoked a bulb with a friendly fiend. Blaze wasn't a heavy user and declined another hit. He didn't forget that Janice needed a car; he *obsessed* about it with busy checklists, countered with arguments against each item, all in his head. But he did nothing. He was distracted when Baxter asked his glass monkeys to clean up his kitchen and everyone scampered around like Merry Maids in a neatnik hurricane. It wasn't just the papier-mâché mess, but Baxter's cabinets had to be organized. Blaze unpacked coffee filters, for filtering red phosphorus, and these had to be stacked in short towers and weighted with empty jars so they wouldn't spill loose. Jars and funnels, clamps and hoses, containers of lye and acetone, blister packs of Mini Thin and Sudafed, hundred count boxes of kitchen matches and all of Baxter's pharmacy bric-a-brac, beakers, stirrers, colanders and everyday kitchen gizmos, cluttered the table and every available counter-top, and these items needed to have their rightful cubbies so Baxter wouldn't waste time searching for what he needed. Jugs of Clorox,

Liquid Fire and Red Devil lye had to be carefully nestled side by side because their corroded caps didn't fit right, and spillage was eating the linoleum. No one could walk from the stove to the sink until empties were discarded and Baxter asked Blaze to carry buckets of corrosive goo to dump at his burn pit behind the house, well out of sight. Along the way, Blaze noticed baby monitors duct-taped in the tree branches, positioned so that Baxter could hear if a car drove up behind the house or if someone was snooping. Blaze told Baxter, "These are too easy to find. Why not just hang out a sign! You should hide your walkie-talkies inside bird boxes."

"Bird boxes? Shit, Einstein, that's good. Why didn't I think of that?" After helping with the cleanup, Blaze sat down with the little girl to play a game of Connect Four. He didn't think it was safe for her to be so near Baxter's chemical stash, so he took her into a back bedroom. The girl kept winning every round, and Blaze was manic as he sorted the little plastic disks for another challenge. Smoking meth had sliced his cortex into paper-thin slivers of skittery insights, brain blips, and egghead ideas that kept circling back again. He worried about Janice's phone call, but his theories shivered from woman to woman. He obsessively defragmented his sphere of feelings about Janice, April, Lucinda, cutting and pasting. He backspaced, erased, edited, and reformatted. Lucinda, April, his mom.

When the flour paste was dry and the tortoise was ready, they painted it. "This is kind of green, isn't it?" Blaze said.

"Turtles are green," Baxter said.

"This is kelly green," Blaze said. "It's unnatural."

The little girl looked worried about the bright paint. Blaze tried to reassure her. "You'll have the best frickin' turtle in the world," he told her.

It was two a.m. when he finally got a lift to the barn. He had a burning, empty stomach. If he ate anything he would instantly de-food. He was spracked and jittery, and it didn't help him when he saw his father's pickup nosed beside April's kitchen door. He felt a hot little wave creep across his bladder. Her house was dark, but her bedroom window glowed willfully.

When he couldn't find Townsend in the barn, Blaze tried to get his thoughts in a huddle to conjure up an alibi for his dad. Okay, his father was at the farmhouse to fix April's toilet with the handle that had to be jiggled a certain way. Blaze remembered it took a delicate touch. Okay, his father was over there to adjust the temperamental thermostat. In December he'd trained her how to tickle it correctly, but women always needed another crash course. Okay, Townsend was at her house to collect the glue traps he'd given April to catch the field mice in the cellar. Women don't like to see mini rodents cemented to the traps, their little furry forms still writhing. Blaze invented scenarios that excused his dad, but he knew it was bullshit.

His dad was shacked up with the neighbor, plain and simple.

Feeling insulted by the two of them was the extra nudge he needed to go ahead with his scheme. Blaze found his father's car keys still in the Tundra. He sorted through its crowded ring to find the little key to the mini vault. To open the safe, he needed both a key and the combination. He'd have to get Townsend's Timberlands.

Blaze pushed open April's kitchen door, making sure it didn't creak. He removed his Nikes on the jute mat and tiptoed in his socks to the bottom of the stairs. He didn't hear anything. The house was as quiet as an auditorium after ushers have pushed the carpet sweepers and the ticket booth is locked. Showtime was over. He didn't like to imagine the first act or its grand finale.

When he climbed the stairs he saw the bedroom lamp still burning, but the couple was conked out. Townsend snored, lying flat on his back, against doctor's orders. Stomach acid would burn a hole in his throat if he didn't sit up. Blaze hoped it would sizzle like Baxter's Red Devil lye.

April was curled on her side, entwined in a swirling green sheet from the waist down. Bare-breasted, she looked like a mermaid beached beside her hoary pirate. In his meth fever, Blaze's sweat evaporated turning his skin cold. The boudoir seemed hazy with dry-ice smoke. April didn't belong beside his father. He didn't know what to feel about the two-tongued professor. Townsend wasn't supposed to be there either.

In this very room, his childhood had been stolen and perversities had been fostered until fully formed. Here he was tortured with nurture and his manhood was twisted out of his own hands. It was useless to fight visions of Janice. Janice was an eternal flame.

He had to get out of that room.

He found the Timberlands at the end of the bed. He forgot which boot had the combination to the wall safe, the left or the right. He took both.

Chapter Twenty-Five

At daylight, the dogs started barking. The embrangle-ment roused April, and the previous night flooded back. She remembered Vivien Leigh in *Gone with the Wind*, in the morning-after scene, when Scarlett wakes up in her bed pleased and perky, after getting banged by Rhett. The vision made her face burn. As Townsend had made love to her, she was pleased by his performance, and she told him so.

"You're not so bad yourself. You've got expert-*tease*," he joked.

She was relieved to remember that Townsend had left her bed, walking home in his bare feet.

The racket continued outside.

Two dump trucks had pulled up beside the sludge pile. Townsend was operating one of his glossy bucket excavators, digging into the hateful compost. They were making a dent in the mountain. She could have pinched herself. The dump trucks were being loaded up! They were hauling the scourge away.

By moving the sludge, he hoped to seal the deal. When he left her bed he had joked, "I'd lose my boots again, anytime you want to."

Suddenly she heard him holler to the men as he shut off the excavator. He jumped down from the seat. Townsend had uncovered an object in the sludge. April was surprised to see the pedestal mirror half-buried in the crud. She watched Townsend pull it free in two broken pieces, its glass in jagged slivers. Townsend stood beside the lonesome heirloom, his hands on his hips. He appeared to be truly miffed.

April thought that of course Blaze had done the vandalism, but then she remembered Janice. Whoever had destroyed the mirror, it was a fabulous display of hatred for its garish symbolism. Townsend piled its damaged pieces to one side, and climbed onto the loader again. All morning she watched the dump trucks being filled. She noticed a few of the provost's store-bought daisies pulverized beneath the wheels of the trucks. The daisies in smithereens had iconic importance to her, equal in force to the shattered mirror at the Sand Bar lounge or to the heirloom oval broken into silvery sticks.

Late in the morning, April received a phone call from the dean of academic affairs, Betty Clark, herself. "We need to have a conference, April. Can you make it at three today?"

She told Betty Clark, "It's Saturday. What's so important?"

"There are issues we have to discuss. It's to our advantage to address these complaints without delay."

"Complaints from where?"

"The provost has been approached by a student, Taylor Moffett, who insists we investigate a particular incident—"

April understood that Mirhege might have seized on her difficulties with the Beautiful Boy just to add another layer of damage to her record at the college. The boy expected an E-ZPass to his degree because of his grandfather's financial power and Mirhege might have seen how to use the boy's complaint for his own campaign against April.

At Sinclair that afternoon, April sat down at a conference table with Mirhege, Betty Clark and the handsome student. Mirhege whispered to her, "The dog is still missing." She looked at him and shrugged, her mouth in a pencil line.

He handed her a folder of color Xeroxes with a picture of the Irish setter. The poster said the family was offering a $500 reward. "We've got the East Side plastered. Maybe you could go up to Federal Hill after the meeting?"

"I have to get back home to fold laundry."

Mirhege couldn't believe she wouldn't help out when his pet was still AWOL. But he said, "Thanks for coming in on your day off. We've got a ticklish situation, and we'll need your help, April."

April was surprised to see that the meeting had not been called because of the snipped harp strings.

They were talking about Milt.

Mirhege asked the boy, "Did Professor Phelps threaten you with an incomplete for the semester?"

"No, I had those incompletes already. He said he'd *fix* my grades if I'd go to Key West on spring break."

"You mean if you didn't take the vacation with him, the incomplete would remain?"

Betty Clark told April, "It will help to substantiate the complaint if the student has previously sought guidance from other faculty about the problem. That's why you're here, Miss O'Rourke."

"Wouldn't that put me at fault for not reporting it? If a student confessed this to me and I did nothing?" She would not help them destroy Milt. "Are you saying our lawyers need me in order to fire Milt?"

"April, it might do him good to take stock," Mirhege said.

"I don't think Milt's going to switch teams," she said, "even if you try to fire him."

She saw that the provost seemed pleased to have a sexual harassment complaint thrown on the table that didn't accuse him. It was a serendipitous dust storm that he hoped would defuse any accusations April might have had hurled his way

The meeting with the dean presented a prism of simmering injustices to one and all—but there would be no medical leave or Continuing Ed drudgery for her. And in turn, the provost expected to be released from any repercussions or future retribution.

April wanted to say, "So, that's the way to spell chicken, huh?" but she said, "All you need is for me to say Taylor Moffett had complained about Milt?"

"And then we can proceed," Betty Clark said.

"April, you know that student never complained to you about me," Milt said.

She touched his arm gently. "They want me to say he did. Then your ass is grass."

"They want to fire us."

"You and me?"

"Not you, April. This is a witch hunt. They want to purge queers from the faculty, any which way. It's about the budget. Everything is money to them. They're not just singling me out. They've been fighting with Charlie. He's pressing them to put his partner on his HMO, and they're going to have to eventually. It's already law in most jurisdictions, Jesus Christ. But I'm not asking for extra benefits. Not yet."

"Did you invite Taylor Moffett to go to Key West?"

"Who invited who, you mean? That kid was trying anything not to get an F."

"Milt, have you been sending me these wacko e-mails?"

"Honey, I know what you're thinking. It's not me. Riley had hangers-on. He left behind the broken-hearted. Mike Black is who you want."

This was too much information, all at once. She shook her head as if trying to release a swarm of bees. "Mike Black? He worked with Riley at Blue Fang. Is he the birthday boy in the video?"

"What video?"

"I didn't order it from Netflix, if that's what you mean."

She realized that Mike Black might have created the website for Marlboro Coffin Supply. He could have shot the Endless Pool video with Riley's floating shirt. April said, "So it was Mike Black? He came over to the house wearing Riley's T-shirt."

"He's getting therapy now. I told him to talk to you. He needs to try some kind of twelve-step Sex Addicts Anonymous program. I guess he's still working up the nerve to see you. But April, do me a favor."

"Like what?"

"Tell lover boy to drop this Taylor Moffett thing."

"Of course, I will. I'm behind you."

"If he doesn't back off, you and I go in there, together, and we talk to Betty Clark about Perv-pro.

"Kind of a three-way draw, you mean?"

"That's right. We tell Betty Clark about *him* and let her decide how the muck trickles down."

Chapter Twenty-Six

After Blaze grabbed the boots from the foot of April's bed, he tiptoed down the stairs, almost weightlessly, and crept back to the barn. He left the big trophy door propped open with a can of primer so he could listen for his father walking in his sock feet. Blaze didn't think he'd leave his mermaid before dawn.

The dogs circled his legs, whining, as if they hadn't been fed. So he had to stop what he was doing and scoop a couple mounds of Dog Chow right onto the floor when he couldn't find their bowls.

He tried to read the smudged combination written on the tongue of Townsend's right Timberland, but the ink had smeared. Worst of all, Townsend never closed off the top of the circle when he wrote a nine so it often looked like a four. The combination to the safe had three figures that could be either-or. So Blaze would have to alternate, back and forth, between both numbers until he hit it right.

He stood before the little vault. He rubbed his hands on his jeans until his palms burned. He inserted the key, and then he pinched the dial between his thumb and pointer. He turned the knob a frozen fraction, and another fraction, halting at the first number. It wasn't as simple as a bicycle lock and was even worse than the maddening combination on his high school locker which had always required several, repeat attempts. As he concentrated, he kept seeing April's gorgeous hipline as she was lying on her side in bed. Her figure, in repose, was like the woman in a velvet painting at the Hilltop Tavern.

He was disgusted with her. If his father had planked her, her prudish holier-than-thou routine was a crock! Turning the dial, he remembered the way it had felt to roll the little wheels of the Matchbox VW over her white body.

Meth hiccups made him shaky, his fingertips slippery with sweat. To calm down he went to his Dell to e-mail Lucinda. He had to convince her he didn't have an STD. Janice was trying to keep them apart. He was surprised to find mail waiting for him, but it wasn't from Lucinda. He didn't give his dad's e-mail address, sleepcreepleap@comcast.net, to just anyone. The subject line said, "Looking for Blaze." The note said:

> how ya doing Blaze? just got out. Greylock, eat me! back in Lex, now. got my own apt above my mom's garage. come on down! let's party.
>
> newty.

He was glad to know his friend was home in Lexington, despite hearing that Newty's mom still had her talons on him. One day he might go see him. Instead he wrote to Lucinda, "Pack some stuff. Not too much. I'll buy you whatever you want. We're flush." He went back to the vault and started over. He pressed his ear to the slick stainless door, hoping to hear the tumbler, like in those noir *It Takes a Thief* flicks when there's a close-up of a safecracker. In those movies, the antihero always gets lucky and walks away with the cash or with a diamond as big as a crab apple. He listened for the metallic click. He heard nothing but the roar in his ears from the white critty he'd smoked. Janice's desperate cell phone message still bothered him too.

He was getting nowhere. Then the door popped open.

Inside the cubby he found three spiral Domes, other plastic notebooks, and manila folders. The real loot was stuffed in three oversized zippered bags, like the vinyl pouches that the Dunkin' Donuts manager had used to drop off a day's receipts at the after-hour deposit box. Blaze brought all three pouches over to the plywood counter. He chose one of the purses and tugged the zipper. Blaze watched its seams peel open. It was thrilling, almost sexual. At RITS he'd learned the expression "meat wallet" when homeboys described pussy.

The bills, all hundreds, were so clean and crisp, the wad had to be dirty. Townsend had organized packets of 10,000, a hundred hundreds in each, sorting these with flat rubber bands. The money was divided into thirty separate bricks—ten blocks in each pouch—and Blaze tried to do the math, and guessing it was more than a quarter million. Blaze unsnapped the rubber bands and counted out about 4,000, peeling the hundreds from separate hunks so it wouldn't be discovered. When he put the pouches back in the vault he saw some unfamiliar certificates and bank items he wouldn't know what to do with. Some of these had Janice's name on them.

He took only the folding money.

Blaze showed up at Baxter's double-wide again. If his mom wanted a car, he would rent one from Baxter. The sun was just rising and Baxter didn't seem to know that Blaze had ever left the party with so many chalked-up believers still milling around. As Blaze unclipped the little packet of cash Baxter said, "Whoa, rain maker, where'd you get that?"

"Got lucky."

"We'll make a deal on a whole gram! Why not?"

"Don't want dope, I need a car." Blaze dolefully counted out some bursted Benjamins with reverence for his father's obsessive affection for his money.

"Which car you want?"

"Which one has air in the tires?"

Baxter told Blaze he could "rent" whatever car he wanted. "We try harder," he joked.

Blaze wanted to get on the road, but Lucinda hadn't answered his message. He refused to believe she was banging

Biggerboat and was through with him. He was pitched off his happy feet, feeling lower than he had felt for months, lower than his bad spell at Greylock. Depressed like this was a bad time to visit Janice, but when he was dejected he felt like some Janice, despite the lies she had told Lucinda. Each time he thought of going over to the A-frame, he saw Janice's silk panties sprinkled across the floor like delicious rosettes of white frosting or dollops of glossy meringue.

He might decide to see Janice or try to find Lucinda. He kept changing his mind's mind. So he wasted another whole day with Baxter.

Chapter Twenty-Seven

By late afternoon, Townsend had stopped working on the sludge pile and suddenly it was quiet. April looked out the window to see that most of the hill was gone. Townsend was at the pasture fence, huddled with his black-market dump truck drivers, handing out their pay. She watched him divvy up the cash parsimoniously with painfully dramatic flicks of his wrist, counting out large bills one at a time, as if he were pulling off his own five fingers. Happy to be paid, the men patted the horses who had thrown their heads over the fence.

Then April heard the short little chirrups of a police siren. A cruiser pulled into the drive, announcing its arrival in polite bleats, its blue lights churning over the barn.

Every time she looked out her window, something more absurd was happening.

Blaze was still unaccounted for, and she was certain that the authorities had come to collect the kid for something he had done. Two officers got out of the front seat. They walked over the muddy apron and approached the men standing with her neighbor. Some words were exchanged, then, without ceremony, an officer pulled Townsend's hands behind his back. Townsend was getting cuffed.

The police were arresting her one-nighter right before her eyes.

Townsend didn't resist. His shoulders slumped and he shifted his legs in a tight box step to regain his balance as they twisted his arms behind him. The truck drivers rubbed the horses' muzzles as if their lives depended on it, as the other cop wrote down their names. For now, the police only wanted Townsend.

April tumbled off her back steps and charged over to the cruiser. She saw Townsend sitting in back. He looked at her with a mixed-up grin, half wounded, half cynical as if he couldn't be sure she wasn't in on it.

She asked an officer where they were taking him.

"He gets booked. Then we see."

April said, "What's going on?"

"Like I said, we'll see. It's district court. We close shop at four o'clock. No night court in Westerly. The judge goes home. He's got a new bride, you know. So hearing's probably not until Monday."

After Townsend was arrested, April didn't know what to do. When her phone rang she expected to find her neighbor on the other end. It was Mirhege. He started to tell her that the setter had been found at a shelter in Woonsocket. "You don't need to worry about putting up any more posters. Everything worked out."

She didn't tell him that she'd tossed the color Xeroxes in a trash bin. His dog's whereabouts were silken worries to her. He said, "I had a meeting with Professor Phelps. You don't have to worry."

"You saw Milt?"

"It's all taken care of."

She said, "So we're square? You've got the dog. And I'm appointed chair of the department?"

"That's in the works. I promise."

"A promise? From you?"

"No, listen, I've had a change of heart, April."

"Where'd you get a heart?"

"No, I'm serious. We're on the same page."

"And the book is closed."

"Behind glass. At the athenaeum."

She had rushed off the phone when a vehicle turned into the driveway. She hoped the police had decided to return Townsend to his front door. When she looked outside she saw it wasn't a police cruiser. The prowler had returned.

She watched him climb out of the driver's seat. She didn't expect to recognize him—but she knew him. The sheet cake boy was standing there, in the flesh.

April met him on the path. "I'm Mike Black," he said. "Milt said I should come see you."

"Milt sent you? You mean the e-mails? That's you?"

"I didn't mean to scare you."

"Hell-o?"

April looked at his face. It was crumbling, the way a toddler tries not to cry when it's lost in a supermarket. He was very young. They all looked like babies to her. "You and Riley?" she said.

"We got a place together. He even brought some of his stuff over. But *you* were holding us up." He sniffed and cleared his throat. "I've still got the apartment. Now it's just a castle in the sand." He wiped his weeping nose. His eyes looked hollowed out, as if he didn't get enough sleep. So, this was him. The stalker she had feared, trying to make her heart melt.

He told her, "If Riley had told you about me, I wouldn't have felt so jealous. I mean, you and I, we're *equals*, really. I wanted to talk to you at the funeral—"

She didn't remember seeing Mike Black at the ceremony.

"The box didn't fit the hole. I couldn't believe it," he said.

Of all the images April could never dispel—the stone baby, the mitten that belonged to her father's mistress, the Playhouse Cottage rolling away, even the pink sheet cake the color of dyed carnations—it was the picture of the oversized coffin that she wanted most to forget.

Mike Black said, "When his coffin was too big, I thought Riley was making a joke about it! A last laugh. On us."

"It wasn't Riley's fault. I bought the wrong size," she said.

"Sometimes he could be so mean," the boy said. "He could have told you about me."

He looked into her eyes, begging her to side with him.

She understood that these weeks of harassment had been spawned by his bitterness. His unrequited love for Riley was one thing. Anonymity was worse. It cuts deeper, stings longer than loneliness. Loneliness stems from a togetherness that's been uprooted. For some reason Riley had not cemented the togetherness connection with Mike Black.

With all her years as a teacher, April had become used to her role as a surrogate therapist, or even as a surrogate mom. "You're right, Mike," she told the boy. "Riley should have told me about you."

Chapter Twenty-Eight

Blaze grabbed a set of car keys from a bowl by the door as he left Baxter's gymkhana. He went outside. He sat down in a beater. The keys didn't fit. He climbed into another tank, and into the next one, until he tried a relic with mismatched fenders, and the ignition cranked successfully.

When he showed up at his mom's, he saw her van in the driveway with its hood propped open. He saw its battery was gone, just like she had told him. Seeing his mom's engine block without a battery gave him an uncomfortable sensation, like seeing a cage bird with its wings clipped, or a balloon tangled in power lines.

Janice came to the door. He saw her puffy face and understood why she'd missed work. She was so beat up he hardly recognized her. She was still in her fluffy slippers. A bottle of J&B on the counter looked like she'd already gotten to most of it. She told him, "See what he did to my car? The prick. Well, come in and take a look at this." In the kitchen he saw her computer monitor had been smashed and the keyboard was in two pieces, as if John Two had snapped it in half over his knee as easily as a vanilla wafer. "He says I was flirting with one of my horse show dads. So he thinks he'll wreck my picture files—"

"Says you were flirting?"

"He always does."

"Well, were you?"

Her shoulders slumped. "Not you too?"

He leaned closer to look at her text book contusions.

"I don't want your opinion," she said. "You don't look too good yourself. You're white as a Chink whore."

He saw spaghetti sauce congealed on the kitchen curtains and corked into the screen. He saw it on the ceiling. She hadn't bothered to clean it up since she flipped a saucepan in self-defense.

She was holding the classified section in one hand. She told him, "I'm looking for an apartment."

"You want an apartment?"

"Maybe. I don't know."

"Good idea, an apartment. Dump the ass-wipe," he told her. "Get out of here. I'll help you."

"But this *Providence Journal* is old. Can you check the tube outside?"

There were at least three newspapers stuffed in the box and others tossed on the ground, still wrapped in blue plastic bags. He found the latest edition and left the others scattered.

They sat at the kitchen table. She leaned on her elbow and held her chin as he circled entries in the *Pro Jo* with a pencil, but he didn't know what to mark. The listings were repetitious; the real estate jargon spilled from one column to the next. Having had one or two hits, or however, of meth made it impossible to concentrate and he started second-guessing everything listed. But he was getting into it. He imagined setting up house with Janice. He read the descriptive details, couplets and words that seemed almost like some kind of secret code he didn't really understand. "2 bed." "Historic District." "Parking." "Hook-ups." "Bus line." "Near Hospitals." "Washer/Dryer." "Den/office." "Eat-in Kit." "No pets." "Pets okay." "First and Last req." And on the next page: "Studio." "Skylights." "Big yard." "First Floor." "Hard Floors." "Wall-to-wall." "Heat and Water." "*No* utilities." "*All* utilities." "New deck." "Section 8 Okay." "Move in NOW."

He said, "This one says 'White-Glove building.' What's that?"

"It's got a doorman or something. I can't afford that." She told him to go back through the columns to find "immediate occupancy," because she wanted to clear out as soon as possible, even better if she could get a place before John Two got home from doing overtime on second shift. Blaze found a good listing, that sounded just right, but then he started second-guessing that one and looked for something else.

"Here's a good one in Peacedale," he told her.

"Peacedale? Sounds nice," she said with bite.

"No, be serious. Maybe they can meet us after hours and show it to us. I've got the cash for your first and last. And you'll need to get a U-Haul."

She said, "You've got money?"

"Went into the safe last night," he said, unable to stifle his braggadocio.

"No shit?" She awarded him a little credit. Flattery was usually something she'd give only in dribs and drabs. "How much did you get?"

He unfolded a big clump of hundreds. Almost forty hundred-dollar bills were hard to keep rolled and shoved in his pockets, and when he was digging it out some of the cash fell at her feet.

"You can't keep that wad in your jeans, are you crazy?"

"Enough for you to leave here before that gorilla comes home."

"Us versus him," she said. She didn't sound convinced yet.

"You *have* to leave him."

He collected the scattered bills. When he looked up again, he was surprised to see waterworks. With tears streaming she said, "You'll help find an apartment for me? Really?"

"For us," he said, casting a line, to see if she'd nibble.

"Go in together?"

"Why not?"

She ripped the classified section in half and it drifted to the floor. "No, honey, I'm not your problem. And you're not mine."

"Who says?" He'd always felt he had caused his parents' divorce. As the unrivaled center of his mother's attentions, he was propelled into a world of narcissistic triumph and heady self-confidence. They had crossed a line that could never be erased, but he didn't blame her. All their opponents would have to fight them as one. If Janice had hooked up with the monster John Two because she was trying to die for their sins, Blaze was going to stop her.

Blaze pushed her into the bedroom, shoving her in front of him. She didn't resist. "Get what you need for tonight," he said.

She laughed at his man-handling. Her cynicism made her eyes well up again.

Blaze rifled through her bureau trying to find some clothes, tossing her mismatched socks, her jeans, and a shaggy sweater onto the bed. He didn't know what a woman wanted for a spontaneous one-nighter. "What's this?" he said, finding her eye mask.

"I can't sleep without it."

Okay, she might want to have her eye mask, her sleeping pills, or her feminine products. He'd let her collect these personal things herself. In her top drawer he found the little gun, wrapped in the toe of her panty hose. He plowed his whole arm into the tight sock to pull the weapon out, but it snagged the mesh. Inserting his arm into the silky tube gave him a pulsing wave low in his abdomen.

"We're getting out of here. Tonight," he said. "We'll go high style. I've got money to burn."

She sat down on the bed and crossed her arms. "You're a pawn. Wake up and smell this shit. Your dad's just using you. He let you get his money just to bribe me. He thinks I'm coming back."

He sat down beside her and grabbed her elbows. He thought he recognized a reddish palm print where John Two had grabbed her throat. "He's right. You're in danger. You're my mom."

She read his face; everything written there she had written herself. She said, "Don't look at me like that."

"You should see what I'm seeing."

"No bones broken."

"Not yet."

She wouldn't be force-fed sympathy. She leaned over and pecked his cheek, an invitation that she offered, then instantly dismissed.

Mixed messages were her strategy, her forte. He knew how to read them like a blind man with a sixth sense. He pushed her down on the coverlet and kissed her puffy lips.

"Ouch," she said and she tried to sit up.

Her moodiness wasn't new to him. Her melancholia and guilty indecision were always the preamble; she'd pretend at least once to try to douse it before the session got underway, but then she would spark. He unbuckled his belt; he kept probing her mouth with his tongue as he kicked off his pencil jeans. April and Lucinda were not in his mind. "Not worth the detour," Townsend often said, when he didn't like the movie, or when the menu at a new restaurant didn't live up to its advertising slogan. "Eat at Terranova's, where the meat falls off the bone." When Janice was in front of him, Blaze felt that all other female distractions were not worth the detour.

Believers forget their secular lives when they're welcomed back to the altar.

He fucked her. Crystal enhanced his man-child prowess, but he didn't need drugs or extra testosterone to partner him when he was with Janice. Her tenderness for him had a built-in authority that triggered his conveyor-belt reactions in a familiar *Charlie and the Chocolate Factory* production line of everything that happened next. There was no stopping it now. The headboard thumped the wall with an accelerating percussion, making a Santa's workshop racket.

Janice had second thoughts, and she bucked to free herself. "We can't do this," she said. Blaze never felt more alive or any safer *anywhere* than the way he felt when he was making love to his mother. He recognized that their exalted status was tenuous, contingent, and fleeting, but that insight only increased his potency. Janice pounded her fists against the mattress on either side of her hips, only half-heartedly. The cast-iron cat jiggled, creeping across the top shelf. Blaze didn't notice until the doorstop hit the pillow beside her head, spewing a few loose feathers. Janice shrieked at the comic close call, but again she told him to stop.

Blaze shoved the cat out of the way, smearing stove black on his mom's pretty pillow slip. He kissed her to shut her up.

Without knocking, someone crashed into the kitchen, banging the door into the pedal trash can. It rolled across the linoleum like a hollow drum. It had to be John Two home from work early. Blaze jumped to his feet with his full erection. He raked the sheets and blankets to the floor searching for his jeans in the tangled percale.

A figure stood in the doorway.

April had walked into the mural. She covered her face and froze.

"What the hell is she doing here?" Janice said.

Blaze couldn't find his clothes fast enough, embarrassed that his cock had not yet absorbed the insult.

April turned her back to them and stood like a pole. She said, "Your dad's been arrested. They took him in a cruiser. We have to go down there and get him."

Chapter Twenty-Nine

Blaze never came home. April decided to drive over to the A-frame to beg Janice to come with her to collect Townsend at the police station. April didn't want to have a one-to-one with the cops. Together they could find out what was happening.

She'd never been to the A-frame but she'd seen the Hippy Haven south of town. It wasn't hard to miss. She recognized Janice's house when she saw a structure that looked like a mini IHOP. She didn't expect to find Blaze. He'd been missing for almost two days and she thought that he must be over the state line, nuzzling with Lucinda.

Finding him in bed with Janice, April felt her throat closing up. She walked back to the kitchen. Spaghetti sauce was smeared on everything, drying in lacy crusts. She found a sponge in the sink and started scrubbing tomato goo off the window sill. She rinsed the sponge and tackled a dab of greasy glop on the wall. A sane woman would have left the premises. April couldn't stop wiping the counters. She remembered Blaze telling her, "That rag has to keep moving."

Janice followed her, cinching her bathrobe. Janice said, "What are you doing? Washing up? Leave that mess to me. You say he's with police?"

"That's right."

"They find out he cooked the books at Diggs & Snyder? Is that why they got him?"

"No clue. What do you think?"

"He'll talk his way out, nothing to worry about."

"They cuffed him and took him away. That's nothing compared to what we've got here."

Janice stared at her. "It isn't what it looks like."

April said, "Looks like *Deliverance* to me."

Janice said, "Are you some kind of wannabe bitch from DSS? What do you know about us?"

"I know you've got a son. You don't know how lucky you are."

"You don't have your own kids? So live with it."

April said, "Some people might have a medical condition." She was ready to explain her close call with her phantom baby, but she couldn't bring herself to admit it.

Janice looked surprised, as if the lid had popped off a can of fluorescent tennis balls. She tried to gauge whether April was just a busy interloper, a barren yuppie mid-lifer, or some kind of egghead lunatic she should feel sorry for.

Blaze came into the room. Pretending to take control, after he'd been seen with his pants down, he said, "Ladies, calm down. Relax." He sounded just like Townsend. And the women winced at the tragic recognition. April couldn't look at him. She lifted her chin and stared at the refrigerator magnets, not really like a spurned lover, but like a preschooler who hasn't been chosen by a hopscotch partner.

Janice told him, "She's losing it. Maybe it's that sludge you've been talking about. It's making her hallucinate, right?"

"I saw what I saw."

Blaze said, "Got a glimpse, eh? I told you it's more than *you* can handle." When his emotions were crisscrossed and confused, his meanness emerged on top.

Janice said, "We should go down to the station? But I'm not walking in there. I don't want them asking those stupid questions. 'Do you feel safe at home? Do you get hit all the time'?"

April saw Janice's puffy face. She was amazed that a woman in that condition had wanted to open her legs and that Blaze could have done it when she looked like ground hamburger. April told Janice, "It's time for you to get out of here."

"That's the plan," Blaze said, "You're slowing us down."

April said, "Where are you going?"

"Get your stuff," he told Janice.

Janice sat down in a kitchen chair. She told April, "Maybe you should go into town with him and see what's happening."

"Not leaving you here," Blaze said. He grabbed a big brown paper shopping bag that was tucked beside the refrigerator. He walked into the bedroom to gather his mom's things. He folded her sweater and placed it in the bag. On top of that, he nestled the precious door stop, believing it was important, like a coat of arms that should go with them everywhere, but it was too cumbersome and he removed it.

He grabbed the revolver from his mom's underwear drawer and nosed it into his pocket.

He came back to the kitchen and told Janice to find her coat. He told April, "We'll have to use your car. The van is dead, and my car might not be registered."

"Since when do you have a car?"

"That's a fiend-mobile you don't want to know about."

"It's what?"

"A pipe bomb on wheels. Trust me."

The three got into the Camry. Janice and Blaze were in the front seat and April sat in back. She didn't miss the absurdities unfolding. Suddenly she was one of them, they were a threesome, but she was the outsider. Her authority had evaporated and she sat like a kindergarten moppet in the back-seat of her own car. She'd never sat in the back since she'd brought it home from the dealer's.

Blaze was behind the wheel. Janice kept telling him to slow down, just as April had done the night they vandalized the harp. Janice didn't know about April's twisted bond with her son. April wanted to tell Janice about snipping the harp strings—now that's a first date worthy of chick Lit or clit Lit. April was thinking she could tell Janice, "I have my claim on him, too." Blaze had sung the chicken song for April. He wrote a poem for her: "Who will be the lover of that woman on the bench? / If she wants to hurt someone, she can use me." Of course, he could have written that poem for Janice, how would April know? All right, she thought, she could tell Janice about Townsend "losing his boots" at her house. Townsend had pursued her. He had chased the Playhouse Cottage as it disappeared up the highway. When it came to the Townsend men, April had earned her keep.

Townsend was the maestro conducting the whole production, even when he wasn't present. He was holding the baton. She hoped he'd figure out what to do about everything happening to them. She was certain he'd get the members of his tribe in hand—and she was one of the family now too.

Blaze pulled into the visitor parking at the public safety facility. In an adjoining parking space there was a big white van with official markings on the driver's door. The truck was from Clean Harbors, a hazmat environmental cleanup company. Then April recognized one of Townsend's dump truck drivers, standing outside the front doors, having a smoke. Blaze said, "Something's up. That's not just a coincidence."

"Maybe they came down here to bail him out?" April said.

"I don't know. More likely he's been pinched too. One of the drivers had bounty hunters after him."

Janice said, "Your dad knows how to pick 'em."

"He tried to get Mother Teresa, but she couldn't drive a diesel. First thing," Blaze told Janice, "go in there and report that John Two stole your battery."

"I'm not doing that."

"Tell them he stole it. That's not just vandalism, that's larceny."

"You would know."

"They'll go after him when it's about a vehicle."

Janice sank deeper into her seat, pushing her sun glasses up the bridge of her nose. "So you go in there, not me."

With a long history of local law enforcement busybodies dropping by, they weren't happy to walk into the police station; they were paralyzed. April agreed to be the go-between. She jumped out and walked up to the dump truck driver. "What's happening?"

"They picked us up at the Hilltop. Kyle's in there now. They want us to tell our separate stories, not be in there together."

"They arrested you too?"

"We're not booked. But Townsend's made a mess of it. He told us it was okay. I didn't think so, but he said we had permission."

"Permission for what?"

"To off-load in Dobyns Quarry."

"You dumped that sludge in the quarry?"

"Fifteen loads. Not in the quarry, exactly, but there's a spillway right there. A ravine where they toss old refrigerators. We told him that there might be some kind of 'Safe Harbors' type problem with Dobyns Quarry. The quarry's fed with spring water. That's conservation land. It might be a federal thing, you know?"

An officer came out to round up the driver. April asked him, "Can I see Holt Townsend?"

"He's in there with counsel. Not a good time. Hearing's

next week. But we've got feds to deal with. Fines, paperwork, red tape like you never saw. And there's townspeople already calling with complaints. Their nature trail is out there at Dobyns Quarry. Your pal's in for a tar bath."

She walked into the station. At the security desk, she had to speak to an officer through a reinforced speaker hole in the bullet proof Plexiglas. "I need to see Holt Townsend, is that okay?"

The officer told her that she'd have to wait until after the police interview.

She nodded, but just the same, she started down the hallway to find Townsend. The cop picked up his telephone.

She tried a few doors until she found him at a conference table with a uniform and two suits. April recognized that one of the men had been Townsend's lawyer at the closing for her house. The other stranger was talking like some kind of hazmat preacher or EPA Nazi. His shoes weren't even muddy so he probably hadn't been down to the quarry to inspect the sludge himself. He was some kind of top-brass official. She recognized his face from other disciplinarians she'd known. Her high school's assistant principal had always worn an unrelenting expression. A uni-brow above his eyes made him look like he wore two frowns. Townsend stood up when she came into the room, happy to see her. He told her, "As a kid I learned a lesson, but I guess I forgot. Taking a short cut through a bumpy pasture, you can lose your muffler."

"Taking a short cut?"

"Boils down to it," he said.

She understood that he'd dumped the sludge into his own lap, so to speak. But he'd done it because she had asked him to move the pile. He didn't seem to hold it against her. She said, "I can give you a ride home. Will this take long?"

The real estate lawyer told her, "It's pick-up sticks. Just some paperwork. But he'll get back tonight."

She said, "Okay, I'll wait."

The lawyer said, "Sit down. Won't be a minute."

The officer said, "Don't be so sure. This isn't so simple."

The hazmat official said, "We're here to ascertain if there's been a federal violation."

The lawyer told Townsend, "Judge won't hand it over to feds. He'll whack you with community service. Put you out on the road in a yellow vest for everyone to see. That's what people want."

The cop said, "We've already heard from Ducks Unlimited and the American Littoral Society. They e-mailed some expectations."

"So we make a donation, too," the lawyer said.

As the hazmat guru was filling out forms, he explained a history of bad deeds by the likes of people like Townsend. He told them about the Ivory Coast disaster, where people had died and hundreds had fallen sick from toxic sludge dumped illegally. In Umbria, an Italian farmer had purchased "fertilizer" to spread on his fields. After the first hard rain, the run off seeped into the creeks. The ponds went black. Fish started to float. The farmer said, "I see my land dying before my eyes." Then, there were the Frank sisters. Susan Frank, a New York City port official, and her sister had contracted family-owned barge companies to dump sewage sludge at a federal dumping site, a hundred miles out to sea. But to save costs, the sisters encouraged their kin to dump the sewage in New York Harbor and had fouled local waters. "These are just a few stories that got some attention. I guess you didn't read about them?"

April remembered her suspect headaches, but if she was taking sides, it wasn't for her neighbor that she felt indignation. Government lackeys were more condemnable. The hazmat official was straight out of a Gogol story and listening to his officious babble refurbished her intolerance.

"I'm just a small operation," Townsend was saying. "I wasn't thinking, long-term, about the quarry. So I'll pay any fines. Tomorrow I'll get the boys to come back to clean it up."

"If it's a hazmat violation, if its toxic materials, then *we* do the cleanup."

April said, "So are you through with him?"

Townsend said, "There's a lot of red tape. You'd think I was buying a car."

The lawyer said, "Yeah, just make sure it's a flex-fuel or hybrid model to please Mr. Green Jeans here."

Townsend told April, "I'll get a ride. Don't wait around."

Chapter Thirty

Blaze drove the women back to the Greek Revival.

"Are we here?" Janice said, with rising alarm, as she looked out the car window. She was being returned to the house she had escaped from the previous year, but at least it wasn't her current hell-hole.

Blaze took the shopping bag of her overnight clothes and steered Janice inside. April went around turning on lamps. She flicked each knob or pulled a little chain and the light bulbs bloomed with a rosy light. April always bought expensive soft-pink bulbs that gave everything a yummy glow. The house was throbbing with warmth. In the kitchen, Blaze ran the tap, filling her coffee carafe with water to make a new pot. Janice had come into the parlor, plopping down in April's van der Rohe Barcelona chair. Janice didn't know that the chair was a treasured specimen prized by the finest collectors. It looked beat up to her, but she pulled her shoes off and tucked her feet under her.

Janice said, "Tell him I don't want coffee."

"Do you want tea? I've got Irish breakfast or Celestial Seasonings?" April was feeling a giddy surge with her sudden hostess responsibilities. Hearing Blaze banging kitchen drawers in search of spoons, and Janice saying, "Uh-oh, he's going to rearrange your cupboards and you'll never find anything," the place seemed to come alive.

She had a houseful now.

"Tea or coffee?" she asked Janice again.

Janice said, "That's going in the wrong direction."

"O-hhh," April said, "well, I've got something else."

"I'll take lots of something else. What's in stock?"

April opened a sideboard and showed Janice the fancy bottles. Janice said, "Got J&B? Nope? Okay, give me that Dewar's, then."

"That Dewar's will *do* her," Blaze warned, leaning out from the kitchen.

April handed Janice the bottle and went to get a glass. Blaze came back with coffee for himself and for April, and the three of them sat in the living room.

They tried to pretend April hadn't barged in on them at the A-frame. Janice had seemed so tiny at that instant, like a child herself, centered on the overstuffed mattress, her hair fanned across the pillow. April had felt a wave of sympathy for her, remembering Janice's story about finding her mother frozen in the pile of blue snow. These blue wavelengths were somehow the cause and effect behind everything that might have happened to Janice. And they'd infected Blaze. The odd phenomenon spilled across April, too.

Janice said, "Second shift gets off at ten-thirty. I'm not there, he'll put it together."

April asked, "Your pipe fitter?

Janice said, "My what?"

"John Two, you mean?" April said.

Janice shot Blaze a look. Since when did everyone keep a numerical accounting or know how many men she went through?

April didn't like the idea that John Two might show up.

"Stay away from the windows," Blaze said. "Maybe turn off all these fucking lights. Christ."

April never thought she'd be asked to have black-out curtains for somebody else's problems.

Blaze said, "We'll handle it."

With so many hostile intrusions, between the provost, the police, and her stalker, April hadn't factored in the beefy boyfriend. Trying to keep it upbeat, she continued her Betty Crocker routine. She didn't recite Betty's motto "Once a week, a meat loaf in every oven," but said, "I've got cookies, do you want some?"

"I've taken a vow. No Pepperidge Farm," Janice said.

"Yeah," April said. "Me too."

Blaze went into the kitchen and came back with a carton. He stacked a tower of cookies on both his knees, and the women watched him pop them in his mouth, one by one.

"Kids," Janice said, "can do what they want."

"Yeah, but we have to watch the carbs," April said, choosing to align with Janice, at least on this one account, but Janice didn't keep it going.

After refilling her glass more than once, Janice said, "I think I've got a headache. Do you mind if I lie down?"

April was surprised to see Janice get up from her chair and go to the stairs. She took her shopping bag of clothes, with her eye mask, and climbed to her old bedroom without any hesitation.

From the landing Janice called to April, "Got any Advil?"

"It's in the bedside table," April said. "Or in the medicine cabinet." But April was frozen in her tracks. Janice seemed to be settling in for the night as if this were a bed and breakfast.

Waiting at the bottom of the stairs, she heard Janice go into the bathroom to pee. She didn't even close the door. It wasn't the same tasteless affront as when April's father had left the door open, parading his wares. Then she listened as Janice climbed into April's own four-poster, hearing the intimately familiar way its bed springs creaked. Janice called down to them, "Shit, there's no room for me with all these fancy shams she's got. You poor girl. 'Satin sheets to lie on, satin pillows to cry on.' Remember that one, Blaze?"

Blaze came up beside April. "Don't mind her. It's good if she gets some sleep. She's a sweetheart in the morning when she wakes up."

"I guess so," April said, but she had trouble imagining her caustic houseguest in a sunny mood.

"She'll go right out," Blaze said.

"Okay. What do we do with you?"

"And you."

April heard a shift in his voice. The man-child, half lost, half found, was back in practice. It was the never-ending predicament she had heretofore prized.

She had Blaze to herself. She would have to think fast.

He stretched out on the fainting couch, his head in her lap. He looked up at her face and told her, "That tiny little horse I brought you, its name was Goliath."

"No kidding?"

"Since when do I kid you?"

"You're never not doing it. But that's a big name for a little horse—"

"You like big, don't you?"

She shifted her legs, shoved him, to warn him off that barstool banter. "So are you moving out of the barn, going back to your mom?"

"She's the one who moved back."

They heard a car enter the gravel drive. In a moment, the kitchen door rattled as someone entered without knocking. Blaze jumped to his feet, ready to confront the pipe fitter, but Townsend popped his head into the living room.

"They let you off?" April said.

"Chinese fire drill," he said, his summary of anything over-the-top stupid, and especially when describing the bumbledom of law enforcement.

Blaze said, "They pin you on a Superfund site violation or because you hired those nitwit parolees?"

"Hearing's next Tuesday. Have to pay a fine. Fifteen hundred max, they tell me."

"Could have been worse," April said. "Are they just being nice to you?"

"They have to support any idiot stupid enough to start a new business in town," Townsend said.

"Then they must love you," Blaze said.

April began to talk a mile a minute, almost spilling that Janice had come down to the station with them. Blaze interrupted her. He told Townsend, "We should feed the horses. The dogs need to go out." April realized that Townsend had not been updated about the stolen battery, and if Janice's van wasn't outside, of course Townsend had no idea Janice was in bed upstairs. Blaze didn't want him to know.

Blaze said, "I'll feed the horses. You better take care of the dogs before they get into the sack of Chow."

"You left that bag on the floor? It's not stowed in the Tuffy?"

"I guess I forgot," Blaze said.

April imagined the dogs going wild, tearing up the house. She said, "Better hurry. Can I come? I'll help."

Townsend said, "You want to feed the critters? Okay. You two take care of the horses and then we'll go to the Sand Bar."

"Where that mirror exploded?"

"You have to overcome your superstitions." He crushed her in his bear hug. He hadn't changed his clothes since moving the pile of sludge. She could smell the dank soup soaked into his pants cuffs. With Townsend's arms around her, she remembered the warmth she had felt in her lap, where Blaze had rested his head. She had to choose. Choose now.

They went outside. Townsend entered the barn to feed the dogs, and Blaze pulled April by the elbow and took her to an outbuilding. He flicked on the overhead light. Bales of hay were stacked shoulder high, but he brought her over to a massive bin filled to the brim with molasses sweet-feed. Its startling perfume overwhelmed her. Slightly fermented, it smelled like brandy-soaked fruitcake.

"Go ahead, try some," he told her.

She said, "No, thank you. I'm not a horse."

"The horses eat better than I do," he told her. He pinched a smidgeon of the candied horse feed between his fingers and held it before her lips.

He waited.

She nibbled the morsel just to please him and spit it right out. She rubbed her tongue with the back of her hand. If Blaze was trying to indoctrinate her in some kind of voodoo, she'd have to put a stop to it. She told him, "So you aren't going to tell him about Janice?"

"What do I tell him about *you*?" he said. He wanted her to make a pledge to him.

She said, "Don't imagine there's something to tell. Get that out of your head." She was thinking that the last thing Blaze needed was to hop from mommy to mommy. He should get out of East Westerly as fast as he could.

"Hand me that bucket," he said.

She gave him the bucket and watched him scoop sweet feed for the two horses.

He rationed it out to the horses, and then they met Townsend in the driveway.

As Blaze walked up, Townsend saw him looking over at April's bedroom window, just a stolen look, yet Townsend recognized his son's body language. Blaze walked with a hip-locked gait, not a swagger exactly, but his secret was on the surface, plain as day. Townsend said, "What's going on? Is Janice at the house?"

Janice wasn't peeking through the curtain, staring down at them, but she might as well have been.

Townsend said, "What's she doing here?"

Blaze said, "She finally left that fuck."

Townsend straightened up, trying to contain himself. He was bouncing on the balls of his feet like a can of spring snakes had popped open in his spinal column. "You mean she's come home?"

Blaze said, "Just here overnight. We're getting an apartment."

Townsend turned to April. "Are you running a hippie hostel or something?" Townsend was surprisingly charged up. He'd always wanted Janice to return to him, but he didn't want her deciding *when and how*. Mostly, he didn't want Blaze to be acting like Lancelot. Townsend should be the white knight. And he didn't like to think April was taking sides with Blaze, assuming her role as handmaiden to him.

He started toward the farmhouse.

Blaze blocked him, side-stepping in sync with him. "Leave it alone," Blaze said. "It's chill."

"Get out of the way."

They started swinging at one another, and it looked like a repeat of the Bobcat confrontation, when John Two went crazy. Blaze shouldered into Townsend, knocking him off balance. Townsend fell backwards onto April's stoop where he sat for an instant like a dazed shopping-mall Santa. He stood up. He told Blaze, "You think she's *your* problem? That's where it goes south. You idiot."

"Get the fuck out of here," Blaze said.

"Haven't you had enough, yet?"

Blaze didn't say.

"Mister 'First and Last Chance.' Mister 'One and Only.' Okay." Townsend turned to April. "Let's go."

Blaze saw what was happening. His father was backing off about Janice because he had April in his pocket. April had moved behind his dad, wrapping her arms around his waist. She peeked over Townsend's shoulder, watching Blaze, the way women look at something that makes them squeamish— road kill, an airsickness bag, a spider's web. His chances with April had been ruined when she walked into the A-frame unannounced and saw him with Janice. Janice capsized all his relationships. She'd blue-screened Lucinda, lying about STDs. He even thought of the girls he didn't want. It didn't matter which one. Janice tasered him from afar.

Townsend told him, "Hell. Why don't you come with us? We'll order some nachos or a pizza." The Sand Bar offered bottomless Cokes like at the Hilltop, and he tried to bribe Blaze with a meal. Since his son had become his rival, Townsend liked to picture him in a kiddie bib. "It's got that all you can eat menu. Come on, let's get dinner."

"I don't want sloppy seconds," Blaze said. He turned his back and walked away into the dark.

Chapter Thirty-One

Blaze listens to Townsend's truck accelerate down the road. He enters the house and climbs the stairs to the bedroom, like so many times before when he brought Janice her Rolling Rock stubbies. But his legs are rubbery and don't belong to him now.

April has made her decision. Blaze has to admire his dad's finesse, but he should have known not to trust the neighbor. On April's desk he notices a stack of her school papers, and resting on top are his own pages. The love poems he gave her. She had marked the stanzas with a red pen, with some brackets and a couple crossed-out lines.

He stands at the foot of April's bed, a mammoth Restoration Hardware reproduction, with an overstuffed mattress, quilts and pillows stacked high, like the towering four-poster in "The Princess and the Pea." Janice is wearing a pink T-shirt from a 5 K run for breast cancer. She never volunteered for women's causes, and the jersey is just a freebie. She's had no trouble falling asleep. Her mouth has dropped open and he gently tugs her chin up with one finger to close her lips. She swallows once but doesn't wake up. He remembers a scene in the original 1933 King Kong movie when the ape checks to see if his nemesis, the T-rex, is really dead. Kong scissors the monster's pointy snout open and shut, testing its jaws, to make sure its chops are fatally broken.

He's thinking that Janice is the nexus of his unclaimed urges and units of perversity, the Aprils, the Lucindas, the plague of honeyed contagions that were spawned by the throbbing queen.

He could put a pillow over her face.

Seeing Janice asleep in April's collection of fluffy squares and shams, with piping along the edges, rattles him. His English teacher once recited a poem about death: "In my beginning I got up from a bed in which I did not lie down, and in my end I will lie down in a bed from which I will never get up." He thinks of all the fortunes he won before childhood had a vanishing point. The cake batter spoons. The brindle puppy. The scrolling Christmas lights that advanced from twinkle, to flash, to chase! He thought of the motherless baby lambs that he fed with a bottle each spring. They imprinted on him, not as their master but as one of them.

He crawls onto the fluffy pallet beside his mom, and spoons her.

His forty-eight-hour jitters have started to subside. He closes his eyes. He's falling asleep in wide circles, winding down, the way a dreidel wobbles before it tips over.

Familiar nested scenes unfold; then his nightmares shift to sweet dreams about Baxter's little girl and the kelly-green tortoise.

John Two grabs his forelock and pulls him out of bed, ripping the roots of his hair.

Blaze yelps, fingering the torn patch at his widow's peak.

In an instant, Janice wakes up. She climbs onto John Two, clinging like a papoose. She screams at him, "Don't hit Blaze. Don't hurt him! I'll come home—"

The pipe fitter elbows her and she falls on her tailbone. "You. Sick. Slice," he tells Janice, disgusted with her and amused at himself.

She springs up again. She grabs a heavy text from April's writing table, an infinite tome or dictionary, a doorstop in and of itself, in which April has underlined entire sections.

She wallops John Two. The book only glances the rind of his skull, and he bats her away. He isn't fazed by her and he's able to maintain his low level of conscious thought. He stands with his feet splayed, but he isn't giving up. He stalks Blaze around the foot of the bed.

Blaze pulls the revolver from his tight jeans, spilling his pinch of hot cash. John Two seems delighted to see the crumpled hundreds.

Blaze levels the gun at the pipe fitter, where the man's paunch protrudes, square as a box.

"Look at you," John Two says. "Mr. Big Stuff."

It doesn't go by Blaze that both the older men in his life

had used a similar honorific to address him, and it wasn't out of respect. He shows the gun to John Two, waving it back and forth in his face. "See? Carry it anywhere," Blaze says.

"Yeah, right. Armed and dangerously fucked up."

Blaze has to laugh.

Janice tells him, "Don't point that at anyone."

Blaze steadies the gun, balancing the grip on his other fist.

"Aren't you important," John Two says.

Janice tells Blaze, "Is that uncocked? You're scaring me, now."

"Fuck him," Blaze says.

He sees that Janice, too, is backing away, using delicate heel-to-toe reversed steps. Suddenly his little cage of paradise unlatches, abandoning him to his own resorts. Unconscious damages stack up: his Marlibubarbies and Little Hens, the *All Smiles* at the bottom of Chapman Pond, his libido animalis, un-tethered and alone.

The little revolver has a recoil. Rod and Gun Club weekenders complain that the model has a wobble—it doesn't hold steady. Blaze shoots and hits the wainscoting behind her legs, splintering the wood. Janice shrieks like the noisemaker in a Happy Bomb firecracker. He fires again into the fortress of goose-feather pillows on the floor beside John Two. The pipe fitter pogos to the bedroom door, pivots, and ducks away, taking the stairs.

It's snowing specks of down when Blaze tells Janice, "Okay, he's gone. You don't have to go with him."

He tosses the gun on the bed.

She reaches for the revolver. She points it at him. She says, "I've got three more rounds, you know. Baby, get out of here."

"I won't," he says, "without you."

Janice says, "Leave now. Don't let them get to say we killed each other."

"We're getting an apartment, aren't we?" he says.

"Look. This shit has to stop. We have to move on."

"What about the two-bedroom in Peacedale?"

She tucks the gun under the hem of her T-shirt, aiming its icy nozzle against her breast.

A red mist peppers the wall.

Blaze sees her pink jersey instantly drenched. She crumples to her knees, her spine still straight, the way a demolished building pancakes floor by floor without tipping over.

He runs to her side and she flops into his arms, her head falling back on her shoulders. He's surprised to see such a dreamy look on her face—the same way she shuts her eyes and smiles when he washes her hair. He tries to help Janice onto the bed, but she stands on her own, tipping backwards. She tells him, "Get off me. I'm doing it myself."

She sits on the edge of the mattress. She gathers her bloody shirt to look at the pulsing entrance wound, high above her belly button. Blaze kneels down beside the bed. She drops the hem of her shirt, protecting him.

He tells her, "I'm calling nine-one-one." He spins around, but April's phone is missing. When he yanks open the bedside drawer the little flower car spills to the floor. He flies down the vertical stairs to the kitchen in one furious leap, sliding on the throw rug at the bottom. In the kitchen, he punches three numbers and tells them to come. The operator says, "The computer lists two residences?"

"It's the white house next to the barn. The Greek Revival."

"It's a-what?" The operator asks him to slow down. She tells him to repeat the address.

"The place with all its fucking lights on."

He returns to April's bedroom. Janice is curled on her side on the bed, cooing sugary groans and griping. "Never saw so many pillows," she says, and "Don't like this busy wallpaper. Do you?" She's sputtering, she's coughing. She twists with dagger-pains, pulls her knees to her chin then scissors her legs out straight again. She paws with her arms, with stuporous, primitive reflexes. Blaze doesn't know what to do. He doesn't recognize the near-death posturing, when someone's extremities try to crawl away on their own from the death throes of the victim.

He drags her onto his lap, her lovely body suddenly quiet. She seems more weightless each second, more fragile, her pale skin as translucent as the sylph decal on a vintage beer bottle. Bright dahlias and vines creep across the bed sheets. He cradles his mom in their red garden until he hears sirens.

Moonlight falls over him, a white rectangle, from the little window in the roof. His scalp still throbs where it was gouged.

He thinks of his friend's garage apartment where he can hole up, and he remembers Newty's rhyme, "I one my mother. I two my mother. . . ."

Wet, red florets bloomed on the top sheet, her body still warm when he left her.

He doesn't wait to insert the fuse under the dash, and he's driving without any lights. He pulls onto the road as EMS turns in, almost clipping him, and laying on the horn. They're too late. He drives in the dark through the hamlet of East Westerly. He stops at the Mobil Mart. He finds the needle-nose pliers and leans under the steering wheel. He centers the silver fuse. Its bitty teeth sink tight. The lamps bloom until every wicked thing is in high definition.

He jumps out of the car to fill the tank. As the numbers are flipping, he shoves Janice's revolver into a trash basket beside the pump. He removes the nozzle from the Camry and inserts it into the trash hopper. He keeps it spurting until he's pumped almost a gallon. The basket leaks, fumes are drifting, but the other stalls are empty. The cashier inside is clueless, reading a fanzine at the counter. Blaze shoves the nozzle back on its hook.

He gets behind the wheel and circles to the other side. He lights a Kool, inhales its icy flavor, and flicks it into the soaked trash container. He floors it.

The barrel drum shoots up and explodes. Pieces of burning trash catch along the awning making a tent of flames. Even the paper towel holder ignites. The bouncing can sprays gasoline across the macadam, a carpet of fire, little fingers crawling to the curb. But he's already down the road, one mile, then two.

In the sky, the moon bullies the stars and satellites. A full moon means nothing to a boy with no mother.

Chapter Thirty-Two

Two long tables were dressed with billowing white cloths in April's back garden. In late July, the tea roses were in second bloom. Townsend had sheared the privet hedges, squaring the crown and corners, using a spirit level, making architecturally perfect monoliths. For a formal picnic, April had brought out the china, real flatware, and her crystal wine flutes. Her old-fashioned ice cream social had escalated to a glorious affair. Townsend had bought her an automatic ice cream freezer and for the past week they had worked together making home-made batches from scratch. Peeling peaches, pulping fruit, mashing blueberries, they created different sorbets and rich full-butter fat flavors that they decanted into tubs and stacked in the freezer.

April had invited many of her colleagues from Sinclair. She didn't include Mirhege, although he had fast-tracked her application for the chairmanship position, trying to smooth things over. She looked forward to beginning her administrative duties. Along with her teaching responsibilities, she'd have office hours at Sinclair from nine to five. The work would be good. Milt arrived with his current boyfriend, whom he had met at a ballad bar, and the two were moving in together. She had also invited Mike Black after meeting with his therapist. The doctor had told April how Mike had improved after confessing to her. April made a special attempt to give Mike a tour of her perennial beds, careful to recite the flowers' names in Latin, but she couldn't resist repeating, "Don't you just love it that this one's named bee balm, and that one's called bugbane?"

Townsend had included a few of his pals from the Hilltop. One geezer showed up dandified in a seersucker suit. Townsend had also invited some customers he'd grown to like, or from whom he wanted further business. April's birthday bash was a big success. Townsend was her co-host, happy that April had graduated to the Leap stage with him. He toasted her, with mock formality, when she cut the birthday cake. She was forty, at last. She decided to have a laugh about it.

That morning she had visited Blaze at the ACI.

After Blaze had transformed the Mobil Mart into a drive-through barbeque pit, the state had tried him on an arson charge and convicted him as an adult. He was sentenced to five years. Seventeen-year-olds were no longer held at the youth facility. With a deficit in Rhode Island's budget, holding seventeen-year-olds among the general prison population saved the state the money it costs to keep pampering them at RITS. Ten other states tried kids under eighteen as adults;

in Connecticut they're just sixteen. Blaze turned seventeen in June. Left uncuffed after his hearing at the courthouse, he had escaped from a transport van, and from there Blaze graduated to belly chains.

To get on his visitor list, April had had to be cleared by a process of red tape called a CORI report which proved she was a reputable college professor with no criminal record. They asked for her social security number and made a Xerox of her driver's license. The visitor form asked if she was a friend or a family member.

At the kiosk that morning, a corrections officer had said, "You his mom? No? You his *step*mom?"

"I'm on his list, aren't I?" she said. "So what's the problem?" She didn't want to be reminded she had no blood ties to anyone. Ever since that night, whenever she thought of him, she remembered how he had fed her a pinch of sweet feed, as if in some kind of pagan rite.

"Not related?" The CO looked at her. Women friends. He'd seen all shapes and sizes, and often-times these gals were rivals. Cat fights erupt in the waiting room, when ladies arrive all at once to see the same boyfriend. First they had to take off all their rings and jewelry, even their earrings. They stored their pocketbooks, cell phones, and outer layers of clothing in a locker. It cost a quarter to get the key. They had to remember not to wear an under wire bra, because it set off the alarm when they got wanded by security. Visiting hours were only one hour, twice a week. Women had to sort out who gets to be first to go into the cubicle. It's a constantly edgy hierarchy. The corrections officer thought that April might be a headache like that. He'd have to make a note about it. Then he saw that Blaze had no other females on his list.

"Next-door neighbor," she had said.

April was faithful and visited twice a week. Townsend sometimes came along, but he can't stand seeing his son locked up. "When he sees it's bad for me, it makes it worse for Blaze," he told her.

"He wants you to come," she said.

Townsend blamed himself. Blaze always tells him, "It's a bummer if you bring that in here."

April was sunny. She picked up the telephone receiver, wiping the mouthpiece with her sleeve, and said "How you doing Blaze? You look really good!"

Blaze has one hour a day to lift weights. He'd increased his repetitions and his strength improved. His biceps were hard apples, his chest was broad. He wasn't surprised to see that some of the equipment was embossed YORK BARBELL. There's nothing much to do in jail but bulk up. A girl came twice a week to teach a creative writing class. In another six weeks he'd take his GED exam. He had his everyday problems when he's ripped into and befouled.

Repetitions.

Judge Welsh used to say, "Pretty boys are fish food." Blaze survived by inventing self-esteem loop-holes with each assault on him.

He waited for April's visits. She pours forth, for an hour of pure chatter, like a spring rain on the tin roof of the barn.

After Janice was discovered in April's four-poster, police traipsed through the house and bedroom to complete their report. They took photographs of blood spatters, and collected slivers of wood from the damaged wainscoting. They apologized for rifling through April's bureau. Before it was discerned that the death was a suicide, a TV news spot had prematurely announced that the event in East Westerly might be the result of a "love triangle," with a local man at the center of an escalating battle between his ex-wife and April. The women had been seen arguing at a local tavern, just the day before.

April remembered when Janice had ranted about such gossip, and had rambled on about a witch getting crucified for spreading rumors. The DA's office concurred that the victim had taken her own life and issued an official press release.

Townsend invited April to stay with him in the barn while police were in her house. April spent a few nights, although he hardly talked. She felt lopped off, like an extra pillar within his tattered acropolis. He had loved Janice. April was his second choice, but she understood that he'd suffer with that distinction more than she would.

The police had finished their procedures at the Greek Revival and April thought she could go home, when a white panel truck arrived. The truck said AFTERMATH INC.

It was a cleaning service often used by police departments and social services to sanitize dwellings after unattended deaths. They also serviced homes that had been occupied by filthy hoarders, or vacated after toxic meth lab operations. The specialists told April she was still banished while workers used their Shop-Vac and steam cleaners.

The Playhouse Cottage had been transformed. Centered on a little knoll above Narragansett Bay in Jamestown, the chapel was secured on a poured foundation, with appropriate landscaping, common lilacs and frothy viburnum, and it was safely intact in its vaulted domain. It had been re-shingled with white cedar top to bottom, its white trim freshened, and its front door was painted marigold yellow. To their surprise, the cottage was christened as the new offices for the Jamestown Chamber of Commerce and Visitors' Center.

April's Camry had been impounded after Blaze dumped it, so Milt was driving. He parked the car and walked April into the cottage. A gray-haired volunteer sat at a desk and she welcomed them as if they were her long-lost children. She offered candy from a milk glass bowl, telling them that the sweets were made by a local chocolatier. April accepted a piece. The chocolate tasted slightly metallic or tinny.

Aerial photographs and reproductions of antique maps depicted the beautiful coastlines, out-croppings, and clusters of islands sprinkled across Rhode Island waters that give the state its storied name. Racks of tourist brochures and real estate fliers were everything you'd expect to see in a resort town's visitors' den.

The little shrine hadn't changed very much. April remembered the exact corner where their honeymoon bed had been shoved against the wall, and she knew exactly where the kitchen table had hugged the sunny bow window. An antique corner cabinet had not been removed. It was now used to display seasonal and municipal bric-a-brac instead of the stacks of rosy willow-ware china that April had once adored. She easily pictured the pattern, but Riley's face didn't materialize. She no longer felt so haunted by his oversized coffin. April had accompanied Townsend to Janice's funeral, and her simple pine box, with weepy knot holes, was fresh in her mind. April was pleased to see that the Playhouse shrine was being maintained, despite its secular purposes. It was never again to be a haven for new lovers or newlyweds. That claim was hers alone. Townsend had promised her a weekend at the Cuddle and Bubble. He was making a joke, but waited to see if she liked the idea.

"Okay, I've seen enough," she told Milt.

"Ready to go?"

"And we never have to come back. I promise."

AFTERMATH INC. had scrubbed her woodwork and floors, but her mattress had been ruined. April ordered a new Beautyrest from an outlet called Sleepy's that guaranteed same-day delivery. From her bedroom window, she watched the delivery men loading the stained mattress onto their truck. Free mattress removal was part of the deal. As the truck drove away, she looked over to the pasture fields. The sky was busy with turkey vultures swinging in wide circles, a common sight. The Audubon's annual Christmas Count was proof that vultures were doing fine, coming back to southern New England after a couple of decades when their population was thin. She was surprised to see so many of the gawky free-loaders.

In the field, the white-faced horse was down.

She had often seen the horse named Jack resting at midday. Townsend had told her a three-legged horse needed to take it easy. Horses usually nap with their heads up. The freak horse was dead-still, its body stretched out on its side, cheek to the earth, its legs stiff.

The vultures rode the air drafts, their circles sinking closer. The vision was heartbreaking, but April had invented it.

The horse stood up, shaking its withers.

Chapter Thirty-Three

Blaze thinks of Janice, scene by scene.

He likes to remember when Janice took him fishing in Townsend's classic Tyee rowboat. Blaze had friends who had let him borrow their Seadoos and WaveRunner jet skis, but Janice complained that they were gas guzzling and made a racket. The *All Smiles* was whisper quiet. The sun was shining, on the first really warm afternoon of the season. Janice brought a pleated umbrella and a picnic basket with ham sandwiches, wedges of lemon sponge cake, and for him, a party- size bag of chips. She made him lug a plastic bottle of fresh-brewed sun tea. That week a social worker had come for a home visit and had suggested that Janice do something special with Blaze. Janice had the idea to take the dinghy and go jigging for trout. In the late spring, the water was still cold and the fish were slow, when they schooled just six to twelve inches off the pond floor. Hopping the jig along the bottom, using a light action rod, was the best way to catch them.

Janice was business when she was jigging. But this time she had dressed in girly clothes. She wore a tank top and a short ruffled skirt. Her pleated umbrella reminded him of a Victorian PBS mini-series where men are supposed to be gallant and take the oars. Not only did Blaze have to do all the rowing, but she asked him to tip her jig with a crawler leech or dead minnow each time she brought it up again, although Janice had never before been squeamish. She had always baited her own hooks. Until then.

They had a couple speckled togues in their bucket and had been jigging for an hour when Janice put down her rod, tucking it under the bench. She climbed over to sit down on the floor boards of the dinghy, leaning back against his legs. As she rested her head against his bent knees, he kept his rod bumping. She said, "Isn't this nice?"

He said, "Only if you're going to do it the way I like."

"You know I will." She squeezed his ankle.

"I mean under the broiler. With lemon and mustard."

"Oh, is that what you mean?"

He shifted his legs. "You're kind of messing me up," he said as he jigged his line again.

"Do you think so? I messed you up? It takes two, you know."

He recognized her shift in tone was dangerous. He had already worried about her ulterior plans when, before they shoved off, she had made him carry an old blanket, a shabby relic from the house. Its ripped hem dragged after him like a ratty umbilical line until she told him, "Right here." He unrolled the blanket on the grassy bank to let it warm up in the sun.

When he didn't answer now, she tipped her head back in his lap and looked at him. She was pretty, he thought, even when her face was upside down. She started to peel down her Lycra tube top. She liked to soak up rays bare-breasted.

He said, "Don't do that, okay? Do you mind?"

"I guess you want me to pay for a tanning salon? Out here, it's still free," she said. "Last I heard." She covered herself again.

Even so, he stowed his fishing rod, and started rowing. "We're going in," he told her.

"We haven't had lunch," she said, sitting straight up.

"Not hungry." He hurled the picnic basket over the gunwale, strewing sandwiches and pieces of lemon cake.

He dropped the jug of tea over the side and watched it sink, shoot up again, roll over, and float away like a buoy.

"Jesus! Are you crazy? You're wasting our lunch." She stood up and tried to reach for the basket, but the boat rocked with her weight.

"Sit down," he said. "You'll tip us."

She leaned over the side, paddling her arms to get the basket. She leaned far out, balancing on just her hip bones. She acted theatrical and stupid, on purpose, until the little boat popped over, throwing them into the pond.

Blaze surfaced and looked for Janice. She was treading water, laughing like a teenager. The trout were lost, but their bucket was bobbing nearby. The rowboat floated face down.

When Blaze tried to flip it back onto its keel, it was difficult to budge, as if he were fighting a gasket seal that glued it to the surface. And with its solid oak ribs and fir thwarts, it was much heavier than fiberglass models. Again he tried to right it, but it was like an overturned bathtub. Its bow started to dip.

Janice made it worse. "Snapping turtle!" she shrieked when she saw something in the reeds. She swam to the boat and tried to climb on board its overturned hull.

"It's going to sink!" he screamed at her. She was frantic and pulled herself out of the water. Under her weight the water slurped above the rub rails and rose higher, sloshing across the brass keel strip. Blaze got her to calm down, pulling her off the hull. But the dinghy was locked under the surface. It nosed into them like a manatee. Both oars had floated away in opposite directions.

Blaze found the painter, hoping to tug the boat to shore, but it was dead in the water. Janice said that they couldn't tow it without one of them getting drowned.

She said, "I know you loved the *All Smiles*. Your dad will hire someone to pull her up."

"I guess it's not going to happen any time soon."

"Probably not."

"It's lost."

"I said I was sorry."

Treading water, their limbs entangled, her silky legs scissoring against him. They moved apart again, up to their chins in the icy water. If she'd capsized the boat on purpose, to further his baptism with her, being pitched into the drink together was the common denominator. Just then, the *All Smiles* suddenly turned, rolling back onto its hull under the water as it finally went down. He watched the boat sink deeper beneath glassy planes, without them.

Janice was shivering, self-consciously. Sinking and bobbing. He promised that he'd wrap her in the furred wool blanket when they climbed out. They started swimming again. He slowed his pace because Janice used the sidestroke and couldn't stay abreast of him. He encouraged her to keep paddling. When she panicked, Blaze told her, "Focus! Focus on the shore. . . ." He could see its green bib spread open.

Author photo by Nancy Crampton

Maria Flook, a 2007 John Simon Guggenheim Memorial Foundation Award recipient, is the author of the nonfiction books *New York Times* Bestseller *Invisible Eden: A Story of Love and Murder on Cape Cod* and *My Sister Life: The Story of My Sister's Disappearance.* Her fiction includes the novels *Lux, Open Water,* and *Family Night,* which received a PEN American/Ernest Hemingway Foundation Special Citation, and a collection of stories, *You Have the Wrong Man.* She has also published two collections of poetry, *Sea Room* and *Reckless Wedding,* winner of the Houghton Mifflin New Poetry Series. Her work has appeared in the *New York Times Book Review, The New Yorker, The New Criterion, TriQuarterly,* and *More Magazine* among others. Maria Flook is Distinguished Writer-in-Residence at Emerson College in Boston.

BOCA RATON PUBLIC LIBRARY

3 3656 3009308 0

Flook, Maria,
Mothers and lovers /

Dec 2014